Cyber Cinderella

Cyber Cinderella

Christina Hopkinson

5 SPOT

NEW YORK BOSTON

Warner Books Edition

This Warner Books edition is published by arrangement with Piatkus Books Ltd., 5 Windmill Street, London, England W1T 2JA.

5 Spot, an imprint of Warner Books, Inc.
Hachette Book Group, USA
1271 Avenue of the Americas, New York, NY 10020

Printed in the United States of America
Originally published in England as *Izobel Brannigan.com*
First U.S. Edition: August 2006
10 9 8 7 6 5 4 3 2 1

Library of Congress Cataloging-in-Publication Data

Hopkinson, Christina,
[Izobel Brannigan.com]
Cyber Cinderella / Christina Hopkinson.—1st U.S. ed.
p. cm.
Originally published: Izobel Brannigan.com, 2004.
ISBN 0-446-69716-8
1. Identity (Psychology)—Fiction. 2. Single women—Fiction.
3. Web sites—Fiction. I. Title.
PR6108.O65I98 2006
823'.92—dc22 2005052119

Interior design by Nancy Singer Olaguera
Composition by ISPN Production Services

To Alex and William Carruthers

Acknowledgments

Huge thanks to my first family: Anthony, Sylvia, Francis, Charlotte, Edward and Marie Hopkinson.

To Arabella Stein of Abner Stein for taking me on and for all her enthusiasm and encouragement, and to Karen Kosztolnyik for her transatlantic editing and cheering e-mails.

Cyber prince Scott Bedford (whose work can be found on www.scottbedford.co.uk) designed www.christinahopkinson.com and www.izobelbrannigan.com. I'm grateful, too, to my favorite photographer, Andy Lane, for the portraits.

Gratitude and apologies to Nicola Usborne and Rose Else-Mitchell, New York dwellers from whom I've stolen anecdotes and attitude.

Most of all, thanks to Alex Carruthers for the support without which I would not be able to write.

Cyber Cinderella

Chapter One

I was bored the day I Googled myself and found the site devoted to me.

Friday afternoon in the office was dragging and I'd run out of other people to Google. So I put my own name into the Internet search engine www.google.com and there it was: www.izobel brannigan.com.

Let's get one thing straight: I'm not a celebrity or anything. I'm sure Britney Spears might occasionally Google herself and find the millions of sites devoted to her. If I had inputted the words "Kylie's bottom" or the "meaning of *The Matrix,*" myriad tributes would have spewed back at me. They are worthy of Web interest.

But not me. Far from being a celebrity, I don't even think I'm celebrated enough in my own life. I'm not one of those people whose birthday is commemorated with a vast surprise party and a postman lurching under the weight of good wishes. I remember other people's names more often than they do mine. I was too embarrassed to put an update about myself on Friends Reunited because I've achieved so little in life. I never have exciting invitations in the post or messages on my mobile.

It's not always been this way. I had thought I would be celebrated, feted, adored. I had so much promise in my early years.

If English single-sex grammar school had yearbooks, then I would have been "the girl most likely to succeed." At least I like to think so.

But I'm thirty and I organize publicity for other people and not for myself. I'm not even particularly celebrated in the field of PR. No Institute of Public Relations Excellence or PR Week Awards for me. Thirty: what had I thought I'd be doing at this age? I didn't ever think I'd be like my mother and have two and a half children by this milestone, but I might at least have had a career to speak of instead.

Definitely not a household name. In fact, quite literally, I am nameless in my own home. My boyfriend George always refers to me as sweetheart, poppet or angel-girl, a habit he's developed over the years to avoid ejaculating the wrong name in a moment of passion.

So, I was surprised when my name came up upon Googling myself. That sounds rather obscene, doesn't it, to self-Google: something that is inappropriate office behavior. I suppose it is a bit masturbatory, but if clients are allowed to snort drugs in the toilets of this office I don't see why I shouldn't indulge in some harmless auto-Googling.

*

I remember the first time I heard the word "Google" used as a verb, about a year before. It was at a dinner to force us all to like Frank's girlfriend Camilla a bit more than we had done first time round. It was significant for another reason—I think it was the first time ever that someone had remembered me and not the reverse. I have a kind of inverted amnesia that means I'm cursed to recall all the names and faces of everyone I meet. This should be to my advantage but instead people look upon me as a sort of stalker and feel an innate superiority that they should be more memorable than I am.

"I always Google prospective boyfriends," said Camilla that night. "I Googled Frank and I liked what I saw."

"You what?" asked my friend Maggie, who preferred to goggle and to ogle. "Sounds absolutely disgusting."

Camilla gave that Mitford-girl laugh of hers. "No, I mean Google. You know, put their name into google dot com, the search engine, to check them out and see what things they've done in their life. Nobody in New York would dream of going on a date before checking out their net status. You can find out so much about someone by what their online appearances are."

"Like what?" said Maggie. "You're more likely to get some American name-alike than anything of any real relevance."

"No, really. Googling is like reading someone's CV before offering them the job. You find out when they've been mentioned in the press, if they've spoken at a conference or written a book. Frank's contributed so many interesting articles to periodicals that I'd never have known about otherwise, would I, darling?" Camilla stroked the brilliant essayist's face. "Clever Frank."

"No, clever you," London's leading academic crumpet replied.

"No, you're the clever one, with all those letters after your name."

From Google to gag, I thought, as I struggled to keep my food down in the face of the banquet of banality. "I'm not sure," I said at the time. "I think it's a bit creepy. It's judging someone on superficial criteria. It's all about their media profile, isn't it, or what level of fame they've achieved. It's like saying that someone evicted from *Big Brother* matters more than a cure for cancer, just because more people might be Googling Jezza or Ped or whatever they're called. It's all about a very shallow definition of worth and about ephemeral profile."

"Hark at her, the PR girl," sneered Frank. "Haven't you just described the very essence of your job?"

I ignored him and continued addressing my remarks to his girlfriend. "What happens if you're not a celebrity, if you have none of this sort of fame? Are you devalued? Can your worth be measured by how many sites a search engine can throw back about you?"

"But everyone does feature," insisted Camilla.

"Yeah, yeah, fifteen minutes and all that," said Maggie.

"No, not that sort of fame," she corrected. "But everyone has a place on the Net, don't they? Every one of us must appear somewhere or somehow. It's terribly democratic. You could always make your own site if you didn't, just so you could be there. And it gives us bits of information that you wouldn't know otherwise. Like . . ." She paused and looked at me. "The fact that you and I were at school together."

"Were we?" I was shocked, not just by the revelation that this alien girl with the Received Pronunciation could have hailed from the same provinces that I had, but that she had remembered me, and not the other way round. "Did you find that out online? Wow, I'm sorry, but I don't remember you."

"Well, you wouldn't, would you? You were three years older. You always remember the older girls from school and not the younger ones. You were, like, so old."

"Strange times," said Maggie, "when the older you were, the more desirable you were."

"And anyway," continued Camilla, "I'm just using it as an example of the sort of information you could find on the Net. I'm afraid I didn't remember you, actually, nor did I find you online, just that girl in your year, the one who became a porn star."

"Astrid Tickell. Or Anne as she was then."

"I was with the old gang last week, you know, the St. Tree's Tasties as we were referred to by the boys' school. Anyway, they remembered you."

"They?"

"Becksy, Kitty, you know, the gang. Amazing that they should have remembered you, your name and everything. Like I said, you always remember the old ones, don't you? They thought you were quite cool. Of that time. They said you were kind of punky. Fancied yourself to be the girl from *The Breakfast Club.* Good look."

Tinkle, tinkle, tinkly laugh, joined by Frank's guffaw, the one that could project through academic amphitheaters.

"I'm afraid I don't think I remember the St. Tree's Tasties. Did you wear, like, baseball jackets with that emblazoned on the back?" I said.

I'm glad I didn't remember them, because they sounded like a bunch of evil little pixies in their bottle-green uniforms, no doubt hiked up to reveal perfect skinny legs. At the same time, I felt grateful to them for knowing who I was all these years on. I was somebody then.

*

After that night, I'd Google everyone I met and even those I hadn't. I could whittle away whole afternoons in the office in this activity. I Googled George and I Googled his potential replacements. I even Googled myself intermittently and would usually get the unrelated names—the American genealogy sites and conference roll-calls. The search engine would presume that I had spelled my own name wrong and would ask me, "Do you mean Isabel Brannigan?" No, Izobel, I-Z-O-B, as I was already used to saying.

Until the day I Googled myself and there it was: www.izobelbrannigan.com. And, for good measure, izobelbrannigan.co.uk. I know I'm not unique, but the way of spelling my Christian name is. My father insisted on naming me after his dead mother; my own mother insisted on making it differently dyslexic. She had aspirations for me even then.

"Under construction." That's what the page said, and I felt then that it must be about me and my life. "Under construction," ill-formed, incomplete, chaotic, that's me. I'm thirty and I still don't know what sort of woman I will become. A bad-tempered and bored one, certainly, but am I going to be a mother? A career woman? Career woman with children? Or just another woman with a boring job and a good-time boyfriend?

*

"Hi," I called out to George above the stereo that blared out to the visual accompaniment of the news on mute.

"Hello honey, how was your day? Mine was a shocker. I was forced to go out for lunch to taste revolting peanut-butter-flavored martinis. Nuts are not the new gin, I'm telling you; I had to have a couple of classics just to wash the taste away. And a few sneaky lines with John. I tell you, the peanut butter got right up my nose."

"Great."

"Still don't feel tickety-boo to be honest. I think you and I ought to go out and wash away the taste with some good Italian," George continued in that 1940s voice of his.

"Something happened to me today."

"Really, sweetheart? Why don't you tell me over some supper at Ravioli? And if there are any big launches you think I should be attending. We haven't had a big old launch party for ages. What good is it, a journalist going out with a PR girl, if there are no parties to go to? We haven't had a really good evening at somebody else's expense since that vodka thing."

I sat down and turned the stereo off. George was a decade to the day older than me, but insisted on playing music at loud levels of teenage noise. I could think only in silence and I needed to think now. He poured me a glass of wine. It's one of his domestic fortes.

He was half-bagged but his suit was well cut, ensuring that he retained an ill-deserved elegance. He looked smarter after a hard day's office drinking than most men in their interview suit. With his slicked-back, mildly receding hair and handmade Lobb's shoes, he resembled a Second World War spiv. George has the look of a man who is either upgraded to first class or thoroughly strip-searched by airport customs, never anything in between.

"Something weird happened to me today," I told him.

"Weirder than peanut-butter martinis?"

"I think so, yes." The wine warmed me, as did George's hand stroking my hair.

"I'm agog, poppet," he said, moving his hand across my chest and undoing my shirt buttons.

"I Googled myself."

"Well, hello . . ."

"I put my name into a search engine and a site came up."

"Hmmm." He had graduated to thigh-fondling.

"Don't you think that's weird? There's a site devoted to me. To *me*."

"I don't have the faintest idea what you're talking about."

"A Web site. I put my name into an Internet search engine—you know, it's like a directory of the Web—and there's a Web site about me."

"Sexy girl that you are, was it a porn site?" he asked while pushing my bra up so I achieved that attractive four-breasted effect, with the real ones squashed by the empty cups of my north-migrating lingerie.

"Seriously, George." I wriggled away. "It's freaking me out. It's a site. For me, about me, done by someone for me, and I've no idea who or why."

He looked bored. We had the symbiotic relationship of a PR person and a journalist so that when I demanded rather than gave attention, it transcended the rules of our professional lives. "What did it say, then? What did it say about you?"

"It said 'under construction.'" That means it hasn't been built yet, but it's going to be. Someone's bought the address of my name and everything."

George laughed. "Silly sausage, it's probably not about you at all. What a delightful little idiot you are."

"But it is, it must be. Why would there be a site registered with my name, with the funny spelling and everything, as the URL?"

"You what?"

"The URL, the address of a Web site."

"You mean its e-mail number?"

"Don't be disingenuous, George, it doesn't suit you. Do you have to be such a Luddite? Or should I say 'laddite,' given that you're happy to indulge in most things that lads do, pubs and women and the like?"

"Laddite, I like it. Masculine men who rather than going for gadgets and all things electronic are maintaining a stand against the tide of technology. You are clever; I can feel an article coming on." He scribbled the word "laddite" across a gas bill that was my responsibility to pay.

"You're not answering my question," I whined. "Why on earth would there be a site with my name as the address?"

"And you're not answering mine. Why on earth would anyone create a site dedicated to you?"

Why indeed?

*

George was right, of course, it had to be a coincidence. There must be someone who did spell their name the same as I did and who had the same surname. I had heard there was a trend in America for giving your children normal names with abnormal spellings, Emalee, Aleksandra, Rayshelle, that type of thing. Maybe Izobel was now one of them and the site was just something whipped up by some expectant parents in the Midwest. It was a more logical conclusion.

"Phew," I said to George. "What a relief. I was really spooked. I thought I might have a stalker or something."

"My poor angel-girl, you're a bit upset that there's no site about you."

"No, of course not. I was really freaked. It would have been terrible, having someone think so much of you as to create a site all about you. God no. Like getting an anonymous Valentine card, should be flattering but it's just annoying and weird. I'd hate it, really I would."

"Well, my darling, you may not have some stupid little site," he said. "But I can give you something so much better." Here we go, I thought, sex as the answer to all, but he surprised me. "Instead of a site, a spa!"

"A what?"

"A spa weekend at Britain's finest luxury hotel, courtesy of yours truly. With a Michelin-starred restaurant attached."

"You can't afford that, surely?" I said clapping my hands together with excitement. "When? How are you paying?"

"Aha, there's the rub. I'm doing a piece on it for the travel section. Well, I might do, if I can be bothered." He looked at me proudly.

Aha, I thought, courtesy of some poor sap of a PR girl like me who will have proudly announced her coup to her clients. He'd get all this for free and I'd pay for the extras like the bar bill, which would come to as much as I'd ever spent on a mini-break anyway.

"Great. Thanks, George. Much better than a creepy stalky site thing."

*

I had thought a site dedicated to me might make George reappraise me. We'd been together for both too long and too short a time to make grand gestures. I was even almost tempted to hire a Web geek to make up a site for me so that I could pretend someone worshipped me, that I had one fan, and to show this to George, to prove him wrong and to whip up his ardor. This being, I suppose, the twenty-first-century version of sending flowers to yourself to make the boyfriend jealous.

"George," I asked one evening soon after. "Am I your number one? The most important person in your life?"

"Naturally, darling, my number one grown-up girl anyway. Of course, Grace is my number one number one. I'd be a monster if it were any other way."

Grace. The divine Grace. Beauty, intelligence and saintliness in a pert six-year-old package accessorized by Gap Kids. He'd once said he'd kill himself if anything were to happen to her. "I'd get over you dying," he had said to me, "but one never gets over the death of a child."

That's the trouble with going out with a man with offspring by another woman. The one person who should put you above all others has the most horribly valid excuse not to. And even to question this principle is to be the wickedest common-law stepmother in the history of fairy tales. Stepmothers are very much maligned, generally, I would think, as I'd read another bloody boring story to a demanding child who was not only not mine, but belonged to Catherine, the woman I most resented in the world.

I phoned Maggie.

"Do you think you're number one in Mick's life?"

"I suppose so, though I don't know for how much longer. When the baby's born, I'm sure he or she will be my number one. And Mick's. Are you asking who you'd pull out of a burning building first or who you like best?"

"I don't know. It would just be nice to feel like you're number one in somebody's life."

"It's not the charts, you know. It's not that simple. And this week's number one in Mick's life, pop pickers, is Maggie, closely followed by Mick's mum, but with the six-month-old fetus poised to make the highest new entry."

"I know, I just don't think I'm anybody's."

"Could be a good thing," she said. "Christ, I'm my mother's and I'd give anything not to be. The top of her hit parade should be my father. More like the top of her hit list. It's horrible being her number one best friend, daughter, quasi-lover, receptacle for all her hopes and dreams. Every morning she phones me. I told her not to use my work number as that was for work calls so now she phones me on my mobile, or 'portable telephone' as she calls it. I told her only to use that for emergencies, so now she prefaces every message with 'It's nothing important' in this really sad and passive-aggressive way."

I couldn't see Maggie's mother creating a Web site devoted to her daughter. She was of the generation that still talked to answer-phones in the third person: "This is a message for Maggie, tell her that her mother rang and that I miss her very much."

"At least you've got two people who put you top, and a third on the way," I retorted.

"Izobel, we are all the protagonists in the movie of our own lives." Maggie was a TV drama script editor both professionally and emotionally. "In everyone else's you're just a bit part—the wisecracking best pal, the mother figure, the girlfriend, the nemesis, doesn't really matter. You're only your own number one."

"But shouldn't I be surrounded by best supporting actors?"

"Yes, but supporting, secondary. There's only one star in your life and that's you. Don't rely on anybody else to give you applause."

"But as I'm going out with someone, though," I asked, "shouldn't I expect George to have me played by Julia Roberts in the biopic of his life? At least, have almost equal billing?" I decided not to tell her about the Web site. Not yet anyway.

"Yes, but would she be in a cameo? Or do you really think that George thinks as much about you as you think about yourself? We're all pretty solipsistic in the end, aren't we? In George's film would the actress playing you get nominated in the best actress or best actress in a supporting role category?"

"I'd be below the barmaid in the credits."

Maggie laughed, though I wasn't actually trying to be funny.

*

I felt that my life was far from being an epic. It was a low-budget short, made by students and lacking real plot or narrative arc; one of those ones where amateur actors shuffle around bemoaning the state of the world without anything really happening. All the audience would be talking through it just waiting for the arrival of the main attraction.

Chapter Two

I checked the under-constructed www.izobelbrannigan.com intermittently, but then I checked a lot of sites at work. I saw *The Apartment* recently and I wondered what work there had been to do in an office before the advent of computers and e-mail.

One day, though, www.izobelbrannigan.com was different. It was there. My site had flickered into life, dormant but now animated, a fairy-tale princess awoken with a kiss marked "Put Live."

And it was *my* site. There was no doubt anymore. It was my site and it was all about me. In the center of the screen in Arial 24pt bold, a couple of paragraphs about my life. Or at least my life as imagined by a *Hello!* features writer crossed with an adulatory adolescent boy.

"This site is dedicated to the life of Izobel Brannigan, who rocks her own world and that of those around her. Born 1973 (she's a Pisces), she went to St. Teresa's Grammar and then to the University of Sussex, where she read European Studies and Good Times. She's now cutting a swath through the glamorous world of the capital's public relations industry."

It went on: "Enough of the past. But what next for Izobel and www.izobelbrannigan.com? We want to make a site that's every bit as crazy and dynamic as the woman herself. Over the coming months, we'll keep you informed of all her antics and her ever-changing world. And we'll be throwing in a few secrets that maybe she wouldn't want out there! Keep logging on!"

Nobody described me as "cutting a swath" through anywhere these days. Not even me in the third-person commentary about my life I'd run through my head to a John Barry soundtrack when trying to cheer myself up.

The site was nice-looking; the stalker knew his stuff when it came to the Web. It was only a one-pager, but professionally executed. The background was an attractive shade of blue and the logo "Izobel" in large squashy letters, like comfy sofas, ran across the top of the page. That was nice of them, I thought, to have taken the trouble to fashion a logo out of my name. It looked like it was underlined in navy, but on closer inspection I made out the words "her site her world" in an angular script, like the border on an Egyptian tomb.

Eliminating all doubt about which Izobel the site was devoted to, there were a couple of photos set at jaunty angles and with fake crinkled edges, as if this was not the Internet but a page from an old-fashioned scrapbook or photo album. The text was in a yellow box, to look as though a Post-it note had been randomly affixed to this commonplace book.

One photo was of me from school, a blurred thumbnail from a group shot. My face was so fat in those days. When people try to flatter women by saying they've the body of a sixteen-year-old, they're clearly not referring to mine at that age. And the hair. Why did I ever think it was cool to have a bleached spiky fringe? I remember how I used to tie it up in a sausage of elastic bands each night, like a unicorn's horn, and then release the vertical plumage in the morning.

Then there was another photo, a more recent one. I couldn't work it out at first; eventually, by looking at the clothes I was wearing and the background, illuminated by a flash, I realized that it was taken at a party to celebrate somebody's thirtieth I'd been to about six months before, held in a club. I was wearing a one-shouldered top and a pair of satin combats with heels in an effort to practice what PR people and magazine editors were encouraging mortals to sport. I like to think I'm quite street: High or Bond, depending on the mood. You could see my nipples. I'm sure you couldn't on the day, so at a guess they had been digitally enhanced.

It was a typical party picture: I had my arms around two friends and was doing that glowing overarching smile of the mildly tipsy while my eyes had been flashed up into a demonic red. My chin was tipped downward, as it was in all photos taken since I had realized as a teenager that if I didn't do that, it looked like I had a goiter. Of course, the flip side was that it meant that the dark rings around my eyes were more prominent, but this was the lesser of two evils.

Dark rings around the eyes were not something that Maggie and Frank, the friends I was embracing and learning on, had to worry about in this photo, for they had little black strips across their eyes to protect their anonymity. The effect was sinister, as if they were MPs partaking in an orgy splashed across a tabloid newspaper, or the innocent victims of a kiddie porn ring, while I was the leering perv they'd been taught to call "Uncle Tommy." Stalker–Web site maker clearly didn't see why my anonymity should be protected in such a way. Instead the bare facts of my life were broadcast across the whole wide world.

Whose party had it been? Some friend of Frank's? Must ask Maggie, I thought, not that she'd be able to remember any better than me. I'm sure if her eyes had been visible they'd have had the enlarged pupils of the totally boxed, her irises like the glow of the sun being eclipsed by the full moon of her pupils. It must have been before she was pregnant. Or at least before she knew she was.

There was a ticker running along the bottom of the site. "Coming soon: a message board where you can talk about what Izobel means to you. Live chat too." I waited for the next installment to shuffle across the screen, very slowly, for it was an arthritic ticker. "Sections on her family and friends." All with blacked-across eyes, no doubt. "E-mail alerts for her birthday and breaking news." It continued to meander. "Future attractions: Izobel-themed ring tones and faceplates. Comps and prizes galore!"

I rang Maggie. "Whose party was it, you know the one where you wore a boob tube thing that kept on slipping down? The thirtieth. Some bloke."

"That narrows it down," she replied. "I no longer go to many thirtieths anymore. Do you know, I've been invited to a fortieth. A fortieth! Can you imagine? I can't believe we're entering the age of *Big Chill* and no longer *St. Elmo's Fire.* This year marks the specific point at which we become nearer to forty than our teens."

"I suppose so."

"Amazing."

"Yes, amazing, how strange, we're so old, but whose party was that thirtieth? The one in the club place where we only had a cordoned-off bit and all the other normal punters looked at us as if we were cattle at an agricultural show?"

"Friend of Frank's, wasn't it? Some bloke from the university who he works with. Economist, I think. It must have been around seven months ago as I was worried that I might have already been pregnant then, but the scans reckon it was about a week or so after. I can't imagine a time when I wasn't pregnant. It seems like a different age. How I miss drinking. And the rest."

"That's right." I remembered now. The host was a goodlooking man called Robert who I would have lunged at had I not been conscious of the fact that he was having a party in a club, was far too pretty and wore a very tight T-shirt. "Bob was his name."

"Hot Bob, we liked him."

"But he doesn't like us, does he? I remember thinking he was hot but maybe no ladies' man. I think he was wearing lip gloss."

"No, don't be old-fashioned, Iz. He's straight. I think I remember Frank telling me about some dodgy business with one of his female students."

Would I want Hot Bob to be my stalker? I wouldn't mind, though I thought it unlikely. But whoever had created the site must have been at the party and must have taken a photo of me. I needed to get the list of invitees from Hot Bob. Not that this would be definitive. After all, I had been there and I had not been invited directly.

I e-mailed George triumphantly.

Subject: Me.

Hurrah, I was the subject of an e-mail to George. Now there was a first.

"Please look at www.izobelbrannigan.com. Let's discuss later. Love you, I."

Ha, I thought, he said no one would devote a site to me, that I was unworthy of a stalker, but he was wrong.

A stalker. I felt my face flush and bright red hives slide down from my cheeks across my chest.

"You all right, babe?" my colleague Mimi asked without bothering to hear the stammered reply.

"Fine, fine, yeah, fine."

I wasn't. A stalker, I had a stalker. I was like a weathergirl or newsreader without the blonde highlights, cropped Meg Ryan haircut or perky personality; just the creepy man watching me, taking photos of me, devoting a site to me. George was right: why would anybody devote a site to me in an adoring way? It had to be malevolent.

I felt my cheeks. They were still hot, as was my forehead. I knew that I'd look terrible; I always did when I got this sort of reaction, piebald in pink and purple hues. I breathed in through the nose and out through the mouth in a yoga-type way in a hopeless attempt to calm myself, before going into a meeting with a new client.

I'd find my stalker. Or was it my admirer? When did one become the other?

*

I switched on my ancient desktop computer when I got home and watched it crank up in its decrepit fashion. At every command, it would whir alarmingly in a way that I think my brain does when asked to do anything logical. I could feel my head making those sort of strained noises once again as I attempted to compute the odd events of the day.

It was my flat and my computer, but George's mess. He maintained that it was bohemian and I was bourgeois, yet his wardrobe was always kept as immaculately as an expensive boutique. The rest, with its ashtrays and saucepans, with its blurring of kitchen, living room and bathroom, was the student accommodation that George might have lived in if he had ever bothered to go to university two decades previously. I suspected he would feel differently about the tangle if it had been his flat. Or our flat, perhaps. Moving to somewhere bigger was on my list of things to do, but the set-up with George had never seemed permanent enough to merit a conversation about our arrangements. Instead of living together, we were living in layers, with my stuff at the bottom and his possessions floating on the surface, like scum at the seaside.

My computer finally blossomed and I looked at izobelbrannigan .com. The site hadn't changed in the hour and a half since I had last looked at it. A little less professional-looking, transposed away from the flat monitor of my office computer and now framed with the ugly off-white of a cheap PC. The ticker still ran and the

Izobel logo still flashed hypnotically. I was still flanked by friends with black strips in place of eyes.

I waited for George to come back. Where was he? I phoned his mobile and it clicked into its familiar voice mail. "Hello, darling, leave me a message." Everyone was "darling" to him. I waited for my phone to ring back with news of where he was, for the computer screen to flicker in recognition of a mobile sounding nearby. I got bored with watching the endless groundhogging of the ticker going round and round and eventually switched on the TV for some trash that was little more interesting. The site had ceased to exist for me until I could discuss it with George, to get his appraisal, approbation and, I hoped, his appalled reaction that someone could be covertly threatening his beloved.

There's that old philosophical question about whether a tree falling in the forest has to be heard by someone to have truly happened. If I were that person hearing the tree fall, it wouldn't have happened until I'd exaggerated the story of its demise, found a punch line, practiced the anecdote, dressed up in a new top that was appropriate for its content, told at least three friends and then e-mailed a couple more about it.

If the site was that poor unfortunate tree, then it was live but had not yet come to life. Not until I'd shown it to George. Where was he? I felt like I was that tree falling with no one around to catch me.

I left him another message; no response followed so I resorted to desperate measures with my third call. "George, ring me quick. I'm in a bar with free cocktails; they'll have run out in an hour." Even the promise of a sponsored event did not induce him to ring me back. He must really have been in a place with no network coverage.

I didn't get to show it to him, at least not that night. He didn't ring but came back after I'd gone to bed, with the tinny tomato smell on his breath that showed he'd been drinking to excess. I always think of George when I smell a past-its-use-by-date tube of tomato puree.

"I rang you," I said sleepily, grumpily, turning my back to him.

"Sorry, sweetheart, the batteries had gone on my phone. Damn annoying to have missed out on the jamboree. What sort of free cocktails? Gin- or vodka-based?"

"Seriously, I was worried. I called you again after that. I thought something awful must have happened to you."

"What is this?" He picked up the phone set by the bed. "Your umbilical cordless phone?" Then he laughed at his joke. "Oh, that's good. I think I can feel an article coming on. The way women use new gadgets and new technology to be ever more old-fashioned and clingy with their menfolk."

I couldn't be bothered to discuss the new technology that was my site.

The next night was his visit to "Gracelands," as we euphemistically referred to his Saturday and one-weekday dadly duties with his daughter. For some reason, the trip with her and her friend Phoebe on a press freebie to *The Lion King* entailed everybody sleeping over at Phoebe's mother's house. A slinky single mother at that, with the embroidered-cashmere-cardie sort of name of Lulu. There was a production line of women like that at Grace's private day school, flinging out mummies called Minty and Cressie and other edible names at the gates. They lionized George whenever he went to pick up Grace from school, as if he were the priest in a convent or the jumbo-jet pilot amid a giggle of air hostesses.

By the time I eventually showed the site to him it no longer seemed either significant or sinister. Needless to say, he had ignored my e-mail entreaty to check it out.

"Look," I said, trying to retain the triumph of being vindicated that I had felt on first seeing it. "Can you still deny that it's a site about me?" I watched as its photos filtered down into view, the slowness of my home computer artificially creating suspense and the sense that something momentous was being unveiled.

He scanned it quickly. "Nice schoolgirl photo, darling, wish I'd known you then."

"Don't be disgusting. You'd have been in your mid-twenties."

He glanced at the screen again. "They don't see fit to talk about the love of your life now, though. Where's the stuff about Izobel's handsome gentleman caller? And it's really badly written, isn't it? 'She rocks her world.' I think we need to find a half-wit illiterate American teenager and then we've got our man." He chortled at his own wit. The crime of the perpetrator lay in his poor use of English rather than in his creepy intrusive tendencies.

"But don't you think it's odd?"

"To use rock as a verb, yes terribly."

"Don't be annoying, George. That it exists. That there's a site devoted to me. Your girlfriend. If anybody should be creating a cyber-paean to me, it should be you."

"Don't hold your breath."

"I wasn't going to, because if I held my breath until you praised me I'd die."

It was just a turn of phrase, but I felt sick talking about death, now that I had a stalker. I imagined the site perp to have a grotty bedsit somewhere plastered with blurred photos of me and cuttings from the *Arlington Crow,* my parents' local paper, where the fact that I had been in Knightsbridge with my mum one hour before the Harrods bombing was considered worthy of the front page.

I sat down, defeated, while George started surfing the Net.

"So how did you find the site?" he asked.

"I Googled myself."

"Hmmm, sounds kind of kinky," he slobbered. "Can we have some mutual Googling later?"

"I went to the search engine page like this." I waited as the site flickered into view. "Then put in my name." I began typing I-Z-O-B—when George interrupted.

"Put in my name, go on, put in my name. Google me, baby."

"I've done it before; it's not that interesting."

"Go on, Google your one and only."

I typed in George Grand and hit "search." "Have you ever thought, George, that this isn't about you?"

He watched the screen, rapt, as he never normally was by the "thing they call the World Wide Web" as he insisted on referring to it.

"This isn't very good," he judged as links to a few desultory articles by him chugged into view. "This is no better than the cuttings system at work. I don't want stuff *by* me, I want stuff *about* me. This is all about some Victorian actor, not me. Why not? This person was born in eighteen seventy-four—I'm not that bloody old. Look here." He shoved a clammy finger onto my screen, leaving a moist smudge as his footprint in the sand. "This is about someone who isn't even called George Grand. It's about someone called George and someone else called Henry Grand. It's just stupid. Stupid Internet thing, World Web rubbish." He flounced off the chair and threw himself onto the sofa and the waiting TV remote control.

"George, for fuck's sake." He lifted his head to look at me quizzically. "It's not about you. It's about me. There's some nutter out there who clearly thinks about me more than you do and you're worrying about your Internet profile. What are we going to do about it?"

"Create a site about me. That would raise my profile."

"For Christ's sake."

"I was joking," he said grumpily.

"This is not a laughing matter. We've got to find out who's behind this site. Someone has taken the trouble and taken the photos to make a Web site devoted to me. Don't you think it's a bit odd? Don't you see, we've got to find out who it is and to stop them. It starts out innocently enough but what if I don't respond? How will they react? By following me? Attacking me? Killing me?" My voice was squeaking.

"I think you've watched too many women-in-peril films. Or been talking to that bloody Maggie again."

"George," I screamed. "We've got to do something."

"*We*," he emphasized the word, "don't have to do anything."

"Too bloody right," I replied, calmer or exhausted, I wasn't sure which. "But *I* do."

And that was that. We then had more to drink followed by sex, our twin hobbies, the panacea for all ills of the world. George was very lazy except when pouring drinks and pawing me.

It might seem strange that we should make love when I produce so much bile and fury toward him, but that was our way. I never understood why relationship experts said that sex was a barometer of the health of a relationship. If that were the case, then George and I would be the Joanne Woodward and Paul Newman of coupledom. But we weren't. Sex was not the barometer of our relationship, it was the Band-Aid. Have an argument, have sex. Have a problem, have sex. Get bored, have sex. It was the grout that kept the tiles of our relationship together and without it they would come tumbling down. I could not help but suspect that behind those slabs of physical intimacy there lurked some major subsidence. For now it was hidden, storing up its problems for later.

*

I was still irked by George's indifference to my little tribute site when I got an e-mail from him at work.

"Check out www.izobelbrannigan.com now."

I smiled. George was now sexy, fun, life-enhancing George once again and I forgave him the fact that he had reacted to my site as if it were no more than spam e-mail.

I logged on.

I was surprised by what I found.

I logged on again. Same response: "The page cannot be displayed." Page can't be displayed? That was worse than being "under construction." I was no longer "found." I was lost. I could hear George's sneers about the supremacy of print media. "You don't turn over the pages of a newspaper to find a blank page with 'the page cannot be displayed' across it, well do you?"

Had I imagined it all along? No, George had viewed it, albeit in a perfunctory fashion.

I sank back, disheartened. My little time of celebrity was over as soon as it had begun. "Phew," I practiced saying, in readiness for seeing George, "what a relief the site's disappeared. Now I don't have to worry anymore." And he would draw me to him and tell me what a silly bunny I'd been to make such a big fuss about it in the first place and then we'd have sex or go to the launch of another restaurant doomed to the lifespan of a fruit fly.

If only I had at least saved the page or printed it out. Now I had nothing except the fact that George would feel like he'd been proved right and the disappointment of having gone from nonentity to notoriety back to nonentity again in but a week.

The phone went.

"All gone now," he boomed.

"Hello, George."

"What a lot of fuss about nothing. I'll make it all better tonight. What are we doing?"

"Fiona's company's doing a launch for a cigarette company. In Soho."

"Free fags?"

"I guess so. It did exist, didn't it? The site, I mean, I didn't just imagine it."

"What site?"

"Don't be a jerk, George. It's still weird and there still is a stalker person out there who made it even if I can't see it anymore."

"I really think you ought to stop worrying about it and tell me where the party is. What kind of fags anyway?"

I looked at the screen and with my free hand went to refresh the page once more in a pathetic gesture of hope. Control R. Refresh. If only I could do that to my life.

I couldn't refresh my nonvirtual life, but it had worked a miracle on the site. It was back. And with a new addition to the ticker: "We're sorry for any inconvenience to Izobel fans who may have been trying to view this site today. We've had technical difficulties that are now fully resolved. Izobel and her site can now keep on rolling!"

"George, the site. It's back. It's working again."

I could hear a sigh on the other end of the phone mutate into a cough. "Fantastic news," he said in a voice that suggested it was anything but.

Chapter Three

Life ground on in its dull and dulling way: frottaged by flesh on the Underground, shocked at the price of a frothy coffee and slumped in the office. Every day was the same, yet every day more irritating than the last.

Every day, I'd be struck by the way that my place of work was like one of those grand houses whose perfect Georgian facade only conceals chaos and architectural incoherence beyond. The clients saw shiny flagstones and meeting rooms with flowers in. I dwelt in the back room of the overcrowded offices covered in redundant piles of newspapers like the house of a crazy person. There mobiles would make their unharmonious chorus of tunes distorted into an indistinguishable blur of grating sound.

In the office, I'd flick through the papers, skipping the politics and getting straight onto the gossip and "Your Life Is Incomplete Without . . ." sections and would discuss how fit/unattractive various celebrities were and which of them were sporting collagen/breast implants. After that I would get down to the real business of reading the horoscope that appeared in the paper George worked for. I'd sigh as Pisceans were once more advised to show financial prudence and were never promised love or luck.

Every day these things would irritate me anew and yet nothing was ever fresh to me. The only things that could penetrate my jaded self were those that depressed, never those that delighted.

Except for my site. It didn't gladden, exactly, but it had excited me, piqued me, intrigued me. It was the first time something different had happened in the two years since I had got together with George. Curiosity expanded and swelled inside me, filling my brain like one of those new foaming cleaners that billow down drains.

My PR missions of getting a plug in a daily or sucking up to the junior fashion features accessories editor at *Vogue* were even more desiccated of their meaning. My relationship with George was still lubricated by drink and sexual pleasure, but dehydrated of the sap of emotions.

The only thing that meant anything to me was finding out who was my cyber-admirer. Or virtual stalker. Whatever you wanted to call it. I didn't even know where to begin in my quest and was convinced I needed to call in an expert. Not a real live policeman, but the next best thing: someone who had worked on TV police dramas.

I invited Maggie round for supper.

"Mags, can I just show you something on my PC?" I asked her before she'd even got her coat off but after I'd poured us both a glass of wine, a marginally smaller one for her in deference to her distended belly. She held it protectively, the belly rather than her glass of wine, in a gesture that I guessed she had copied off actresses playing pregnant women, who'd stroke their fake bellies and fake babies, rather than as a prenatal instinct.

"What Internet delight? Woman eating her own feces, man having sex with a chihuahua, George Dubya . . ." she posited.

"Not exactly."

I clicked the mouse so that the screen saver of George and me on holiday melted away to unveil my site.

Maggie frowned, then giggled, then frowned again. "Bizarre bizarre bizarro. What a funny home page or is it called blogging these days? This is your Web log. Why have you done that to Frank's and my eyes? And I'm sure my nipples didn't show as much in that top. When did you do this? Can you do one for us? Mick's on about creating one for the fetus and putting photos of the birth on it and stuff. Why do you talk about yourself in the third person?"

"Because I didn't create it. What do you take me for?"

"You did once send yourself a Valentine."

"One, I'm not weird enough to create my own tribute site. Two, I'm not technically capable of creating one. And three, I never sent myself a Valentine."

"True to the first two of those statements." Maggie folded her arms around her chest. "So if you didn't make it, who did?"

I shrugged and my stomach cramped. She read the text that floated in the middle of the screen.

"It's anonymous? That is so creepy."

"Is it? Or is it flattering?" I asked hopefully.

"No, it's creepy. It's weird and stalkie and strange. We've got to find out who's behind it."

"We?"

"Of course. I haven't script-edited two dozen episodes of Britain's favorite midweek long-running police drama for nothing, you know. I bet I can work out who's behind it."

I hate myself. For being the sort of person to auto-Google and for being the sort of person to cry when anybody's nice to me.

"Iz darling, don't cry." Maggie never did. She was one of the people who'll jab you in the cinema and say loudly, "You're crying, I can't believe you're crying," as you snuffle at the bit when John McClane meets his radio buddy at the end of *Die Hard.* "Really not a crying matter," she said on seeing me dripping from both my eyes and nose. "You're only letting them get to you with this site if you cry. This is so weird. I can't get my head round it."

I wasn't upset. I was relieved. Maggie was taking me and it seriously. "Thank you."

"For what?"

"For thinking it's important."

"But it *is* important."

At that moment, I heard the familiar jangle of the wrong keys being put in the slot by George. He took the kitchen exit off the hall before coming into the sitting room, vodka in one hand, cigarette in the other. This left none free for giving us the finger on seeing us hunched at my computer.

"For Christ's sake, you're not still banging on about that bloody Web site."

"Piss off, George," said Maggie, whose spleen was undiluted by the fear that George would leave her and she'd be left alone for the rest of her life and never have sex again, as mine was. "And don't put that filthy fag near me."

"You can piss off, poacher turned gamekeeper, it's my house," he replied.

"No, it's not. It's Izobel's."

He was derailed by the truth of her comment and retreated into the tiny Formica-covered cave that passed as a kitchen in order to avoid us and to shout at Radio Four.

"It's always the boyfriend," hissed Maggie to George's departing back and the whiff of exclusive gentleman's cologne that he left in his wake.

"Always the boyfriend what?"

"You know, when they have these appeals on the news and the reconstructions on *Crimewatch* and the boyfriend cries and says, 'Please, please, if you know anything about my girl, then for God's sake come forward,' and you're like, 'poor chap,' and he's the murderer all along. Do you remember that couple in the Scottish Highlands, when he claimed a big dog had come and mangled her, the beast of Glenbogus or something? Of course, it turned out that he'd insured her about a week before and done away with her. He even faked fang marks on her flesh."

"I'd rather you didn't compare this to a murder."

"Or like with that French woman," she continued in a whisper. "First suspect was that nice banker fiancé, then all her exes."

"I'm really not happy with that analogy either. Anyway, it wasn't any of them in the end. It was someone completely unconnected, a random stalker man."

"So they say. Still, unlikely in your case, unless you've noticed one?"

I often have the sense of being watched and often I am, but only by me, Izobel Brannigan, who catches sight of my reflection in shop windows and captions the look with a series of flattering phrases. "No, I don't think so."

"So, George is still our first and top suspect."

We looked toward the sound of a radio comedy show being berated by George.

"No," we said in unison. What was it about my boyfriend that made him the last person to be first suspect?

"Well, maybe he is," said Maggie as if sensing my dejection.

"George can't connect to a site, let alone create one."

"He might have paid someone to produce it."

"Ha," I hissed back. I was about to retort that I'd have known if that was the case since he'd have to have borrowed the money from me in order to do so, but I stayed silent. The moneylending would remain my guilty secret. The sub-editors at the paper had a joke that they were thus named because of the amount of money they had to sub the editor of the "Life Itself" section. They would at least be paid back eventually, though. With money "borrowed" from me. "Anyway, why would George do it?"

"He's planning on proposing and one day you're going to fire it up and it will say 'Izobel will you marry me love George'? Or something."

"But it's not his style. George is all about extroverted, crowd-pleasing gestures, 'public relationships' if you like. He'd never do anything covert or secretive like that." Or costly.

"Good point. We need to do a psychological profile of the person behind it, our site perpetrator, henceforth known as the perp." Maggie grabbed a piece of paper from the printer and wrote "Suspects" in her overblown italic calligraphy at the top. "What do we know about the perp? First that he's a stalker, which means he probably already shows some obsessive-compulsive tendencies and sociopathic leanings . . ."

"Such as?" I asked. "You don't even know what that means."

"Yes I do, it's stuff like collecting train sets, heavy drug use, drinking, violence toward women, washing hands a lot, switching lights on and off. Probably got mother issues, we should check out anyone whose parents divorced or whose mum bolted as a child. Or whose mother is overbearing and loves them too much. Also anyone with a history of unstable relationships with women. Which, given that our first suspects are anyone you've gone out with, figures."

"Thanks."

"Second thing we can assume is that they know something about computers and new media. Either that or they know someone who does. Or can pay for their services."

"I don't feel we're really narrowing it down here."

It was as if Maggie had pressed the button on the remote control that made my voice mute as she ignored my comments. "Number one as previously discussed," she intoned, returning to her list, "George Grand." She pulled a face as she wrote down his name. "Sociopathic tendencies? Heavy drinking, some drugs too, addictive personality, can't give up smoking."

"Hasn't tried."

"Issues with mother . . ."

"No he doesn't, he's lovely to his mum."

"Like a Kray twin," Maggie remarked. "What I was going to say was issues with mother of his child. That's fair, isn't it?"

"Wouldn't he create a site about her then, I mean Catherine, rather than me?" I felt sick to even think it. I'd always suspected that George thought more about Catherine than he ever had about me. I caught him once with photos of her and Grace spread out across the table while he dripped tears and vodka over them.

"Possibly," said Maggie. "If it's not the boyfriend, then it's someone who was a boyfriend, so now it's on to the 'ex files,' to use a crappy magazine-style headline the likes of which George is inexplicably paid good money to come up with."

Now it was my turn to pull a face, both at the lameness of her pun and the thought of having to trawl through the motley crew of past boyfriends, a group of men whose arrogance outstripped their eligibility.

I always wondered whether there was a sexual and marital IQ, made up from a series of calculations based on a person's physical attractiveness, ability to quip, status of job, baggage and finances. I thought mine was mildly above average but decreasing all the while (age, disillusionment, professional failure). The MQs (marital quotients) of my partners, on the other hand, bordered on the subnormal. If ever a sudden burst of fortune sent them soaring, then we'd always split up soon after. Either I was always down-dating MQ-wise, or my MQ was a lot lower than I supposed.

"Suspect number two, Frank," continued Maggie.

"No," I said. "Really, such a long time ago, surely he doesn't count?" Although his MQ was at least quite high, subsequent boyfriends had shown a marked depreciation over the years. "I'd call him a present friend rather than an ex-boyfriend."

"They all count," she said firmly. "How long ago, how long for?"

"Second year of college, early nineties, for about eighteen months, a couple of years maybe."

"Long enough to gestate. Twice."

"But we didn't. Only stagnate and realize that we were always going to be better off as friends than lovers." This was true, though there was that little part of both of us I liked to believe felt we could do a lot worse than end up with one another in our late thirties. "I don't think he's my cyber-stalker. He is besotted with Camilla."

"I do think people should have arranged relationships," said Maggie. "But arranged by their friends. I'm sure we'd do a lot better for him than her. She's so Gwyneth, isn't she?"

"I think Frank's always favored those ethereal, barely-there girl looks. I think I was too fleshy, too earthy for him. He always used to clutch my thighs with the surprised look of a bachelor left holding a baby, like he couldn't comprehend these rolls of fat. I was a chunky statue; he wanted a mere sketch of a girl, a watercolor woman."

"Vapid."

"Yes," I said smugly, Camilla-bashing being one of my favorite games. "Straight hair, straight legs, straight attitudes. I really can't see him holding a candle for me. I can't even see him holding a bike light."

"You were a good couple though," said Maggie. "The four of us had a laugh together. Why did you chuck him?"

"I didn't chuck him."

"That's what he says."

"It suits Frank's doomed romanticism to think that, but it's not true. I always thought we'd get back together at a later date anyway, but I think he's in it for the long haul with Camilla. Which means he's not our cyber-man."

"But now I think of it, he was definitely at Hot Bob's party, wasn't he?"

"He's in the photo."

"Exactly, that would explain how it came to be in his possession, wouldn't it?"

"George was there too. I think. Free booze and all that."

"Aha. Two very likely suspects. Who next? Spanish Artist?"

"Or Foreign Correspondent or Married Man or Toyboy?"

"You have gone out with a lot of nouns, not names."

It's true. Do I go out with caricatures or do I caricature those who I go out with? "I do it for you, Maggie. Where would you be without my sexual shenanigans? You'd never have stuck with Mick all these years if you hadn't been able to live vicariously through my anecdotes. Or should I say anecdates? Romantic incidents experienced purely for the benefit of being able to turn them into a good story for you."

Maggie laughed. "I do think I've had more pleasure from some of your stories than you got from the sex itself."

"Undoubtedly," I replied sadly.

"Speaking of which, let's get on with the list." She was irritatingly gleeful. "What was Picasso's name, then? San Miguel or something?"

"Pepe," I corrected. "My little Pepito. He was small of stature."

"I knew it was the name of a drink. What about him? I did an episode once where the baddie was a Spaniard. Or maybe a Colombian, something like that. We got lots of viewer complaints about it afterward, though, saying it promoted the idea that all Hispanic people are drug dealers. Still, doesn't mean it can't be your Pepe."

"Pepito, no, I can't see it. His English was a bit rubbish for starters."

Maggie reread the text on the screen. "But don't you think the prose style of this is exactly like somebody who's learned their English from bad pop songs? 'Izobel rocks her world,' can't you just hear that in a Continental accent? I don't think it's enough to dismiss him."

"He was playing around with electronic art and installations and stuff when we were going out. Last time I heard of him, he'd gone back to Barcelona on yet another obscure artistic scholarship."

"He was funny, wasn't he? What was his full name?"

"Pepe or Pepito Gomez Gomez."

"So good they named him twice. Just his name alone is hilarious."

"That's the joy of funny foreign boyfriends. Every incident's an anecdote. Ah, the paint-splattered sex, the Spanish-intonated orgasms, the Kennington squat. And the fact that he had green teeth and bones due to some bizarre TB-related calcium deficiency that his peasant mother suffered in the time of Franco."

"Love it. He's *so* a possibility then, especially with what you're telling me about him doing electronic installations. Surely this is just the sort of postmodern rubbish he'd come up with."

"I can't see it." I really wasn't sure that any of my exes had even loved me at the time, let alone were composing computerized paeans to me years on. "I doubt it. We had what he referred to as a '*relación abierta,*' an open relationship. It sounds better in Spanish, less car keys and seventies, but whatever way you look at it, it was license for him to shag every art-school floozy who dribbled paint and saliva in his direction."

I could barely remember what he looked like, only those devilish jade-colored teeth and the fact that he'd say words like *"cojones"* a lot, which gave the sordidness an exotic glamour. "If

Pepito was going to build a site, it would be to all the girls he's loved before, not to just one of them. Least of all me."

"I like it, a sort of Tracey Emin's tent crossed with Julio Iglesias crossed with the Internet. Perhaps he's doing that and yours is just one in a sequence of electronic installations to all his lovers. I'm putting him on the list. I think you should Google him and see if he's still doing cyber-stuff. It's the best lead we've got so far. Virtual art."

"Virtual arse more like."

"I am trying to help you, Izobel," she said sternly and then did that stomach-rubbing thing again, as if to emphasize her emotional maturity. "Where's the Foreign Correspondent these days?"

"Wherever war and pestilence lurk."

"Does he merely follow misery or actually bring it with him?"

"I don't know. Either way you'd fear for your life if he ever rocked into your neighborhood press club."

"And Married Man?"

"MM is still MD, though no longer of my heart. I'll find out what he's up to as he's about the only one of them who'd have the finances to do my site. Though I can't see a motive."

She sat up with a jolt and exhaled as if baby Maggie-Mick had just given her a penalty shoot-out winning kick. "Of course, what about Elliot?"

Elliot Edwards. He was someone who wouldn't be at all shocked to Google himself and find that there was a site devoted to him. In fact, there are dozens. The sort of fans he collected would be just the sort to do fan sites. That's what comes of having a certain obscure (or at least it had seemed to me when we were together) nerdish charm and presenting a television program in which contestants played outsize versions of board games with deviant twists (Snakes and Ladders with real vipers, Scrabble with scrambling, Monopoly with the chance of a night in Mayfair or the threat of a spell in a cell).

"I think he's probably too busy answering all the fan queries on his own sites to worry about creating one for me, don't you?" I replied.

Elliot Edwards, now there was someone whose MQ shot up dramatically after the time we were together. One minute he was the lowly runner in an independent TV production company, the next he was the man behind the format for *Board Stupid* and then the man in front of it (or a giant replica of Dungeons and Dragons cutouts, as the case may be). He was one of those people I prided myself on fancying, thinking that his attraction was far too quirky for normal girls to get and only someone of my kooky tastes would ever favor. Then tarnation, it appeared that all girls think like that and every one of them loves a nerd. My nerd to be precise. I'm always reading about him in articles about unlikely sex symbols. And if I hadn't dumped him then maybe I'd be "the lucky lady who'd bagged Britain's favorite geek." Girls would envy me, people from my past would gasp as they saw me pictured at premieres in long slinky dresses slashed up to the thigh. I'd attend launches without having to organize them myself. I might even have to hire my own PR person . . .

"Yes," replied Maggie, interrupting my reverie. "But it would be ironic if all this groupie adulation had left Elliot feeling bereft and more adoring of you than ever."

Another snort of objection from me.

"Or that because he has fan sites of his own, he wanted to reverse that and place the burden of being fanned onto somebody else, the hunted becomes the hunter type of thing. The way that some celebrities take photos of the paparazzi."

"It's a theory."

"Which is all we've got so far. Anybody else?"

I trawled the mental filing cabinet of scrap that was my previous loves. "William."

"How could I forget? He's super-weird."

"And wired, both drugs and computer-wise."

"Yes, he is. He might be shooting straight to the top of our hit parade."

"Again, not happy with the use of the word 'hit,' Mags."

She ignored me. "What's he up to?"

"The usual—living off his trust fund, playing computer games, taking drugs, living in an expensive mews house. I think he's still nominally doing that PhD in medieval philosophy of science or whatever it was."

"You do pick them."

"Ah, the self-satisfaction of the cozily coupled-up. You have no idea what it's like out there, Maggie."

She laughed, in a frankly self-satisfied way. "Let's recap. George, still number one. It sounds incongruous, I grant you, but love does strange things to people and he does drink too much."

"He can take it."

"Yes, of course."

"He doesn't have a problem."

"What's that," George said on coming through to the living room.

"Izobel doesn't think you've got a drink problem."

"No, of course not, I live right next door to the off-license." Chuckling at his own joke, he retreated to the kitchen once more. Maggie snorted and looked back to her list in disgust.

"Number one suspect, the man without a drink problem, George. Number two has to be William. He's weird, he's wired, he's loaded. Number three Pepito, he's interested in computer art and he's got green teeth, which is kooky. Then Elliot, it's a nice theory and would make the best drama, but I'm not convinced that he sees anything beyond himself these days. Foreign Correspondent and Married Man, search me, I never met the latter anyway, but maybe they're in the running. And lastly, Frank. It does seem most unlikely, although that probably means he's the guilty one."

"Life doesn't follow the precepts of TV drama, Maggie."

"Oh, but it does. It does."

"What now though, Ms. Director? How do I follow this up?" I asked. I now knew how actors feel when they complain of feeling like a powerless cipher for somebody else's vision.

"We investigate our suspects. We Google them, we get in touch with them, we ask them what they're up to, pick up some clues. Have a think about boyfriends you had at school too or anybody else you've been involved with. I mean, you're not seriously telling me that you've only been out with seven men. Then you need to meet up with them and see how they react when you probe them. Find out about their Internet usage and see if they react differently or behave oddly when you do. Also, give them a piece of false information."

"Like what?"

"Something untrue so that only they will think it. Like you're a hermaphrodite or you're pregnant or something. A different piece of information each. Then if it appears on the site, we'll know who's behind it."

"We should also try to get a guest list for Hot Bob's party. That might narrow it down a bit too."

"Will that be shorter than the list of men you've shagged?"

"Ha, ha."

"No, seriously, that's a good idea."

"Thanks. What about school boyfriends? I didn't sleep with any of them."

"Really?"

"It was a long time ago; we grew up later in the country. We were still making wedding veils for our Barbies out of loo paper when I was fifteen." I had always been intimidated by Maggie's tales of clubbing at fourteen and moving in with a boyfriend three years after that. She got it all out of the way quickly, I suppose.

"You don't have to have had sex with them for them to be a suspect, in fact quite the contrary. List thc possible school perps. Smart thinking, partner."

Junior partner, I presumed, the rookie cop to her seasoned maverick of a detective.

"Here we go. What do you want?" Maggie asked of George as he came back into the sitting room.

"To see my girlfriend," he replied and rather flamboyantly groped me.

"Can't you see we're busy?" she snapped.

I wriggled away to the kitchen, leaving them to stew as I marinated chicken breasts and the ideas that Maggie had planted in my head.

Chapter Four

I couldn't face calling up exes, even those who were currently friends like Frank, so I began with George. He seemed a fairly unlikely prospect and one whose movements were as predictable as a daytime soap, with all the shouting and sexual shenanigans included.

Fridays, for example, always followed the same pattern. Having finalized the weekly section he edited (or "put to bed" in journalese; all their parlance seemed to involve sexual metaphors, talk of straps, heads and body copy), he'd go for lunch with his cohorts. The more his newspaper churned out right-wing, anti-drug and moralistic stories, the more he and his colleagues would indulge in all the vices most berated. While the paper raged against asylum seekers, George would score narcotics off illegal immigrants. As female family lawyers wrote of how women are to blame for high divorce rates, the paper would house their adulterous husbands as columnists. Every detox diet displayed was displaced in the offices by the real-life re-toxing of its inhabitants.

Playtime at the newspaper's offices was the laws of the school playground revived. Cocaine had replaced sherbet, and sex in the disabled toilets was in lieu of kiss chase, but there still existed the cool gang (those in features, the columnists and the critics) and the bullied (subs, work-experience girls and admin support staff).

George was in the former and didn't he know it. The disdain which they held for anyone in life who had to pay for restaurants, holidays or toiletries was comparable to an aristocrat's snobbery about anyone who had bought rather than inherited their furniture. The arrogance of George and his entourage masked their jealousy that others could afford to buy what they had to beg for as freebies. And just how useful was a new lipstick-fixing formula to George anyway, other than as a free present to offload onto me on my birthday?

I bunked off work the following Friday, pretending to be visiting clients, in order to get to the paper's offices at lunchtime. I knew he'd be off by 12:30 and was buzzed up from reception by his long-suffering assistant.

"He's not here at the moment," Hettie told me. "Surely you know that by now, Izobel?"

"How stupid of me." I made mock "duh" gestures and slapped my forehead. "You'd think I'd have realized. Damn, how annoying, I need something off his computer, an e-mail he's got with an address on it. What do you think I should do, get him back here or just have a delve round the electronic underwear drawer that is his in-box?"

Hettie laughed. "Do me a favor. Get George back from Friday lunch? He'll have his lips superglued to a martini by now. If I were you, I'd just have a recce round the virtual pants."

Correct answer. I settled myself at George's desk, banking on the fact that he'd be too drunk to question Hettie's tales of my e-mail quarrying by the time he'd got back from his quaffing. I didn't know his passwords so prayed he'd left his computer on in an attempt to make it look like he had at least some intention of returning to work that afternoon. I clicked the mouse and the PC awoke from its sleep, a slumbering cat. Bingo.

First I looked in his e-mail in-box. For what, I wasn't sure. I scrolled through, attempting to look nonchalant yet investigative.

"I'm going for my own lunch now," said Hettie. "Somewhat more modest than my boss's. Are you happy being left here in the corner?"

"Fine, thanks."

The proportion of work to play e-mails seemed to be about one to five. A few desultory ones sent out to chase freelancers' copy, but most were the usual selection of sick round robins, the fixing of pub meetings and scraps of gossip. I started reading all the ones from Catherine, his ex-wife, but realized after a few that they were concerned with child-care arrangements rather than amorous assignations behind my back. There was, though, a defiantly flirty tone to them.

I looked in his e-mail folders directory. No folders at all. His electronic filing was no better than his real-world or emotional variety: all tangled, tortured, torn. I don't know what I had expected, some discreet folder entitled "Izobel's tribute site" with neatly filed correspondence with whoever had created the site on his behalf?

I used the e-mail search functionality and typed in "Izobel." Nothing came up. It seemed that, if he ever mentioned me in e-mails at all, he would not refer to me by my name.

I gave up on the in-box and opened up Internet Explorer to see what sort of sites he viewed. His home page was the Media Guardian. How I loathed the self-referential nature of those working in the media, myself included. I'm sure I saw more column inches about the way that wars are reported than on any war itself. I went to his Favorites list. Again it was a jumble of unfiled and defiling detritus, a commonplace book of new media trivia—a gossip chat room, a games site, mild porn, photos of him taken at a restaurant launch, and various e-zines and online newspapers. I scrolled my way down it to see if www.izobelbrannigan.com had at least joined these far-from-illustrious colleagues. Again, nothing.

I gave it my last shot and began to type the letters into the address bar at the top of the page. One of George's colleagues gave me a slimy smile from across the desk, which I returned as wholeheartedly as I could muster. A random girl hacking into one of the paper's computers seemed to be no cause for alarm.

Into the address bar on the top of the Internet page, I typed an "i" and various permutations of ITV and ITN popped into the previously accessed list of sites that unfurled themselves below the bar, but no izobelbrannigan. This indicated that he didn't go into my site with any frequency, otherwise it would have popped up to join them. I typed "iz" and then the "o" and then the "b." Nothing. This, I presumed, meant two things. First, that he was probably not the instigator of the site, given that he could barely be bothered to look at it. Second, that he didn't give a monkey's about it anyway, not even to have a laugh with his workie friends: clearly it wasn't anecdote-worthy. He didn't even glance at the site at his desk.

I went to "Tools" and "Internet Options." How long did sites remain in his Internet history, I wondered? If it was only a day, then it was possible he had looked at my site yesterday and the day before that. There it was: "The History Folder contains links to pages you've visited, for quick access to recently viewed pages. Days to keep pages in history: 10." Ten days? George hadn't looked at the site for ten bloody days. I wasn't part of his history; was I even part of his present? I counted back. It was about a fortnight since he told me the site was down; the chances were that this was the last time he had bothered accessing my site, my lovely, lavish, beautifully designed site. The tribute to me and my uniqueness and my celebrity in the eyes of one.

Yes, I thought to report back to Maggie, it was unlikely that George was my man.

I was just about to start rummaging round his nonvirtual drawers when my mobile went. It was Mimi from the office.

"Are you monged or something, babe? You've got three boffs in here who say they've got a meeting with you, Candida and Amanda or something."

"Shit, I'd forgotten. Tell them I'll be over in fifteen."

"All right then, doll, laters."

In my excitement at being PR-girl-turned-PI it had slipped my probing mind that Camilla had bullied me into having a meeting to discuss free PR for her new business venture. Ironically, the proposition was something to do with the Internet. I felt that the World Wide Web had truly caught me in its sticky threads. What did I know about PR for the Web anyway? This was always happening, me being viewed by amateurs as a PR guru, when all I could offer them was a bit of common sense and ridiculous costs. Still, I reasoned, I could continue with some detective work on Frank via his girlfriend.

I scooted back to the office with the continual sense of being watched. But then, I'm the sort of self-conscious person who always feels as though I'm in a film or being described in the narrative of the type of novel with embossed lettering on its cover. I have a particularly bad habit of imagining being photographed for one of those articles about what real people are wearing every time I get dressed. For this reason, I can never wear more than one item from the same shop at the same time and always try to include some very costly designer item to "lift" the cheap rest of the ensemble.

Camilla looked as imperious as ever in the office reception area, her yoga-bendy body contrasting with her pointy, precision mind. She was even carrying a Psion in one hand and a yoga mat in the other, as if posing for a feature about women who juggle the spiritual and the professional. She was flicking through one of the glossy magazines that lay shiny face up in the foyer. Beside her and looking eagerly over her shoulder to the pages of the magazine were two girls. They were dressed similarly to Camilla, but their clothes were of decreasing expense and in each case more faded than the last, so that the second one resembled a bad photocopy of the willowy blonde beside her, while the third was so muted as to be a photocopy of a photocopy, where all that had once been sharp and bright was obliterated. She was the sort of person who could commit a crime and no one would be able to create the photofit of her afterward, so unmemorable was her face.

"So sorry I'm late."

"That's OK," said Camilla, which was gracious of her given that I was offering my time for free. "I'm pretty busy with all my projects, but Becksy and Alice are still working full time, so it would be good if our lunchtime meetings could start promptly. Thanks." She brandished the glossy magazine. "We need a piece about us in one of these. Can you do that?"

"That is, I'm afraid, the holy grail of PR, the Herculean task of PR, the glass mountain being climbed in slippers of PR . . ."

"All right, all right, I get the picture. But, like, how hard can it be?"

I ignored her and introduced myself to the girls, Becksy and Alice, I presumed.

"They know who you are," said Camilla. "They were at school with us too. Don't you remember anything? We were rather renowned as the St. Tree's Tasties."

"I'm sorry. You were a couple of years younger, I think," I said to Becksy and Alice.

"Three actually," Camilla corrected to giggles from her acolytes. "There's a whole gang of us Tasties working on the business in fact. It's just like old times."

"I'm not really in touch with people from school," I said. I wondered why; was it because I thought I was above their provincial ways or that I had not reached high enough?

"Ahhh," the three of them said with one voice. "How sad."

I jostled them into a meeting room and determinedly didn't offer them anything to drink. From the lofty Camilla downward, they were smaller versions of one another, like a set of Russian babushka dolls.

"Have you got any green tea?" Camilla asked almost immediately.

"We love green tea," said the medium-size Camilla doll.

I ignored them. "Right, why don't you three tell me about your Internet service, what it is and what your roles are. Then I can give you a few ideas about what PR you could get and how you'd go about it. All right?"

They concurred.

"OK, so tell me about the thing then."

"It's an Internet dating service with a difference. It's going to be huge," said Camilla.

"Gynormous," said middling girl.

"I thought all that sort of thing was over, that it was all dot gone not dot com these days."

"Not in the dating sector, and not with our agency. In New York, Internet dating is massive and it's growing here," Camilla spieled. "The stigma has completely gone these days, there's nothing sad about logging on and loving in."

"It's cool," said Camilla's echo.

I shivered. "I don't know, seems a bit creepy to me, finding love online. You never know who's out there."

Camilla sighed. "That's why people need us, to vet and match people accordingly."

"Would you use an online dating agency?" I asked her. "What about Frank? Does he use the Internet much? Does he ever, like, I don't know, create Web sites in honor of you or something?"

She looked offended. She was chary of me as an ex and I of

her as a present. "That would be nice of him. I'll have to suggest it. However, I can't see either of us using an online dating service. I mean, we're hardly the sort of people that need to."

At that moment the mouse beside her roared, or at least spoke.

"I would," said Alice or Becksy. I didn't know which, the very smallest one anyway. "I think it's brilliant. We will make people happy. We'll get invited to their weddings. We will change lives off-line by what happens online."

I smiled at her. "So, what do you think is so special about your site? What makes it different from the other ones out there?"

Camilla interjected, "It's a dating service with a difference." My God, would she leave it with the sloganeering. "Most online matchmaking services just ask really boring questions about user requirements, but we match people up using whichever criteria they prefer including height, horoscopes, hobbies et cetera. You choose which criteria are important to you. That's new. Loads of girls are obsessed with height, some with money, some with status, some with looks—it's up to you which one you emphasize in your search."

"How do you decide how good-looking someone is?"

"We don't. The other punters do—it's like that Web site 'Hot or Not.' The users give the other users a looks rating out of ten and we collate their scores. Then we can match the hottest with the other hotties."

"How Darwinian."

"Absolutely, though many of them will be unattractive, I'm sure."

"You." I turned again to little one. "What do you think is the big selling factor?"

"Ask me, I'm the figurehead and marketeer," interrupted Camilla once more. "She does all the technical stuff. I'm the spokesperson."

"In new-media-speak we say," said Alice, "that I'm back-end and they're front-end."

"Like a pantomime horse," I observed, to which Alice and Becksy whinnied and Camilla gave her equine laugh.

We droned on for a while, with me having absolutely no intention of doing any free PR for their site and Camilla convinced that it was my patriotic duty to get it a plug in a broadsheet. I was more concerned with interrogating Camilla about her boyfriend's Internet usage.

"Does Frank have an Internet connection at home?" I asked. "George is completely hopeless with anything new-media or newfangled. Is Frank any better?"

"Of course. He's an intellectual, he needs access to other thinkers."

"Do you have fun playing around on it? Is Frank any good at making Web sites as well as accessing them?"

"Frank is brilliant at whatever he chooses to do. Why the interest?"

"Nothing."

It was going nowhere. I knew that I would have to get it straight from the other horse's mouth. I felt very tired and attempted to wrap up our meeting.

"It's really nice to see you again after so long," said Alice in her third sentence of the meeting.

"Oh right, yes, strange, four of us all from the same school in a work situation together. Probably very normal for old Etonians in Conservative Central Office, but doesn't happen to me much. Do you remember me, then?" I tried to be nonchalant, but I was shamefully pleased by the idea of meeting someone who remembered me rather than the other way round.

"You were funny," said Becksy. I decided not to take a woman who still went by her schoolgirl nickname very seriously. Nor one who still hung around in a big girly gang. "Political and stuff."

"Yes, you were. We were a bit surprised," Alice added, "to find you doing this." She lifted her head to glance through the horn-rimmed glasses that slithered down her pointed nose at the framed magazine covers and outsize lilies gracing our meeting rooms. "If you'd said to me then that in fifteen years you'd be doing PR, I'd have assumed it stood for proportional representation."

"I started out doing press for Amnesty actually," I batted. "It's not my fault you need a trust fund in order to work in the charity sector. The wages are so low."

"I'm still surprised to see you so changed. Camilla hasn't changed so much."

"We haven't changed at all," giggled Becksy.

Alice continued. "You were so impassioned. Are you passionate about the politics of heel sizes now?"

If we were still at school, I'd be whopping her in detention at this point. Well, I would be had I been a prefect, but I was seen as too anti-establishment for such giddy responsibilities. Who were these horrid little girls coming in here to sneer at me and my life?

"I do a lot of voluntary work outside of the office," I lied. It really mattered to me not to disillusion my own remembered schoolgirl self nor anyone else who might recall me from that time. I did not want anybody at all to think the worst of me; that was my prerogative.

"Really." Alice was wide-eyed behind those distorting lenses. "Like what?"

I was saved by Camilla, something I never thought would happen. "Is this really relevant? We're discussing our product, not the halcyon days of St. Tree's. Are you going to get us into one of the monthlies, then?"

Becksy giggled at the use of the word "monthlies" in a non-menstrual context and I got back to drawing up a battle plan that could be used in the phony war of PR. I showed them out into the reception area, womanned by a temp in an inappropriate piece of nightwear that fell off one shoulder. She was showing the sort of flesh normally sported by soap starlets on red carpets, to the indifference of the IT systems administrator who was asking her about server room temperatures.

"Who's he?" whispered Alice, pointing at the departing figure of the technical guy, who was only ever flirted with in the disastrous situation of our e-mail network going down.

"He's scrummy," said Becksy.

"Him?" I queried. "He's just the systems bloke. Dan the IT man."

"He's very attractive-looking," said Alice.

"A bit gorgeous," said Becksy.

I grimaced. "But he's a techie."

Chapter Five

Techie, technical, tech, detective, de-*tech*-tive.

That's it. I needed someone technical to help me in my search for cyber-stalker. Maggie was all very well with her in-depth knowledge of the conventions of TV thrillers, but there had to be a more robustly mechanical approach to finding out who was behind the site. For all I knew there was a great big telephone book listing who owns every site in the whole wide world.

I thought about Dan the IT man. I didn't know him; I couldn't ask him. Far too embarrassing. I flipped through my e-mail contacts list. Most of them hadn't yet worked out how to use Video Plus, let alone anything about computer systems. Java for us was old-fashioned slang for coffee, rather than a script for making Web sites; wireless was something that blared out Radio Four. Microsoft Office was as high-tech as it got. Camilla was the only person I'd ever met with a Palm Pilot.

When we were at school, computers were just coming onto the curriculum. Unwieldy monsters with the memory of an Alzheimer's victim and funny green screens that flickered into life by the typing of dyslexic command languages with lots of full stops. How we laughed at the people who were into them, the boys in the next-door grammar who had started their own computer club in a bid to meet girls. The only girls at school who were into computers were super-spods with boys' haircuts, shapeless cords and Guernsey sweaters. We picked our boys' school counterparts via the debating and drama clubs.

The laugh was on us now, I had to concede, as those spods and boffins had made a mint with their software companies and contract work at a thousand pounds a day. Oh to have been that square, I thought.

Oh to have at least one friend among them, I also thought, now that I needed a geek with the first idea about how the Internet worked. Alice, perhaps; hadn't she just said she was "back-end"? What did that mean, apart from sounding rude? No, not Alice, she'd tell Camilla and Camilla would tell Frank and one of my suspects would be tipped off. Too embarrassing, that Camilla should know about the site. I could imagine her having a real laugh about it. Her and Frank in bed together, giggling at my hubristic reaction to the site, speculating that I might be behind it myself.

And lo, my mobile went and Frank's name flashed up on the screen. I did that mobile telephone walk, the one where you slink away from the desk or restaurant table, with a lopsided gait and your phone glued to one ear, speaking in an exaggeratedly hushing voice as you shuffle toward privacy in the most public of fashions. I would eliminate Frank from Maggie's list, there and then, but I didn't want my colleagues to hear of it.

"Just phoning to check that you and Camilla are making good progress." He never used to speak like a lecturer, but now he always seemed to be orating.

"And Becksy and Alice, they came too," I said.

"Yes, Camilla's gang. Of course, I'm pleased that she has so many friends, but they seem to multiply like fruit flies. Becksy, Megsy . . ."

"Mopsy, Topsy and Turvy."

Frank laughed, but these days it was as if he was practicing the function and tape-recording it to play back to examine its effect. "Are you going to get them and their venture into the *Observer* this Sunday, then?"

I tried a tinkly laugh of my own to deflect him. "It's interesting, this Internet stuff," I said. "Do you use the Internet much? For research and things?"

"Too unreliable most of the time. I've got subscriptions to periodicals that I can get online. That's quite useful." He ricocheted back to Camilla's godawful venture once again. "Tell me what you've got planned for my baby's baby? I'm rather hoping she'll make millions and I can retire to a book-lined study on the proceeds."

"I haven't got a concrete plan, yet," I said with an effort at sagacity. "With PR we like to start at first principles and really analyze the proposition."

He laughed once more. Ha, ha, I thought, Mr. Clever Clogs Academic, have a good old guffaw at my fluffy little profession. "No, really," I continued. "We need to think about how people use the Internet and how best to get them to think about dating online. To do this I'm going to do some informal focus-grouping on how people view the Internet. A bit of brainstorming on the emotional resonance of computers. For instance, the television is seen as the friend in the corner of the living room, but what about the connected PC? Is it malevolent, a place of kiddie porn? Or is it something associated with work and so unfriendly? What do you think, Frank?"

"It's just a tool. It's not the medium that counts but the information it conveys. That's true throughout history. Is the radio responsible for Lord Haw-Haw's addresses? Can we blame Gutenberg for *Mein Kampf*?"

"No, you're right, yes absolutely, interesting point." Lord, but he was pompous these days. "But you're referring to a passive user experience, what you find on the Internet. How would you use it to create something? You know, to engage with it more actively. Because, when you think about it, that's what Camilla's lonely hearts will have to do. They're not just looking at a Web site, they'll also be creating their profiles, doing quizzes and getting in touch with other, what do you call them?"

"OnLovers. That's what the site's users will be called. Clever, isn't it?"

"Very. So these OnLovers will have to be willing to use the Web both passively and actively. Have you ever created a site or contributed to a message board, Frank? Would you, for example, ever create a tribute site to a writer or person you found particularly inspiring?"

"Theoretically yes. But, practically? That would be a no." He paused and whistled. "Izobel, I can tell when you're bullshitting. You must be a crap PR person."

"Thanks Frank, you're really making me feel good about my career."

"What. Do. You. Want. To. Know. And. Why. Are. You. Asking?"

I opted for partial revelation. In the striptease of honesty, I was going down to my bra and pants. "I've found a Web site, it's nothing important, but it just says some things about, well, about me and I'm trying to find out who could possibly be behind them."

I might as well have accused him of online bestiality. "What, and you think it could be me?"

"No, of course not. I'm just eliminating you from my inquiries."

"I am eliminated. I should never have been a part of them," he harrumphed. "What on earth are you suggesting, Izobel, that I'm libeling you online?"

"No, of course not. I know it's silly, it's just that Maggie has drawn up a list of suspects and it has to include all boyfriends and exes. She's daft, must be preg-head or something, but I said I'd talk to everyone on it, just to make sure."

"Funnily enough, Izobel, it's not the first way I define myself. As one of your exes. I think of myself as many things, but not as that." His voice was flat but aggressive, the voice I use only with strangers at call centers when I'm trying to get a refund on a train ticket. "I find it somewhat disconcerting that you should do. I'm sorry, Izobel"—stop using my name, I thought—"but it was a long time ago for a very short while. Let it go, Izobel."

"Piss off, Frank. I don't think of myself as one of your exes either."

"Doesn't seem so. Izobel, I've got a girlfriend now, I love Camilla very much. I'm sorry that you don't seem to feel the same way about George."

"Yes, I do, I love him very much. We're terribly in love. Totally in love. We have an amazing sex life actually. He's the best thing that's ever happened to me. Better than anyone I've ever been out with."

"Stop accusing me of obsessing over you then."

"I didn't. I didn't say you were my stalker or anything."

"Writing things about you on Web sites? It appears that you do. If anyone's doing any stalking around here, it would be you, Izobel. I could accuse you of stalking me."

"All right, you're right, absolutely, yes, totally, sorry. By the way," I gabbled, sensing that he was on the verge of de-mobbing the mobile. I looked around for inspiration and found it in the restaurant across the street. "I'm learning Chinese. Yes, I'm learning Chinese. Did I tell you? I'm really good at it, actually. My teacher says I'm up to intermediate standard already."

"What are you on?"

"Book three of the course already."

"No, not that. Why are you telling me?"

"Just thought you'd want to know."

"I'm very pleased for you, Izobel."

With that, my phone fell into silence. It was then it struck me as strange that he never asked me what things about me were said on the Web or which site I was talking about.

I made use of the fact that I was outside to phone Maggie. Really, it's a wonder I manage to get any work done.

"I can't go on," I wailed.

"Neither can I. Blooming my arse, blooming horrible pregnancy. Although actually my arse is blooming, expanding at the rate of a bun in the oven, all yeasty and doughy and mottled. Looks like a cauliflower. Why don't I have one of those neat forward bumps like a model with a football up her sweater? That's what I'm used to whenever a pregnancy storyline is called for."

Of course, this was all rubbish. Maggie looked like a snake that had swallowed a small rodent, all skinny with a slight tummy protrusion. I could swear her stomach was still flatter than mine. Some reassurance later and I got back onto the topic of me, me and my site.

"It's hopeless, this isn't working. If I ask men straight out whether they're behind it they accuse me of stalking them. The guilty one is just going to deny it, assuming that it is one of my exes at all, which I doubt, given that none of them seemed to give a monkey's about me even then and certainly not now."

"How many have you investigated?" she asked, putting on TV tec voice once again.

"Two, George and Frank."

"Well?"

"We can categorically rule George out. I hacked into his computer." The use of the verb "to hack" was clearly erroneous but I liked the sound of it. Made me sound like Matthew Broderick in

War Games. "And the site's not even in his favorites. There's nothing about it in his e-mails and he hasn't even viewed it for ten days."

"Hmm, that would be a good decoy though, wouldn't it?" said Maggie.

"I can't win. If there's absolutely no evidence, you say it's a good decoy. Can't we take people at face value? Does there always have to be a plot twist? By your reckoning, the only way we can eliminate is by actually finding proof positive. It's like when I suspect George is sleeping around. His denials are meaningless. I almost think to find out that he's definitely unfaithful would be a relief as then at least I'd know for sure. And you only feel you know for sure if it's bad news."

"Has George been unfaithful to you, Iz?"

Shit, I'd forgotten that was another of the secrets of my relationship I kept from my friends. "The point is, the only answer to my interrogations that is going to mean anything as far as your plot goes is for them to crumble and say, 'Yes, yes, it was me.' "

"No," she interjected. "Because that person would probably turn out to be covering for the real culprit."

"Either way, I'm stuck because the person responsible is the very last person who'd just come out and admit to it. We know that the whole MO of the person behind the site is one of subterfuge, isn't it?"

"True," she replied. "I am only trying to help you."

"I know. Thank you." At that moment I saw Dan the IT man emerge from the front door of the office. "Maggie, we've got to try a different tack." I said to her. "A simultaneous tack. I'm getting a technical detective to work on this too."

"Good thinking," she said with an aggrieved tone.

I cut through the swaths of huddled smokers crouched around the entrance of our office building, like the supplicant poor man at the biblical gate, to get to my man.

"Dan, Dan," I shouted. He was ignoring me. Arse. I caught up with him and tapped his shoulder.

"Hello, Dan, I'm sorry to bother you, but may I have a minute of your time?"

"Of course you may, but my name's not Dan. Does that make a difference to your request, Izobel?"

"Oh gosh I'm so sorry, how very silly of me." I slapped my head and then segued the gesture into the twiddling of a lock of hair. From what I'd seen of the office manager's dealings with the IT support staff, technical people required some outrageously mechanical flirtation. "Gosh, what an airhead I am. One day I'll forget to get dressed in the morning and come into work completely naked."

He looked skeptical. "My name is Ivan."

Ivan, of course, IT Ivan or Ivan the IT man. That was his name, though one of the assistants called him it-boy on account of him being passably attractive. For a techie.

"Ivan, yes, of course. Ivan, can I buy you a coffee?"

He glanced at his watch. "I've got fifteen minutes between appointments. I need to get over to one of my other clients."

"I thought you just worked at our office."

He looked like it was his turn to hit my forehead in a "duh" move. "PR O'Create wouldn't keep me in chewing gum; my business services about forty companies that size."

"Oh, I see." I feigned interest as we walked to the incongruously greasy spoon that nestled amid the chains of latte purveyors lately embedded in the West End. "What does your business do exactly, Ivan?"

"Systems administration."

Two such dull words, like "mechanical engineering" or "natural sciences." "Really, how interesting. What does that mean?"

"My company makes sure computer systems run efficiently—

we install hardware and software, solve problems, make sure there's appropriate server capacity. That sort of thing." He raised an eyebrow. "You probably think that sounds terminally dull . . ."

"Terminal dull," I attempted to quip.

"But without me, well, me and my team, you wouldn't be able to e-mail or look at the Internet and you'd all be up in arms."

"You're absolutely vital, I can see that." We ordered our teas, both black with sugar. "What do you know about the Internet?"

"What do you know about public relations?"

"Not a lot actually. I see what you mean, that is a bit of a big question, isn't it?"

He grinned. "Well, it's not exactly 'is there a God?' and 'what are we here for?' but yes, it's a difficult one to answer. Can you be more specific?"

"Say there's a Web site on the Net. What would you be able to tell about its creator from its address?"

"What sort of things?"

"Could you find out a name of the person who owned the Web site or where they lived or anything?"

"I could find the DNS servers in Whois and from that the ISP and then maybe a registered name. Or another route would be via the IP address I suppose. Yes, either, although there are no guarantees that it wouldn't be registered under a false name or business name once you'd got there."

"Stop, stop, too many TLAs," I said. "Three-letter acronyms. I have no idea what you mean by IBS unless you're referring to Irritable Bowel Syndrome."

"ISP," he corrected.

"Isn't that when you're psychic?"

"Internet Service Provider. The people who provide access to the Web for users, but also host the sites themselves."

"If the Internet is a town, these are the landlords," I posited.

"Exactly. And IP stands for Internet Protocol and an IP address is a thirty-two-bit numeric address."

I looked blank again. He looked pained.

"That means it's a binary number of thirty-two digits. But that would be difficult for humans to process, although machines would have no problem with them, so it's expressed in a decimal form with dots separating each bit of what would have been the eight-figure binary number. So you're left with something like two-one-seven dot one-seven-three dot two-six et cetera to identify a particular host on that network. It's called dotted quad notation."

I nodded in a way that I hoped communicated understanding. I was trapped in a BBC Schools Science program and I understood it no better than the ones I saw in fifth year.

"So if you get the IP address of a site," he continued, "you can find out who's hosting the site and that might bring you closer to identifying its owner."

"And the D one, DNA or something?"

"DNS, Domain Name System. You've got your IP addresses, but they're totally unmemorable as they're made up of a series of numbers."

"Like phone numbers?" I asked in an attempt to involve myself in this conversation.

"But with periods in. Domain names are made up of words, lastminute.com or whatever, so they're easier to use. So again, if we find the DNS entry we can get the IP address and then the ISP. Then we might find out who's registered the URL." Ivan looked at his watch. It probably had lots of computer data stored in it or something, or a 3D game that he could play across wristwatch networks. "Look, I'm sorry, Izobel, but I've got to go."

"Right, fine, of course." I must have looked disappointed.

"I'm coming into your offices next week—why don't you show me the site you're interested in and I'll see how I can help?"

I thought for a second. Was IT Ivan really the person I wanted to entrust with the quest for the site perp? "That would be great, thanks so much, Ivan." I gave him one of those flirty smiles again and contrived to move from hair twiddling to a coy wave bye-bye. "I'll show you all then."

What a busy day and none of it work-related. The best sort of day, the one that would go quickest. Now it was the weekend. And next week, my new friend IT Ivan would sort it all out for me. I felt optimistic for the first time in months.

George and I never went out on Friday nights; we were too out of drink-sync by then after his mammoth lunchtime session. I was counting on that to delete any memories of Hettie having told him about my forage through his in-box.

I smiled to myself. I'd done that well. I had eliminated him from our inquiries, whatever Maggie said, and I'd done it with almost professional levels of subterfuge. Now I'd recruited a technical consultant for the investigation. I was good, I was damned good. I swung my handbag in the manner of a sixties starlet trotting down the King's Road and being whistled at by men in MGs. I was hot. If site stalkie person were looking at me now, which wasn't improbable, he'd see that he'd failed to crush me. I was strong.

Chapter Six

The phone by my bed woke George and me the following morning. Through the hiss of a bad connection I could make out a familiar voice.

"It's me, Jonny."

"Jesus, Jonny, where are you calling from? It sounds like you're in Beirut." The line had the romantic snap and crackle of an old telegraph wire. I could imagine the Foreign Correspondent wearing khaki shorts and a linen shirt holding one of those phones that come in two pieces, in a dusty bar with an overhead fan. Conchita the local whore would walk past and offer her services.

"Coming into Paddington . . ." He disappeared again. "We keep going through tunnels."

The romance was quashed. He was annoying. Why did he always do this? Ring when actually in London rather than giving a couple of days' notice? And then expect us all to drop what we were doing and rush to him. He seemed to think that we were those dancing plastic flowers, standing still until he animated us into undulating to his tune.

"You're in London. For how long?"

"I'm only in the UK for a couple of days—what are you doing tonight?"

I knew the score. I'd reorder my life to meet up with him only to find that he'd also arranged to meet seven other people and I'd spend the evening talking to a poor sap who'd been at school with Foreign Correspondent about how exciting Foreign Correspondent's life was and how much we all admired him. Meanwhile Foreign Correspondent would only talk to other foreign correspondents and they'd say things like "Eddie! But I haven't seen him since Tora Bora. Didn't he look fabulous in a burka?" and they'd look disparagingly at us civvies, while we tried to pity them their inability to maintain long-term relationships.

Could Foreign Correspondent be cyber-stalker? This could be my only opportunity to find out.

"I can't see you tonight," I said, perhaps for the first time. "But, look, I can be in Paddington in half an hour. Let's have a coffee somewhere near there." I caught sight of myself in the mirror. I was a sight. "Make that three-quarters of an hour. See you."

"Are you going out?" asked George from beneath the duvet.

"Yes, that was—"

"You couldn't be a darling and nip back with a couple of cans of Coke. No make that a bottle."

"That was Jonny. Just flying in from the Gulf on his way to Korea or something. Now that's journalism, don't you agree?"

George snorted. "The features desk is the new foreign desk. Hasn't he realized that? Nobody cares about newspaper foreign reports in the age of CNN," he said, mummifying himself further in the Egyptian cotton bed linen. "Make it a family-size bottle would you, my poppet."

"Big night?"

"Hardly," he said.

*

At the appointed venue I saw him. He probably did look very dashing at some foreign press club, but here in a London coffee shop he just looked unfashionable. Living abroad for the past decade had contrived to make sure that his wardrobe was preserved in aspic as that of the generic media man circa 1993—black-zipped, mildly blouson leather jacket, chinos, a pale blue denim-appearance shirt and desert boots. This period piece was topped by a floppy fringe that would have been replaced by a number one crop had he been living in London, especially given the state of his hair recession. Two competing entrances of forehead tunneled into his crown. These A-roads were perilously close to meeting and becoming a great big divided highway of baldness across his pate.

The Foreign Correspondent had once said that his eyes had seen too much destruction. I don't know about that, but his skin had seen too much sun. He had the mottled look of a junk-store mirror, as the boyish freckles became full-blown liver spots.

I continued my snapshot full-frontal attack on his appearance. I had to before we spoke; it made me feel better. It was always the same routine on meeting the brave war reporter: shock at his appearance, awe at his glamour. His personality would make you forget the reality of his face and force you to believe that he was every bit as handsome and airbrushed as the byline photograph beneath his articles on the horrors of war.

His teeth were bad, yellowing and withering, with gums eroding like chalk face. I knew this from having studied them before, not from looking at them anew. Today I couldn't muse on his molars because a surgical mask covered his mouth and nose.

"What on earth are you wearing that for?" I asked by way of a greeting.

He glanced around the coffee room and then leaned forward. "Don't tell anyone this, classified info, but there's a virulent virus that's going to explode in Europe. Of course, you may survive it, but I won't have your Western immunity. I'd sooner jump in a pool full of lepers than walk around London with my mask off."

"I thought these diseases all came from the East, not here?" I said, remembering the last really-severe-terrible-chronic syndrome to have infectiously spread through the newspapers' health pages and plagued their leader columns.

"That's what they tell you," he said knowingly.

"You're such a scaredy-pants," I said and sat down, watching his mask stain yellow as he puffed a tab through it, like that school experiment when we had to examine the nicotine left on a tissue by a mechanically smoked cigarette. He kissed me on the cheek, again with mask intact. It was really rather touching, like we were in one of those pioneering HIV films. "You always have been."

"You wouldn't say that if you'd been there at the fall of Kabul," he replied.

I had never been able to reconcile Jonny's swinging-dick professionalism with his cowardy-custard demeanor. He once refused to go for a walk with me as it was drizzling and he had failed to bring any waterproofs. Forget those men who claim to have flu when they've only a cold—with Jonny it was SARS or pneumonia that was causing his nose to dribble. His paranoia extended to contraception over the two years we'd had sex together whenever he stopped over in London and slept over in my bed. It had been hard to enjoy sex while he wore a condom and I wore a diaphram. He used to try to withdraw on time too, just to make certain. How could someone so internationally brave be such a domestic wuss?

"It must have been amazing," I said on cue. "Is the paper pleased with your coverage at the moment? I'm not quite sure where you are right now, though."

"Journalist of the world. I presume the powers-that-be at the paper are pleased. I felt like I colonized a small corner of the foreign pages and I got a few congratulatory e-mails from the editor. The owner knows who I am, too, especially now that I've been nominated for Foreign Correspondent of the Year. Fifth time running, actually."

"That's brilliant."

"Sorry?"

"That's brilliant," I shouted.

"You'll have to enunciate, I'm afraid. Bullet whistled this far from my ear. Gone deaf, you know." Cue much exaggerated cupping of the good one. "The bullet actually whistled. That's not a figure of speech. Bullets whistle."

"Like milkmen."

He chortled and showed me photos of himself in his new state-of-the-art bulletproof ensemble, which made him look like one of those evil riot cops who batter anti-capitalist protesters at G8 summits. I said "wow" a lot.

I had slept with him on and off for all that time, despite the lack of pleasure involved in the layering of contraception and the fact that our relationship would never go anywhere while he was traveling to everywhere. I had been a stationary point while he had moved around me, yet he had been the sun and my life had revolved around his. The sex wasn't great, the emotional succor was nonexistent, he wasn't an Adonis, and yet I had never questioned why I had been prepared to put up with being somebody's fly-by lay, his woman of the connecting-flight night.

"It might sound really brave, Izobel, but when you're out there, you just don't stop to think. I knew I had to go out and get the story and cop whatever was thrown in my direction."

Jonny never looked so pleased as when there were rumors of a good old war about to start.

"You just do what you have to do, really."

"Well done. If you die, though, whose fault is that?"

"The fault of these damn conflicts," he sighed. "It makes me weep to see small children with their legs blown off. And if we have to die to show the world their plight, then we do it in their service. I'm starving." He looked around. "Is bacon all right to eat in Britain these days? Are pigs affected by foot and mouth? Maybe I'd better just have some crisps."

"We do the PR for that brand," I said pointing to the misshapen crisps. "They really do hand-slice the potatoes. But the tomatoes are oven- rather than sun-dried." It was hard for me to compete with his tales of derring-do. He spent his life flying from war zone to war zone; I traveled by London Underground from zone one to zone two.

"How is the wacky world of PR?" he asked.

"Great, fine." I'd always accuse Jonny of not being interested in me, but whenever he did ask me a question I'd find it hard to answer in anything other than monosyllables.

I wanted to say, Do you know I'm a somebody? A somebody with a tribute site and my very own cyber-stalker. There's someone obsessed with me. What do you think about that? You might have seen fighting in Kosovo, but you haven't got your own site, have you? Well, have you?

But I didn't.

"And life with George?" he continued.

"Fine, great."

"I've been thinking." He looked soulfully out into the socially layered streets of Paddington. "There's nothing like hearing the cries of an injured infant against the relentless baseline of nearby bombs to make you think. In Basra, I saw a man lose his whole family. He wept for them and not for the loss of his whole town. What's it all about?"

I made to answer, but it was rhetorical.

"That's what it's about. It's about family. It's about having children. Do you want to have children, Izobel?"

Was he asking me if I wanted children in general or his children? "Maggie's having a baby, did I tell you that? Makes me think, yes, I do want children, a baby, I suppose, one day. I feel like I'm still a bit immature for it, though, that I'd be a gymslip mother and everyone would look at me and say, 'What's that child doing with a child?' and then I remember that I'm in my thirties."

"Yes, you are. And I am two years older than you."

"You always were." We grew up together, which meant that he was forever imbued with the glamour of the older boy. It also ensured that my mother could rebuke me on Sundays by sighing over the newspapers and saying, "Let's see what our successful friend Jonny's up to this week, shall we?"

"We're neither of us teenagers, then." Except we always were. With him I would always be doing my exams and seeking advice from the worldly boy-next-door about which A levels to choose and what university to put down on my university application form.

"You especially," he said. "I was reading an article on the way here about how fertility plummets at twenty-five, not at thirty-five as previously thought. There were lots of quotes from weeping women who'd mistakenly put their career before caring."

"Why are they always 'career women'?" I asked. "Why not just 'women with jobs'?"

"Izzi, Izzi, Izzi. All teenage girls think they won't be the ones to get pregnant and all thirty-something women think they won't be the ones to fail to get pregnant." He shook his head. "You're not getting any younger."

"Nobody is," I replied. Two can play self-evident clichés.

"Least of all George."

That was true. He was pickling away at an even faster rate than Jonny. The only part of him to defy his age was his cock. That was adolescently priapic, as if he had a portrait of the real thing, Dorian Gray–style, in the attic, as impotent and creaky as befitted a man who drank as much as he did. I felt a vague twinge between my legs to think of it. George had always been my sexual spirit level; Jonny had mere glamour, success and a year-round tan.

"Yes, George is pretty ancient. That's the glory of going out with a man ten years older than you. You'll always be a young thing."

"Don't you think you ought to be with someone you can have children with?" Jonny asked.

"I can. I mean, George has got a proven track record, hasn't he? In Grace? None of us have." As George was fond of reminding me.

"I mean, someone you can have children with on an emotional level?"

I felt my face stipple in shades of pink, like a wall painted with tester colors called Tuscan Blush and Dawn Fuchsia. I'd daydreamed about such a conversation for so long, except in my reveries Jonny would want to marry me and then would whisk me off to a crumbling colonial flat in a far-flung city to drink gin and tonics and help local children learn to read.

I gulped. "Maybe."

"I want to have children, Izobel. Bar girls are all good fun, but not for settling down with."

He sighed and gave a thoughtful nod that suggested to me that his next move would be television. "I want a baby. I was thinking about adopting an Iraqi orphan. There were some very adorable ones, with all their limbs and everything, but who would look after it?" He gave a self-deprecating laugh and his surgical mask billowed like a spinnaker. "You've read the evolutionary psychology, I want to propagate my own genes." Again that rueful self-mocking. "Terribly egotistical I dare say, but a male instinct."

He was broody; I was his brood mare. Was this what he was

suggesting? "It's funny," I said, though not in the remotest sense amused, "how much more broody the men I know are than the women. George wants another one, too, despite already having Grace. He wants a boy this time."

"Don't have a baby with George." He grabbed my hand; evidently the deadly European virus wasn't transferable through skin-to-skin contact. "I've seen life and I've seen death, Izobel, and I want to create life. Create life with me. You could live in your flat with the baby and I could try to spend more time over here. You do own your flat, don't you? I'd support you both, well, contribute obviously, and come over as often as I could. I expect you'd like to continue with your career, but you could visit me too."

"You want me to be your incubator."

"No, no, Izobel, the mother of my child. The mother of our child. And what are we in this world without children? Nothing, nothing I tell you." He really was much better-looking in his byline photo—that was his equivalent to George's preternaturally youthful cock.

"And then you want me to be your unpaid childminder while you swan around the world?" I said.

"No, of course not. We'd be parents together. Think of me as like someone who works on the oil rigs. My work takes me away for intense stretches, but when I'm back I'll be totally committed to our child. I'll be the best goddamned father in the world."

"But that's just it, isn't it, Jonny? You'll be in the world and old baby-mother here will be stuck holding the rug rat."

"I'm shocked," he said, though his employers had dubbed him the Man Who Cannot Be Shocked. "That you should look upon the greatest job a woman can do with such vilification. Your life is so amazingly complete already, is it? That having a baby would distract you from your glittering career and your wholesome relationships?"

I ignored his assault. Didn't he realize that some might say I was cutting a swath through the capital's PR industry? "And how are we going to conceive anyway? You never did like sex without triple protection."

"You can have all the tests. I've thought of that."

"You are very thoughtful."

"Thank you."

"I was being sarcastic."

"Oh."

There was a momentary lull in the conversation. He, I guessed, would be wondering whether I was stable and giving enough to be the mother of his child. I was thinking, What a prat. What a selfish arse. What a solipsistic git. How could I have wasted the creativity of my daydreaming on such a prick? Why did I fancy men with glamorous jobs when the glamour of their jobs means they're either going to be working away or playing away? I asked myself many questions, but not one of them was "Do I want to have this man's child?" I did want to have a child, I realized it at that moment; I wanted one very much at some still-distant point in my life. But I wanted to have one with an equal partner. The prospective men in my life contrived to be both simultaneously superior and inferior.

"No, Jonny. Kind as your offer is, I don't think I'll be taking it up. Sorry, I've got to go now." I stood up, sucking my stomach in and sticking my chest out at the man in the white surgical mask. "Good to see you, though. Best of luck with everything. Hope you find some other mother."

"I'm sure I shall."

As I swung out, it occurred to be that I hadn't interrogated him as the potential father of my site. I turned back and shouted, "You never did know anything about me." He looked confused. "You never even noticed that I've got six toes?"

"Not ten?"

"Six toes on one foot, eleven in all. Everybody knows that about me and you never even cared. It defines me and my whole outlook on life. You cannot describe me without this one fact." With that I stomped each of my five-toed feet and walked out on him.

And then I thought, He's not my site perp. I wondered why I had bothered to use up one of my lies on him. He's yet another of the men in my life who don't care enough to have to take the trouble. He cares enough to procreate, but not to want to create something in my honor.

*

George had wriggled from bed to daybed and was watching a black-and-white film.

"Jonny was a bit odd," I said.

George grunted.

"He's going through some sort of life change."

"Probably realizes that he's not Graham Greene after all."

"Yes, probably." I paused. "He wants to have children."

George chuckled. "Don't they all, these fey little boys of yours. But none of them have managed it, have they? He might be able to go swanning off around the world making money from misery, but he can't find some woman gullible enough to have his children. There's not going to be a lot of your lot's genes knocking around in years to come. I expect I'll be a grandfather by the time one of them shoots in range."

"It's not that big an achievement, you know. Having a child. Any pig-stupid fifteen-year-old can have a baby."

"Well, I don't see any of your friends managing it."

"How about Maggie and Mick for starters."

"Maggie this, Maggie that, Maggie likes my site, Maggie, Maggie, Maggie," he sneered. "You'd have children with her if you could. Are you going to the kitchen, sweetheart?" He shook his glass. "There is nothing in this world that's better than the love of a child, than Grace's and my love for each other. You don't know the meaning of love until you have children. Until then you're nothing. When you see your baby for the first time and she wraps her tiny hands around your finger, then it's you that's born, not them."

Blah, blah, blah, I'd heard it all before. I topped up his glass in the kitchen and wondered, if it were men who got pregnant, whether George would have been able to stop drinking for nine months.

"Come here, sweetheart." George made a small bit of space for me on the daybed and kissed the top of my head between drags of his cigarette. "Do you want a little baby boy then? Shall we make babies right now?"

Two men in one day, I thought.

"We could have a lovely little boy, a chip off the old block."

"Why a boy?"

"Because of Grace. I want a boy with my brains, this time." Not, I thought, a girl with my looks. The beautiful Catherine had bestowed hers on his firstborn.

"I see, and if it's not a boy, you'll bellow furiously about not getting your boy-child like some latter-day Henry the Eighth. 'Where's my son and heir?' you'll shout down the corridors of your castle and keep."

George laughed.

"Except he'd hardly be an heir, would he?" I went on. "Heir to a nice collection of expensive suits and not a lot else." I stood up and surveyed our cramped living quarters, where George's personality was the only expansive thing. "I can't live like this any longer. We can't have a child. You can't have a child. My life doesn't rock. It's rubbish."

With that I walked out, having failed to get a rise out of George, merely a raised eyebrow.

*

George thought it common to hit the town on Saturday nights and have to jostle with the hoi polloi of other nine-to-fivers. We went to bars with free drinks on Tuesdays, not expensive ones at the weekend. Friends of mine were out of bounds too, as eating at theirs constituted a Dido CD on the stereo. Instead that Saturday night we went round to the house of his work colleagues John and Jenny. For some reason eating at theirs was never dubbed a dinner party, it was just supper, more liquid than solid. They drank just as much as George did, but were older and more rancid.

I drank to forget about the site. I wanted to blot out Jonny and the sense of my mortality his proposition had encouraged. Then I drank to obliterate the terrible specter that John and Jenny presented of what my life with George could become, where the only babies were bottles of spirits. Eating supper with John and Jenny was like being trapped in a real-life *Who's Afraid of Virginia Woolf?*

"Where have you left the vodka, darling?" Jenny would spit at her husband as she keeled toward the fridge.

"You know where I put the fucking vodka, darling," he'd spit back at her, "in the fucking freezer where I left it last night," and she'd open another bottle from the plentiful stock.

George and I would never be like that.

Chapter Seven

I had Monday jet lag, not having been able to sleep Sunday night after getting up only eleven hours previously after our grim evening. Since I began going out with George, I always felt like I'd caught the red-eye from New York on Monday mornings. In the two years we'd been together, I had had a couple of killer hangovers a week, each lasting for at least a morning, until the salvation of that moment when you realize that, yes, you were going to be all right. That was a day disabled every single week, a hundred days of our relationship, over three months of scrap-metal head and rubbish-bin mouth. I wouldn't volunteer for a prison sentence of that length, especially not one that involved nausea, crumbling brains and the taste of a small dead animal in my throat, yet that was exactly what I had done.

"Hello, Izobel, good weekend?" asked Ivan IT-boy, who I bumped into in the foyer, raising an eyebrow at my choice of sunglasses. I wore them a) to cover up the bags under my eyes and b) because they made me look like a film star.

"Wild." I felt a need to prove to Ivan how far removed my life was from the presumed tediousness of his. "Yeah. Went to an amazing party on Saturday night, actually. Got a lot of launches this week too. Never stop. Work all day, work all night, really. Don't know when work stops and play begins. Exhausted."

"If you've got any space in your schedule, I'll have some free time this week to help you with that site you were interested in. Do you want to show me your site then?"

"My site? What do you mean, my site?"

"Nothing. The one you were talking about on Friday, the one you want to find out more about. I'll see what I can do. And you'd probably see a lot better if you took those glasses off."

I was too tired to think and at the moment agreed that Ivan, a stranger to me, should become my de-tech-tive. He couldn't be any worse than Maggie or George, could he?

"Thank you, it's kind of you."

"Pleasure."

He disappeared and as if in a revolving door a pair of vaguely familiar figures appeared in the gloom soon after.

"Hello, Izobel," said Becksy and Alice with one voice. I wondered what the lesser Camillas were doing in my office. Through my dark glasses they seemed even dimmer than at my first meeting with them. I could barely recognise them without the presence of their leader.

"Hello, what are you doing here?"

"We just wanted to know whether you had any cool ideas for the PR yet," said Becksy. "We both work nearby."

"Right. Well, no, I only saw you on Friday. Is there a hurry?"

"Kind of."

"We need to raise more capital," said Alice.

"That's not the fun bit. But the PR bit is such fun," said Becksy.

Both Becksy and Alice were barely looking at me, but were glancing round the reception of the building where I worked. Behind the shades, my eyes were narrowing. Strange. "Fine, fine. I'll e-mail a plan over to you pronto. Things are a bit hectic here at the moment. I've got a couple of launches this week alone and some pretty high-profile clients being very demanding. You wouldn't believe how completely frantic things can be in my line of work."

"I'm sure it is. It's amazing that you find time for your charity work on top of it all," said Alice.

"It's exhausting," I said. Sarky cow, I thought.

"Is it political stuff? You were very political at school."

"A bit." Leave, please, I thought, but they continued to look surreptitiously around reception, with Becksy going so far as to start looking down the hallway into the open-plan area in which I sat. Becksy in particular seemed to be wearing more makeup than she had done on Friday.

I got it. "And if you're looking for systems man, he's just left. And his name is Ivan, not Dan. I got it wrong."

They giggled in unison, like a pair of schoolgirls being faced with a sculpture of a male nude in a gallery. I sighed and left them to it.

*

Ivan the Elusive successfully evaded me for the next three days. I felt that I could not proceed with my own line of inquiry until I had discovered whether he could solve my mystery in one stroke.

I checked my site, fearful that it might disappear before I had a chance to show him. Every time the same old site. I was bored with the photos and bored with the ticker that promised so much and yet never delivered.

Then one morning, a change: a third photo and a rearrangement of the other two. The ticker explained: "the past . . . partying . . . PR . . . the many faces of Izobel."

I looked at the new addition. "This cracking photo of Izobel shows her in professional mode." I stared at it. I was wearing an extremely expensive trouser suit. I didn't carry it with ease, but rather as if I was attending a fancy dress party sporting the costume of "modern businesswoman." The photo had been taken at a pitch that we gave at a conference of UK gaming companies. We were trying to win new business. We didn't, as I recall. "We're sure," the text continued, "that her presentation skills are every bit as slick as her appearance."

There had been captions added to the other photos, too, in the form of cyber-Post-its scattered across the scrapbook-like page. They were written in the site's customary gush. "Izobel's not only about work. She has fun too!" was its interpretation of Hot Bob's party, while it judged that "Izobel's school photo shows a fashion icon in the making."

The site perp seemed to have entry points into every aspect of my life. I looked around my office, wondering if the perp could be among my colleagues, all of whom were disinterested females whose idea of techno involved Dutch hard-house DJs. I couldn't shake off the feeling of being watched.

There was another addition. There, in the bottom right-hand corner of the screen, the bit that's obscured when looked at on a small monitor, was a tiny *contact us* link.

I clicked on it. Up popped an empty e-mail message, a new mail ready to be written. In the "To" box, the address mail@izobel brannigan.com presented itself. No clues there. What had I hoped? That the name of the site-maker would appear spelled out in the address?

I filled in the subject box.

Question

And then in the message box beneath it:

Who are you?

I stared at the screen for a while and then pressed "send." I had made contact. There was someone who would read that message and maybe reply to it. I could imagine their fingers typing but not the arms and body that they were attached to.

I waited, all day, checking my in-box with even more frequency than normal. I'd stare at the bottom of my screen, at the tool bar, willing the little envelope icon to appear.

The next day, still nothing. I clicked on the link again.

Another question—urgent

Then I wrote my second message.

Who are you and why have you created this site about me? I demand to know. It's my right to know. Tell me.

Send. It was gone.

*

When Ivan eventually deigned to visit PR O'Create, I grabbed him and bundled him into a meeting room with a PC and steeled myself to show a third person the site. Please let it work, I thought, please let it work. I typed in the URL and as I did so I could see him blinking as he realized the words that I was spelling out.

Carriage return, enter, site.

"This is great," he said, smiling. "You didn't strike me as a blogger."

"A what?"

"Someone who keeps their own Web log, an online diary. Well done, it's not bad. I think blogging's great, such a democratic voice for those who usually go unheard. Good for you. Did you design it yourself?"

"I didn't do this. God no, I don't know anything about the Internet. Why on earth would I keep an online diary? In the third person? What sort of a person do you think I am? This"—I pointed at the screen—"is my problem. I don't know who made it, who created it. Who owns izobelbrannigan dot com."

"I see, someone else made it," he said, with some disappointment. "Then that is weird. Who on earth? Why?"

"I don't know."

"How long has it been up?"

"A couple of weeks. Three, now, maybe. They'd bought the domain name before that, I guess. I Googled myself and this came up."

"More than you bargained for."

"Exactly. I've always thought myself too anonymous, but now I'm too high-profile. Well, not anonymous exactly, I do quite interesting things a lot of the time, but I'm not a celebrity. Though I do know some."

He sat down and read the home page. "So you're 'cutting a swath,' are you? Given that you're in PR, you're certainly not cutting the crap."

"Ha, ha." Cheeky. I was going to tell him to stick it up his modem, but remembered that he was here to help and so put my head to one side. "I'm a bit scared actually."

"I'm not surprised. This is odd."

"That's why I need help."

"Whoever created this site needs help."

"Not design-wise. It's quite good, isn't it?" I said, as ever rather entranced by the blue of the background and the contrast that it made with the almost bleached-out colors of the photographs and the yellow of their captions. My site would make a rather beautiful commemorative tea towel.

He smiled ruefully. "Yes it is. Oh well, that's all right then, as long as your cyber-weirdo gives good design then we needn't worry."

"If I am going to have a cyber-paean, it might as well look quite nice."

He continued to run the mouse over the site, the small arrow of the cursor stroking its page, caressing the curves of my Izobel logo. He then clicked and a white box filled with chevrons and gibberish popped up in the middle of the page.

"What are you doing? What have you done to my site?"

"It's the source code."

If we'd been in a cartoon, his thought bubble would have been filled with "</SCRIPT><NOSCRIPT><A HREF='http:' <TR><TD> class='LSearchText' align='right'>," while mine would have had a great big "?"

"And source code is?"

"The language used to make up Web pages." I couldn't decide whether he was patient or patronizing. "Imagine a page of the Internet being like a painted and plastered house. Looks pretty enough. The programming language is like the bricks underneath the plaster. Without the bricks the house wouldn't exist. Same with the code. What they've used here is HTML, which is not particularly exciting but it's the most commonly used mark-up language."

"Why?"

"It's fairly sensible, logical. The Esperanto of authoring languages."

"I see." I understood all I needed to.

He sucked air through his teeth. Techies really were the plumbers of the office world. Next he was going to tell me that someone had made a real mess of my wiring.

"It's good, it's all right," was what he said.

"What is?"

"The coding. Although a page may look the same, the way that it's coded can be badly done or well done. Sometimes you see some really messy code."

"To use your house analogy, that would be like bad brick-pointing or something. Might look OK, but could make the whole edifice crumble."

"Exactly. Whoever's made this up is either a reasonably proficient page developer or has hired a proficient page developer."

"My site's pretty advanced stuff?"

He laughed dismissively. "Hardly. It's just a basic one-pager. It's not database-driven or using advanced scripting. Your bog-standard teenager can produce something like this." He sneered again. "All I'm saying is that it's not been badly executed."

"How long would it take someone to do?"

"No time at all. Half a day to create once they'd got all the assets."

"Photos of me, you mean. Half a day. That's not long." I didn't know whether to be reassured or offended by this fact.

It seemed a bit autistic to be staring at a page of squiggly code instead of a page containing pictures of me, so I clicked on the background again in order to tuck away his little white box of "source code" and reveal my schoolgirl self once more.

He did that tooth-air-sucking thing again. "Who could have these photos of you?"

"I don't know. One was taken at a party in a club, the other's from school. Then this one"—I moved the cursor to the new one—"appeared the day before yesterday. It's from a big conference, so lots of people could have it."

"And you haven't thought to check whether they could have been copied off the Net?"

"I've been very busy investigating possible suspects by other means, actually."

He opened up another window on the Net and started searching for sites, clicking on them and dismissing them with fevered pianist's fingers. "Where's this St. Teresa's school anyway?" he asked and then punched the name and town into a search engine. "Bingo."

God, he was annoying. He acted like he was top Pentagon programmer hitting upon the evil villain's password rather than a saddo who was quite good at surfing.

"Look. It's your old school site. When did you go there, when were you eleven?"

"September nineteen eighty-four." He didn't respond to my tacit admission of age.

"And here"—he clicked on a link—"is a photo of your year." I could see his eyes scanning across the class of 1984. "Does this look like your lot?"

"There I am," I said, tapping the screen with a pencil.

He flicked between the school page and my Web page. "See, it's the same picture, but they've cut it and blown it up so that it's just of you."

"Is that difficult?"

It was as if I had asked whether the sky was green.

"No, it's very easy." He clicked on the photo and then copied and pasted it into another document. "There, then I'd use a basic photo-editing program to crop it and maybe enhance the colors a bit. A doddle for anyone with even the most cursory computer skills."

"Cursor-y. Ha, ha."

He shook his head. "What it means is that whoever created this site wouldn't have to go far to find photos of you. If they knew where you went to school then they'd be able to do the whole thing in less than a day. I don't know where they'd find the party photo, so why don't you have a think about that."

"Right. But what about technical ways of finding out who they are?"

He continued tapping away at the keyboard and scanning the page. "I'll see whether I can source the owner of the domain name for you. That would help, wouldn't it? A company name or some sort of address maybe."

"That would be great. Thank you." We looked at each other for a second. His mobile went. It was the very latest model sporting a full polyphonic ringtone of the soundtrack to *Gladiator*. He dismissed himself. He was dismissed. He was dissed.

*

I had five incoming e-mails when I got back to my desk, shouting their newness with bold text. One appeared bolder than the others.

From: mail@izobelbrannigan.com. Subject: Re: Question.

My throat was dry and my mouth felt full as if I was playing that challenge when you try to eat five cream crackers in a minute. I attempted to swallow but could not. I typed as though wearing woolen mittens.

Open it, open it. Read the text, just two short sentences.

Don't worry, Izobel. I'm your friend.

Chapter Eight

We were all meeting up for Mick's birthday drinks in the West End. I was early. Others would be coming straight from their offices, but I could never manage to plug that work–play gap between six and seven. I should be the sort who goes to the gym or studies a foreign language in that window of opportunity, but instead I mooch around the shops, not buying, not even really looking.

While window-shopping, I think I spend as much time analyzing the clothes I am wearing as the clothes I might buy. As the site might say, "Izobel's a snappy dresser who today sports a classic look of tweed slacks and cashmere." I looked quite good, I thought.

In an uncharacteristic burst of intellectual hunger, I decided to go to a bookshop and buy some nonfiction. Like those radio stations that play one oldie, one chart song and one new release in rotation, I try to force myself to alternate between trash, classics and fact. I used to read political tracts for pleasure. Now when I reread essays I wrote at university, I can't even understand my own words or theories.

I went to a big modern store, the sort where book-buying can come quite low on your list of intentions, well below imbibing a detoxifying apple and wheat grass juice or reading American

Vogue. I spent at least ten minutes grubbing around the foreign gossip magazines and trying to understand what *escandalo* they talked of, before I felt strong enough to enter the book section of the place that purported to be a bookshop.

My progress through to the floor laden with tomes about other people's lives was impeded by a cardboard cut-out from my own autobiography: a larger than life–size poster of Elliot Edwards sitting inside a Monopoly boot as big as a car, holding a ladder in one hand and a snake in the other. Beneath was the information: "Elliot Edwards will be signing copies of *Board Stupid: Beyond the Boards* in the second-floor mezzanine."

How his success mocked my own lack of it. Sometimes I liked the party piece of I Dated a Celeb, but most of the time I wished he were still a runner as he had been when we split up almost two and a half years ago. How his fortunes had changed in that time; how mine had remained the same.

I wanted to have something new to report to Maggie so I made my way to the book-signing. Did I have to buy the damn book, I wondered; I had no intention of splashing out the £10.99 required to read all about the wacky backstage secrets of the cult game show. I already knew quite enough about Elliot's personal habits. Maybe he would not have so many female fans if they knew that he could only maintain an erection if you talked with awe of his manhood throughout sex. Having to intone, "Oh your big hard dick, oh your big hard dick, it's so big and it's so hard, it's so hard and it's so big" did nothing for a woman's own pleasure. It was almost as unsexy as his tendency to fret about his weight and his ability to tell you the number of WeightWatchers points in a banana. Never trust a man who drinks Diet Coke and Slim-Fast.

He was looking good though, I gnashed as I observed him from a distance. He had that stringy, skinny look that can only come from a carbohydrate-free diet. Evidently Weight Watchers and Slim-Fast had been replaced by the Atkins regime. Just as a protein-laden diet removes anything round from your plate, like potatoes and bread rolls, so Elliot looked as though his doughy softness had been sucked away from his body to leave it vacuum-packed and as if assembled from pure lean turkey breasts and skinless chicken thighs. His sunken cheeks only served to make his trademark horn-rimmed glasses seem even more outsize, as if they, too, were a prop from *Board Stupid.*

I hung back, waiting for the session to come to an end.

"Izobel," he cried when I presented myself. "How brilliant to see you. You look amazing."

Even though he was my squitty ex, I still felt the relief and pleasure that you get from being recognized by someone more famous than you. He was nice, that Elliot, I thought to myself, blushing at a compliment from the mouth of a celebrity.

"Ditto. I saw the posters and thought I'd come and say hello." As if that were a normal thing to do. I wouldn't usually have come along to stand in a line with a bunch of game-show freaks merely to pay homage to Elliot, charming as he could be. I felt like I always do at weddings when you have to queue up to compliment an old friend, just because she's wearing a long white dress.

"That's so kind of you. Thank you. You're probably too busy, but I'm just going to the hospitality room for a drink. Why don't you come?"

"Thanks." The teenagers looked at me enviously. It was as though I were sitting in a swanky convertible with the top down—I probably looked like a prat but I couldn't help feeling that everyone was impressed.

Even someone with the low-grade level of fame of Elliot has "people." In the green room lurked a publisher and a publicist. George only has a publican. I had a lager while Elliot sipped from a white wine spritzer made, I noticed, with only the merest dash of Chardonnay.

"So, how have you been?" he asked.

"Are you wearing makeup, Elliot?" I said, helping myself to the hospitality crisps that he had pushed away.

"No." If not makeup, he definitely dyed his eyelashes. "Enough of me, Izobel, what are you up to? Something very glamorous, I'm sure."

"The usual, PR still. And"—I looked to seize the moment—"breeding chinchillas."

"Chinchillas?"

"Yes, chinchillas. Rabbity things, like great big hamsters, you could have them on the show they're so out of scale. Worth a lot of money." Chinchillas? Why, why, why? I was allowed to make up anything and I made up that. Why hadn't I said that I was George Clooney's secret lover or that NASA wanted me to join the space program? No, I breed squirrel creatures.

"That's great, that's fabulous, how exciting. Wow, you're doing really well. You must be so proud of yourself." He wasn't being sarcastic.

"As must you be," I said. "Your life's pretty good."

"A bit. Not really. It's a lot of hard work most of the time. You're looking fantastic too, Izobel, really well."

"So are you. You've swapped bodies with someone."

"What, me? No, I'm still a bit of chubster. Too much of a couch potato, sat at home watching *The Simpsons.*" He puffed out his chest and pulled in his stomach, glancing at the mirror as he did so.

"Hardly sat at home. I've seen the photos of you—you go to all those celebrity parties."

"Me? A celebrity? Don't be ridiculous. If people ever ask for my autograph it's because they think I'm somebody else. Woody

Allen, probably. I'm just thankful that an idiot like me can get paid for doing something I love."

I'd read that very spiel in an interview with him. "Come on Elliot, don't put it on. You know life's turned out pretty well for you."

"No, really. How are things for you?" he said. "Are you still with George?"

"Yes, I am." I sounded apologetic. There had been no actual overlap between Elliot and George, though there may have been an emotional one. "What about you?"

"Gosh, me? I couldn't possibly say," he muttered.

Perhaps he wasn't yet over me after all. I changed the subject. "What do you do when you're not working? Do you use the Internet much? There are lots of sites about you." I had Googled Elliot long before I had Googled myself.

"Really? I wouldn't know about that. Probably mad people. Can't imagine why anyone else would make a site about me."

"Come on, I bet you do look at them."

He refused to concur.

"Do you know much about the Web generally?" I probed. "You were one of the first people I know to get an Internet connection and e-mail. You used to go to American chat rooms in the middle of the night."

I perceived a blush in those recently sculpted cheeks.

"I know a bit," he said. "Gosh, so little really. I can create sites. Dave and I have been doing a few satirical ones anonymously. Hoaxes and stuff, causing mischief." He looked around. "Don't tell anyone, though."

If in Maggie-world all my other suspects' Internet ignorance made them more likely to be the perpetrator, did the fact that Elliot was so freely admitting to having the necessary nous to create a site mean that he was innocent?

"And we're interested in raising the profile of a manned mission to Mars," he added. "We've got a site about that. They've already been there, you know, the Americans, they're just not telling us. Dave and I have seen the pictures and we want to force them to go public with them."

At that moment a familiar-looking girl approached us. She was small and narrow-backed but with disproportionately large breasts that nonetheless had the mobility of real ones. If her body was inflatable doll, her face was china doll—little Cupid's-bow mouth, round eyes framed with mascara that looked like it had been applied with a spray gun and tiger-striped straightened hair. She wore a tight T-shirt with "Board Stupid Crew" written across it, but the size of her chest ensured that it landed far short of her tight hipster jeans, revealing a flat stomach and high, tiny outie belly button. She could have been a pretty checkout girl from Top Shop or a cover star from a lads' mag. She was, I realized, the latter. One of those male fantasies, the playgirl-next-door, a woman without a surname, one hand pulling her pants almost down, the other fingering her mouth, spatchcocked on the pages of middle-shelf men's magazines.

"Hello, darling," Elliot said to her. She must have a lot of fan sites on the Internet, I thought. "Talitha, this is Izobel, an old friend of mine. Izobel, meet Talitha." He paused. "My girlfriend."

Talitha, yes, of course that was her clearly faked-up name. I had seen her on TV and on those magazine covers. Her face was blank but her body was not, telling men as it did how "up for it" she was. Isn't it depressing how women fancy quirky, nerdy-looking men and these men praise us for our ability to see beyond plastic handsomeness? Yet they repay our lack of superficiality by being more obsessed with landing themselves a conventional babe than their good-looking rivals. The more they portray themselves as dorky, the less dorky their taste in women becomes.

"You're going out with each other?" Elliot beamed at my surprise. "Wow, that's great. How long have you been a couple?"

"A few months." He leaned forward. "Please don't tell the press, they'd have a field day. We don't want the whole world to know." On the contrary, he looked as though he'd like nothing better, and I could start by informing those rugby-playing types he'd been at school with.

Talitha wriggled her freakishly small bottom onto his lap.

"Where did you two meet?" She kissed the tips of his fingers, the ones that created Web sites about Martian conspiracy theories.

"On set. Talitha had a friend working on the show."

"We share a makeup artist," she said, in a baby voice. I shuddered to think of that little-girl voice praising the size of Elliot's cock in congress. "Oh Elliot, your big hard cock, it's so big and it's so hard, oh Elliot," she'd be forced to squeak. Or maybe with a girl as sexy as Talitha, Elliot would not need such continual verbal encouragement to remain constant. Maybe it wasn't his problem, but mine.

"And now we share much more," he said.

"Much, much more," Talitha replied.

I raised my eyebrows and made my excuses, leaving them to swap spritzer and spittle.

"Good luck with the cute little animals," he called as I left. And good luck with yours, I hissed under my breath.

*

I stared at my face in the mirror of the pub toilets. I had scooted into them unseen before feeling able to face Mick, Maggie, Frank and the others in the back bar. It was an OK face, but not so pretty as Talitha's. I had ended up downsizing boyfriend, while Elliot had traded up, if not intellectually then erotically. There would be few men in the world and absolutely no boys who'd choose me over Talitha. I shook my head to try to scatter the image burned onto it of Talitha's tiny little body coiled around Elliot's newly toned one.

"It's our very own star of the Internet," said Frank as I approached their table.

"Piss off." I looked around to see who was here. Camilla sat beside him. Frank couldn't come anywhere without Camilla these days. Beside them was a girl I'd not met before.

"Frank told me that you think he's been writing stuff about you on the Net," interjected Camilla incredulously.

"No, not exactly. It's more complicated than that." Where was Maggie? I needed her help. "And very boring."

"Where's George tonight?" asked Frank.

Piss off, I said, but silently this time. At least I hope it was silent, I'm never quite sure. Out loud I explained, "It's his night with Grace." This was a lie, of course, but it was always a convenient one to explain George's absences from my friends' gatherings. Nobody, not George, not my friends and not me, wanted him to attend them.

"That's his daughter, isn't it? How sweet. How old is she?" asked Camilla.

"Six. Going on twenty-six. The other day I admired her shoes and she said, 'Yes, they're from Harvey Nicks.'"

"Surely not," said Camilla.

"Really, she's so knowing. She met Maggie and asked why she spoke like a man and had a hairy chin."

"I bet you adore her really."

"She's all right, I suppose. Who wants a drink?"

"Becksy and the other one are at the bar," said Frank. "And this is Molly, by the way."

"Another St. Tree's alumnus," said Camilla. "The gang's all here. Well, except Miche."

"And Kitty," said Molly, in exactly the same gushing tones as

Becksy and Alice used. I hadn't realized that some sort of evil Stepford cloning experiment had gone on at St. Teresa's in the late eighties, churning out enthusing blondes with overgrown flower grips in their hair.

"Izobel doesn't have any friends," said Camilla.

"I'm sorry, what did you say?"

"I mean, friends from school anyway." Camilla and Molly put their heads to one side, the same side of course, and looked at me pityingly.

I escaped to the bar to help and to place my own order. It was already crowded with pints, although I had noticed that all the men around the table were already nursing beers.

"Hello," Alice said with surprise, as if these were her friends, not mine, as if she was more than an almost silent faded carbon copy of Becksy and in turn Camilla.

"Hi. Let me help. It's always the same with these blokes, they always like to line up their pints. The way men time their arrival around round-buying and its elaborate rituals makes me realize why they all eventually end up becoming obsessed with military history. They've been practising annexation and stockpiling all their lives."

"You're so right," said Becksy, as I scooped them up. "I've never thought of that before. That's really clever."

"Hardly." I scooted back to the table, not wanting to get stuck at the B-list end of it with Camilla's friends all evening. "You'll never guess who Elliot's going out with now," I said on my return to a captive audience. "Talitha." A few blank stares. "You know, the one who was in that celebrity reality thing and poses in men's magazines and red-tops." Flashes of recognition.

"Urgh," said Maggie. "She's so plain."

"Yeah right," said Mick. "She's hideous. Bollocks, Maggie, she is absolutely gorgeous. Out of two, I'd give her one." All the other men mumbled agreement.

"She is so not," said Camilla. "She's completely nondescript."

"Yeah right," said Frank. "This is why when a woman is described to me, I always ask, is she female-pretty or male-pretty? They are such different concepts."

"Well, I've just met Talitha," I interjected. "And she's both weirdly plain and weirdly sexy. And Elliot is looking like the adolescent geek who's pulled the head cheerleader on prom night."

"From you to Talitha in the space of a few years," said Frank. "Elliot must be gutted with the progress of his life. He probably spends all his time writing stuff about you on the Internet."

"Oh piss off, Frank." This time very audibly. I looked at Maggie and she raised an eyebrow at me and shook her head. "Are we going to eat at some point tonight or are you beer-arians going to do your usual trick of surviving on Guinness alone?"

"Not me," said Maggie. "Eating for two and all that. There's a new-wave Chinese across the road. We call it Fung MSG."

"Iz can order for us, can't you, Iz?" Frank turned to everyone. "Izobel has so many talents, and one of them is that she speaks Chinese."

Maggie raised both her eyebrows this time.

"Mandarin. I'm learning Mandarin," I corrected. "That place is Sichuan, I think. Don't speak that, sorry."

*

I was eating a sandwich alone at my desk, dribbling chicken globules into my keyboard to mingle with the croissant crumble and splashes of coffee that already made a meal of it down there.

"Hello, Izobel." I jolted. I hated people coming up behind me at my desk.

Ivan sat down on Mimi's midget swivel chair at the desk next to mine. "I've been thinking about your site. It's strange." I hated people interrupting my lunch breaks too.

"You're telling me."

"I can't imagine who'd do such a thing."

"Me neither. That's why I'm asking you for your help."

"What else are you doing to find out who is behind it?" he asked. "Besides enlisting me?"

"A colleague and I have put into place a series of investigations." I paused. "We're starting from the premise that the perpetrator is most likely to be someone who has been, er, emotionally involved with the eponymous protagonist of the site. Aka Izobel Brannigan. Aka me. Since adopting this strategy we have instigated such investigations as to the likely responsibility of the respective candidates."

"What on earth are you talking about?"

"We're talking to those people who at some point have been intimate with Izobel Brannigan."

"Your exes?"

"Indeed. As yet these investigations are proving inconclusive but informative."

"Meaning?"

"I don't know, Ivan, I don't. That's why I've got you on board."

"And who are they, your exes? No, don't tell me, I bet they're all men who work in professions advertised in the *Guardian* on a Monday. Creative, Media and Marketing."

"Rubbish. Frank's an academic." With a sideline in radio punditry. "And one of them's unemployed." Though William's dole-queue status was mitigated by the fact of his father being Britain's richest theatrical impresario.

"And the rest?"

"So. What's wrong with working in the media?"

"Nothing, I suppose. It's just that people who work in the media are so self-obsessed and superior. They think that it gives them license to bore the rest of us with stories about their jobs, when really all work tales are as interesting and relevant as the details of somebody's dreams. Boring and meaningless."

"And everybody else is so interesting?" I asked with irritation.

"More so, yes. We don't feel that we can talk shop to people outside our worlds so we make an effort to cultivate other interests and observations. We don't insist on only mating with others who work in the same sector and we don't think we're better than anybody else. Instead we strive to make ourselves better. That's what your lot fails to do."

"It's not my lot."

"All right, everyone you work with, hang out with and go out with. Are you honestly trying to tell me that you're not prejudiced against those who work in banking, or the law, or, God forbid, IT?"

"No, of course not. Now, if you don't mind excusing me, mere technical minion, I have some high-level phone calls to make to journalists, TV producers and editors to discuss glamorous celebrity evenings and the launches of new lifestyle magazines."

Ivan laughed and I smiled.

"And I'll get back to you if the analysis of a technical nature pursued by your IT consultant yields any evidence beyond the merely circumstantial," he said. "Ditto, if your probe of previous emotional involvements proves fruitful."

"Thanks," I said turning back to the celebrity gossip message board I was currently investigating in depth.

Chapter Nine

George was in repose on the sofa, quaffing a lager and watching a James Bond repeat.

"Let's get out," I said. "It's a nice day. Let's go for a walk or to an art gallery or a street market."

"Or one of those other activities as prescribed in listings magazines that nobody but tourists actually does."

"Let's do it, go on, George. It'll be fun."

He faked a snore and continued watching the television. I stood up and he looked at me with interest for the first time since we'd got out of bed.

"You couldn't be a love and get me an ashtray." I ignored him, but he lit up anyway.

I fired up my computer in response to his indifference. I was just like any sad old man chatting to Lithuanian lovelies online because his wife won't put out.

There hadn't been a change since the new photo and the link. I still hadn't heard any more back from Mr. Contact Us via e-mail, despite repeated cyber-entreaties from me. Yet I always opened the site up with a sense of expectation, a hope that this time the mystery would be solved.

"Oh my God," I said on viewing izobelbrannigan.com. "Shit."

George grunted and turned the television up.

"The site, it's changed. My God."

He continued his recital of farmyard animal noises with a snort of derision. "Site, site, shite. That's all you talk about these days. Christ, you've become dull."

"But really, please George, take a look at this."

"You're obsessed with the bloody Internet. It will never replace newspapers, never."

"I'm not saying it will."

"Yes you bloody are."

"Of course not, you can't wrap fish and chips in a computer. Please, George, come and look at this." I dragged him from the sofa. He sat in the chair in front of the computer as I leaned over him.

"Yes, yes, it's your site. Now what?"

"For God's sake at least put your specs on, your reading glasses."

"It's your site, I don't know what else to say about it. I've already admired it and talked about it ad nauseam. Darling." He spat out the last word and replaced it in his mouth with a gulp of his beer.

"But it's different. Look. I've been papped," I said, clicking on the link off the home page that read *photo gallery* and which led to a display of paparazzi-style photos, images of ordinary situations that are usually made extraordinary by those embroiled in them. The page showed familiar papping situations taken with a long-lensed camera, but with an unfamiliar protagonist: me. Me at the supermarket with ten items or less in my basket. Me in tracksuit bottoms blinking blearily, coming out of the flat, not celeb-style on my way to yoga, but wearing comfy clothes in lieu of getting dressed properly. Me at the bus stop, instead of unlocking the doors of a four-by-four as is more common in this genre. Me coming out of the bookshop. Me picking my nose. If that one had been published in a magazine, it would have been in the "Celebrities, they're disgusting like the rest of us" section.

Each had a caption, characterized by the cheery inanity of the magazines I loved to read and the style already pioneered in the rest of the site: "Izobel tries to make sure she eats her five portions of fruit and veg by stocking up on spinach"; "Izobel's not above using public transport"; "Hot picks—sometimes life gets right up Izobel's nose."

What I hated about my life was that it was always the same. The site changed, yet just served as proof of the unchanging nature of my life. It had pap shots of the shopping trips and taking out the rubbish, but not the leading features of marriage, birth or a shiny new home.

"Look, there's me," said George, pointing to a picture of us, not emerging from an upscale restaurant but from a gastro-pub, leaning on each other, physically if not emotionally. As a new trick, his face had been pixelated to become unidentifiable rather than sporting the low-tech black strip across his eyes. "I look like I've got a gut. Do I have a gut?" He sucked in his stomach. "I don't have a gut, do I?"

"No, you're perfect. I don't remember these photos being taken."

"That was on Wednesday," said George, pointing to the one in which he costarred. "Doesn't mention me in the caption, though." He read it out in a soppy voice. "The night before the morning after for Izobel!"

"It never mentions other people. Only me, in fact. I knew it was Wednesday, I just don't remember seeing a camera flashing. Do you?"

"I am a fine figure for a man of my age, aren't I?"

"Don't you remember anything odd about that evening?"

"I barely remember anything about that evening at all, sweetheart."

"Nobody flashed us then."

"I may have flashed you later."

"Think, George, can't you remember anything?"

"I recall having pan-fried calves' liver as a main and a very fine bottle of Barolo."

"Don't you see what this means, George?"

"I'm sure you're going to tell me."

"It means that they're following me. It means that they know where I live, where I go, what I do. They're stalking me, staking me. Scaring me."

"I suppose it does," he said, while continuing to stroke the convex planes of his stomach. "I'm sorry, poppet. Let me make it better for you." He tried to pull me onto his lap.

I shook him off and walked out of the flat. As I stood on the doorstep I looked around, trying to catch a photographer in the bushes or in the building opposite, pointing a long-range camera at me. There was nobody. I was alone. "Izobel emerges from her flat in the fashionable fringes of the throbbing metropolis. What exciting event are you off to, Izobel?" the caption would read.

I went to a café. Those photos, they were my life. A life that involved going to the pub, to work, to the supermarket, to a party. Where was the snatched shot of me giving up my time to work in a soup kitchen or delivering leaflets for a worthy cause? There were no pictures of me holding a placard on a march or helping an old lady cross a road. I did nothing for anybody but myself.

I felt overwhelmed by self-pity, exacerbated by the knowledge that I couldn't let my tears leak for fear of them being snapped with a caption reading: "The secret sadness—we're sure you'll feel better soon, Izobel."

*

I flopped out at Maggie's, while she busied herself around me. I was aware that she was the one who ought to be supine, but I was pregnant with worry. I saw myself as if through a camera's eye, splayed out and pulling ugly, blotchy faces. Every pose I made was now captioned by myself, as if I were a new-wave photographer, turning my life into an installation. This one read: "Izobel gets tired just like the rest of us."

"I feel like it's mocking me, Maggie."

"He, she or they are mocking you. *It* can't do anything. *It* is inanimate."

"Much like Izobel Brannigan herself," I said.

"Come on, Iz, don't be so lumpen," said Maggie, as she plumped up cushions around me. "I'm so nesty nowadays." She flashed the roll call of suspects she had written weeks previously. "You haven't done half the people on this list. Get onto them. This site is making you feel powerless. Well, empower yourself."

I sighed. "I feel like my life is in abeyance until I find out who's behind it. I'm preserved. Or pickled, thanks to George, most of the time."

"You're only stuck if you let yourself be. Pull yourself together." If she'd written that in an e-mail to me she'd have inserted an exclamation mark to convey jocularity. As she was saying it to me in the flesh, there was none. "Elliot you've done, albeit by accident, and we've agreed that going out with Talitha probably keeps him busy enough. Frank is not fully eliminated, nor is George."

I shook my head.

"What about Foreign Correspondent?" she asked. "It's a bit odd that he turns up out of the blue and asks you to have his children just after this site appears, don't you think? Did you even find out which war zone he's on his way to?"

"It's not him. I just know it's not him. He doesn't give a fuck about me. Neither does George, nor does Frank, nor does anyone. I'm all alone, bar stalkie photographer person."

"No, you're not. Don't be stupid. You'll feel better if you do something about it." She looked at her list. "Get in touch with Married Man and Spanish Artist for starters. And William, didn't

I say it was likely to be him? You split up with Frank for him, don't tell me he's meaningless."

"You've never forgiven me for splitting up with Frank, have you? For messing up our cozy foursome."

"For God's sake, I don't give a monkey's about that, I just want you to be happy. And to find out who's behind the site. Perhaps whoever it is wants you to find them."

"What do you mean?"

"Why would they go to all this trouble if they don't want to give you a message directly from them or to let you know how they feel about you? Remember how when you used to send Valentine's cards, you'd make sure that the postmark or some other clue would let them know who you were, if they really wanted to find out? We used to write hidden messages on them in lemon juice when we were at primary school. You'd leave a clue, yet it wouldn't be so obvious that you couldn't deny the connection if necessary."

"Yes, but what are you getting at?"

"That I could've been too lateral about this, assuming that whoever is behind it is trying to cover their tracks. Maybe whoever it is won't deny it if you ask them straight out, because they want you to know how they feel. Or there's a really obvious clue actually on the site. I don't know, like the first letter of every sentence spells out their name, or they're visible in the background of one of the photos or something. Think, Maggie, think," she exhorted herself. "What would happen in a film? You know how you can play heavy metal tracks backwards and they talk about the devil? What if there's some message hidden in the pages? In the code stuff."

"Maybe."

"You need to talk to your technical consultant about that. Ask him whether it's possible to add phrases into the code without them showing up on the page. Hasn't he come up with the goods yet?"

"Ivan. No, he doesn't seem to have. In fact, I feel he's dragging his heels a bit. I don't think he realizes that I can't get on with my life until I find out who's behind this."

"Well, hassle him then," said Maggie. The words "instead of hassling me" were left unsaid. "And take this list. I can remember the names on it, even if you can't. And don't come back until you've investigated them all."

*

I sat in reception of Married Man's office, a TV company. We'd been hired by them to boost their profile just before launching on the stock exchange. We'd boosted that of their CEO as well, while I had boosted his ego by sleeping with him, a man who hadn't had a blow job since Virginia Wade won Wimbledon.

TV attracted as many slips of girls wearing slips of clothing as PR. Both industries, to use Douglas Coupland's phrase, go in for Brazilification of wages: those at the top were buying houses in the South of France, while those at entry level were being paid less than part-time supermarket shelf-stackers. At least waitresses got tips. PR girls and TV researchers got late nights and lecherous bosses.

In the ten minutes I sat waiting I saw so many employees whose faces were full of hope. I listened to two of them, talking loudly and proudly.

"Yeah, the TVR was fabulous, totally dominated the eighteen to thirty-fives in that slot. Thirty-three percent share in fact."

"LE's the way to go, I reckon," replied her lissome friend. "Totally the best people too."

"Have you seen the guy execcing my program? He's an amazing man. And so handsome. Got a girlfriend, but apparently she's really let herself go since having the baby."

They were the envy of their contemporaries for working in the media and herding C-listers into hospitality. I could see that they had a sense of themselves in the third person, too, at the epicenter of crap television output. Don't do it, I wanted to say to them, all jobs are just admin so get yourself one with bigger pay and proper employee rights. Your friends won't envy you when you're unemployable once you have children or want something more from your life.

They were so young—the stomachs were flat and their faces full. Their hipster jeans crept ever more stealthily southward, dangerously hovering above their pubes. Was there some link between the stock exchange and how low trousers were going, as there reputedly was between the market and how high the hemlines of skirts floated?

Married Man was the squire of the television feudal system. He had the wealth to be able to afford to hire someone to do the site. I had looked up his company's Web site and it wasn't in a dissimilar style to mine. It wasn't exactly similar either. I didn't know how I was going to approach him, but I was curious to see him after all this time.

I was gestured into his office, an orange glass pod at the corner of a vast open-plan office. He was wearing a suit. Relations had been brilliant between us when I had only seen him in a suit or naked, both of which he wore extremely well. They had started to go wrong when we made the mistake of going out in mufti. Then he had sported the regulation chinos and Icelandic pattern sweaters of dress-down Friday, just like any other banker in the City at the end of the week. He looked like a middle-class dad about to mow the lawn. Which wasn't so far from the truth.

And he was a banker. I kidded myself that because he had such a thriving company, making such innovative combinations of reality shows and docu-soaps, that he must be creative himself.

But he was Mr. Money while in the next-door podule grubbed MC Creativo. All my lover had cared about were numbers, although some of those included my measurements.

"Hello, Izobel, to what do I owe this pleasure?" He shook my hand for the benefit of the minions on the other side of the glass.

"Thanks for seeing me at such short notice."

"I'm always happy to see you."

We stared at each other and then I glanced away to look at the photos of him with television stars suspended like a giant mobile from the ceiling, and the BAFTAs that lined the windowsill. "It's been a long time, hasn't it?" I said. I couldn't help but speak in the mechanical clichés of a business reception with him. Those or sporting metaphors were his lingua franca.

"Time flies. How long has it been?"

Since I dumped you for your employee Elliot, I thought. "Since we finished work on the campaign and you went public."

"Four years then."

I had loved him professionally and sexually, pinstripes and nudity, but we had never had anything to say outside of boardrooms and bedrooms. His business brain had inspired me into going to bed with him. And I had loved going to bed with him. He was as driven and enthusiastic there as he had been when building his company.

"Yes, four years." Four years since I'd last slept with him. I had adored the way he had talked in bed; he'd tell me I had fantastic "knockers" and use the word unironically. He was a sexual Rip Van Winkle, having been married for twenty years. His carnal vocabulary was straight out of the seventies: it was Benny Hill and Carry On. His tastes were those of a naughty schoolboy reared in a tradition of British smuttiness and good-natured jollity. He made remarks about éclairs and "having it off" and "giving you one." He'd stroke my "fanny" and bury his face in my "boobs."

I'd responded by eschewing utility underwear for lace, satin and garters. I'd worn the sort of transparent negligees not seen since window cleaners did daily rounds with bored housewives wearing naughty nighties. I was starring in a film called *Confessions of a TV Executive* where I was, to use his parlance, always up for a bit of nookie.

He looked at me expectantly. "Well, Izobel, don't beat about the bush. What do you want?"

"Do you have Internet access in here? I feel like I'm trapped in a cough drop."

He spun round his flat screen and clicked on the "E" of Explorer. I could see the home page of his company reflected in his German architect's glasses. They were a new addition. I wondered whether he'd picked up another young lover. He started typing "www" into the search box for that site. Clearly, Web-savviness was something he left to the kids, both his own and those he employed.

"Do you mind?" I asked and captained the keyboard, bringing up my site.

He read it and laughed. "Do you want a photo of me for it?"

"No, it's not mine. I mean, I'm not behind it. I'm trying to find out who is."

"How rum. But how can I help?"

"Exes, they're all suspects," I said apologetically.

"Izobel, Izobel," he spoke very quietly, all the while looking out of his glass cocoon toward the grubs in the open-plan area. "You're batting from a very sticky wicket here. What on earth are you suggesting?"

"I know." I did, Frank had made sure of that. I shrugged my shoulders.

He continued staring at the screen. "I couldn't create something like this myself, could I? The only people who could would be my son or someone I'd paid to do it."

I nodded.

"I've taken some risks but I don't think I'd distract Jakey from his A levels to create a Web site about my mistress. My ex-mistress."

I rolled my eyes. Mistress was an old-fashioned word too far.

"That leaves paying someone. Can you imagine if that got out? What that would do to a man in my position? It would be compromising to say the least, don't you see? Can you imagine what fun *Media Guardian* would have with it, or God forbid one of the tabloids?"

" 'This family man claims to make family entertainment. Instead he spends his time creating Internet filth in honor of his girlfriend,' " I posited as a potential storyline.

"Exactly." He smiled at me. I smiled back. I did like him. I'd forgotten that. Strange that my only experience of adultery should be one of the less shameful episodes in my sexual history. Though his wife and children might disagree should they ever find out. I felt a belated twinge of guilt about them while at the time I had been able to justify our affair quite easily.

"I'm sorry," I said. "I'm just stuck. My life is stuck. It hasn't moved on since I last saw you and then this site comes along. And it's made me even more stuck as all I can think about is who might be behind it. I'm stuck in a stupid job, in a bad relationship, and it's all caught on the bloody Internet."

He leaned forward and whispered, "I'd hug you if we weren't displayed in a glass podule, you sexy gorgeous creature, you."

I did so want to be held by him. He was of the type characterized in gay classifieds as "bear," huge and hairy.

"But it wouldn't do you any good," he continued. "What are you still doing at PR O'Create? It's such a two-bit operation."

"You hired us."

"I hired you. Get out of there and get yourself a real job. Or have some children. Make your life change. Don't wait around for some stupid Web site to change it for you. We in television are finding that all this interactivity stuff is very much overrated. You should be a top striker, not stuck on the subs' bench of life."

"Thanks."

"Now get out of here, before I rip your top off to reveal your splendid boobs to the troops."

*

Bored, I was so bored in the office, but look where getting bored got me. I'd never have found the damned site if I hadn't been so bored. I fired it up once more to search for clues. I squinted at it through half-closed eyes, as if it were one of those Magic Eye pictures they sold on the street and, if I looked at it right, a 3D dinosaur would appear.

What had Maggie suggested? That the perp was revealing himself on the site. I read the text and extracted the initial letters of each sentence. T, B, S. Tony, Toby, Thomas, Tom, Tim; Bill, Billy, Boris, Bob, "Hot Bob" maybe? Sebastian, Stephen, Simon, Sy, Sid, sod it.

I pressed my face up to the screen to check out the logo, fat blobby "Izobel" underlined with "her site her world." Still. That would have been a cunning place to put a clue. But none.

There was a treasure book when I was growing up that had a rabbit hidden on every page. I moved my head away from the screen. Did the arrangement of the photos make up a letter? A "C" maybe? Yes, it could be a C.

I stared hard at the photos individually, pressing my nose almost up to the glass like the academic's children of my youth who didn't have a television used to do outside the rentals shop on the high street. I could make out a figure lurking in the shadows of the pub. I'd have to ask Ivan to do something clever with it, blow it up like they do on detective programs.

Ivan. I hadn't rung him yet. Something was stopping me. I don't know whether I felt bad about hassling him when he was only helping me out, or scared he too would fail to have the answers and I would have run out of options.

I continued staring at the site, my mouth agape, possibly with a faint dribble coming out of it. That's what I felt anyway, idiotic, befuddled and belittled, not beguiled and bemused. I put my head to one side in order to get a different perspective. I right-clicked on photos in the way that I had seen Ivan do. Nothing.

"Hello, Izobel." I looked up to find Ivan by my desk.

"Talk of the devil." I definitely did have a bit of spittle squatting on my chin. I tried to lick it off, but succeeded in making myself look like I was dementedly attempting to lick my lips in a gesture of lasciviousness. And that wasn't the impression I wanted to give Ivan. "I was just thinking about you."

"Why?"

"My friend Maggie reckons that the person behind the site might be trying to hide a clue as to their identity in the site, buried somehow."

"Perhaps."

"Do you remember you got that box full of code up? Could there be additional words in that?"

He smiled. "Of course there could be. I like it. Depending on the code you put around the words, you could put any number of phrases into it and it wouldn't affect the look of the Web page at all. Look, I'll show you."

Here we go, I thought, another science lesson.

"Here's a Web site, for example. And here's its code." He brought up the white box with an ugly typeface filling it. "I could put these words into the code." He typed "my name is Ivan" into it, the sort of phrase you use when testing out pens in a stationer's. "Because of the symbols I've put around it, it won't make any difference to the page at all. It could just be an in-joke between programers."

"Not a very funny one."

"No, of course not. I wasn't trying."

"See if there's anything on my site. Please. Thanks."

Izobelbrannigan.com flooded the screen, soon replaced by its code. He skimmed through the endless chevrons and symbols as if it were the easiest-to-read magazine article and then stopped. "There you go." He laughed.

"What? What is it?" I stared at the screen and he pointed to it with a pen. I put on a serious face as I saw my boss Tracy walk by and look at Ivan and me with barely concealed fury. "Show me."

"Read it."

There, among the technical nonsense, was a sentence in plain English, perhaps a Rosetta Stone that would unlock the meaning of the hieroglyphics. But it might as well have been in Ancient Egyptian for all it meant to me.

" 'Said tree in distress,' " I read out. "Stupid site, what does that mean?"

"I don't know. Does it not mean anything to you?"

"Trees? Ash, oak, sycamore . . . do I know anybody called those names? Or a tree surgeon? No, I don't."

"I don't think it's someone who shares a name with a tree, actually. It looks more like a crossword clue."

Damn, I never could get my head around cryptic crosswords. "You don't by any chance know how to do them?"

" 'In distress' implies that it's an anagram. Of, I suppose, 'said tree.' " He wrote out the eight letters in capitals in a circle on a Post-it note. "Sid someone, do you know anyone called Sid?"

I shook my head. "Or could it not be a crossword clue but a hint that there's somebody called Said? You know, the Arabic name Sa-eeed."

"Do you know anybody called that?"

"No, but . . ." My desk phone made the sound of an internal

call. Once ordinary people could recognize birdsong; now they just know the difference between mobile with message, mobile with call, internal and external office tones and the home phone. Not that the latter rings much anymore.

"Izobel speaking." Each trill had a different response.

"Sorry, Ivan, got to go." I made my way, as requested, into my boss's office, which was enclosed. Open-plan only went so far.

"Come in," said Tracy. Or "Tracy, as in Katharine Hepburn in *The Philadelphia Story* and Grace Kelly in *High Society*," as she was wont to introduce herself. She modeled her clothes on such epitomes of restrained good taste too, never straying too far from black trousers, kitten-heeled boots and a pastel-colored cashmere top. She was my age.

"Izobel Brannigan," she began. "Who are you?"

"Sorry?" I had enough trouble with identities without Tracy adding to the load.

She leaned back and put her muscled arms behind her head. I should go to Body Pump at the gym more often. "You're smart Izobel, who was hired for her way with words. You're lots-of-experience Izobel. You're a-creative-approach-to-PR Izobel." She then switched positions and put her elbows on her desk.

I nodded and mumbled some acknowledgment of gratitude.

"But at the moment, you're distracted-and-unproductive Izobel."

The further forward she came, the more I slunk back, maintaining that force field of distance between us.

"Clients have been complaining," she continued. "Every time I walk by your desk you're surfing the Net. You disappear for hours on end. You miss deadlines. You fail to follow up leads. You haven't placed anything in weeks."

How humiliating that in a profession famed for shirking, I should have been caught out.

"I took the trouble of checking on your Internet usage. Well, my little helper did." Tracy thrust a printout of my Internet history at me. It was like looking at an extended bank statement, a humiliating roll call of your existence that you never thought to see. It was the Turin Shroud of my office life, a negative imprint based on hours on izobel brannigan.com, interrupted only briefly by forays into media sites and gossip boards. "It seems like you spend many hours of company time working on your personal Web site, or blogging as I believe it's called these days. We don't pay you to create your own home page. Though we're clearly paying you too much if you can afford to have all those photos of yourself taken. It's the vanity of it that I find so extraordinary. I don't even have a photo of myself on the company Web site. And this"—she pointed at my sheet of shame—"isn't company business. Have you got something you'd like to say?"

I was silent.

"Take this as a verbal warning." She avoided my gaze. "In the current climate we can't be carrying slackers. See this." She pointed at a pile of papers on her desk. "These are CVs from Oxbridge graduates begging to be allowed to come and work for us for free. Just remember that. And if you've got a problem, then please talk to someone about it. Don't allow it to affect your professional conduct. If you want, you can leave work now." It was almost five anyway. "Use the time to think."

I would think, I resolved quickly as I bustled through the office. I went to my computer and pulled the server support line number off the list of central resources. We had to sort this out once and for all.

As I walked out into the street, the pap caption might have read, "A good day's work: Izobel leaves the West End offices of the thriving PR business."

Chapter Ten

I rang my technical consultant Ivan, who readily agreed for me to come round to his offices just north of Oxford Street, despite having seen me only half an hour before. George was disengaged, Maggie disgruntled and I was disappointed. At least my technical friend still seemed to retain the last vestiges of patience about finding out who was behind the site.

I made my way to an unfamiliar area of the West End, but ten minutes' walk from my office. Its streets were lined with wholesale clothes shops selling the sort of outfits only worn by girl bands: one-shouldered tops, spray-on trousers and six-inch-wide belts, all in fawn colorways. The rest of the area had a vaguely holiday feel, culminating in a crossroads of cafés with outdoor tables, complete with a mariachi band singing "Guantanamera" on repeat, and throngs of people enjoying not being in an office at just after five on a partially sunny afternoon.

I made my way up steep stairs, having waded through the mail almost blocking the door of Ivan's building, letters addressed to fake-sounding businesses with names like "Flair International Fashion" and "ERM Elegant Models." I was stuck in an optical illusion; the stairs went on forever, up and up and up. By the time I reached the top floor, I was doubled up and panting like a pervert.

I almost fell in as Ivan opened the door. He was wearing non-office gear and he wore it well.

"Hello again." He smiled. "I've got a terrible advantage over anyone visiting me. They always look like they've completed a decathlon." He was pressed and fresh. Even his hair looked like it had been steam-cleaned, especially in comparison to mine, which was held up with a rubber band garnished with the strands that it had already ripped from my scalp.

He ushered me into a mezzanine room that was as small as the two computers it contained were outsize. I felt like a twenty-first-century Alice in Wonderland, facing a machine that would be labeled "use me." I could still hear the grating sounds of the band playing from the street, although it seemed as though I had crossed into another world. A world where it was acceptable to have a hand-made poster bearing the legend: "Systems Administrators do it with their hardware."

"Is this your office?"

"Yes."

"Where do all the people sit? I thought you had a team of employees. Is it a team of one?"

"Five people actually. They all work on-site or from home." He shrugged. "There's no point me shelling out for an expensive office when they wouldn't be there most of the time and I've set them up with powerful computers at home."

I frowned. "But how can you tell that they're not slacking?"

"I don't care if they are. They all get their work done, so what does it matter how long it takes them? I trust them and they trust me. No clients ever complain."

I sat down on one of the two swivel chairs placed in front of the computers that were raised on 1,000-page-thick manuals. The two screens faced coyly toward each other and their keyboards jostled for space on the desk. I spread out a hand on each of them and mimicked plinky-plonky electronic music sounds.

"Hey, I'm Jean-Michel Jarre."

"I thought you wanted to get down to business."

"I do. But I'd love a cup of tea. I've just had a bit of a stressful time with Tracy."

He raised an eyebrow. "Did you not get the Choo account? Or you forgot to order the giant penis ice sculpture and mini fish-and-chip canapés for the next launch?"

"Actually, if you must know, I'm about to get sacked as I apparently spend so much time surfing my own site. If only they knew."

"I knew something was up," he said. "Tracy asked me for a server printout of the Internet activity from your computer."

"And you gave it to her? Oh man," I elongated the word. "Couldn't you have faked it or something?"

"No, because that would have been both illegal and unprofessional."

He sat down, fired up both the monsters on his desk and then went to the corner of the room where an ancient plastic kettle sat among mini cartons of UHT milk and café packets of sugar. He made us our teas, black with sugar, without my prompting.

He looked intently at the screens before bringing up a black box with pale script. The box floated listlessly in the middle of one of the vast screens while he drummed his fingers in the one clear space left on the desk.

"What do you want to do? Work on that anagram or see if we can find more clues in the code?"

"I'm not sure. You said something about being able to get the name of the person who owns Izobel Brannigan, I mean, owns the name izobelbrannigan dot com. Can you do that for starters?"

"Find the domain name? I could give it a shot. It's fascinating," he continued. "I can find out so much about the servers izobelbrannigan dot com is using."

"But can you find out who's responsible for it?"

"Possibly." He had become distracted, as if his world had turned into something black and white with strange prompt commands. "If I ping it," he said, typing "ping www.izobelbrannigan.com" onto his screen, "we can see if the packet comes back from a remote server and how quickly it does. Look, nought point six milliseconds. These packets will keep spewing out until I press Control C." Which he duly did.

"Yes, but who owns the site? Who owns izobelbrannigan?" I felt hot and speckled. I had that sense of expectation that can only lead to acute disappointment.

"If I do a traceroute, I can find out the quickest route between the server I use here and the server it uses. Probably via LINX at Telehouse."

I made the face he must have been tired of seeing. I was tired of making it. I felt like I should just keep my hand permanently raised with the words "But *miss,* I don't understand" tattooed across my forehead.

"London Internet Exchange," he said patiently if patronizingly. "It's the largest Internet Exchange point in Europe. Anyway, back to the traceroute." He looked at my blank face and filled in the metaphor. "Like six degrees of separation. It will find the most direct links between servers and sites."

"But what about the owner of the domain name?"

"I'll do a whoislookup."

I liked the sound of that. At last computer language I could understand.

"Let's try on the co dot uk one first." He typed "#who is izobel.brannigan.co.uk@whois.nic.uk" into that strange little black and white box on the screen. These computer commands were contradictory, in some ways so opaque and in others so insultingly simplistic. "Who is" indeed.

"Who's Nic?" I asked.

He looked like I'd asked him who was top of the hit parade. "It's Nominet, the registry for all dot co dot uk Internet names." He shook his head.

"And who owns my site?" I asked as information clattered onto the screen.

He pointed at the information with his pen. "Domain name: izobelbrannigan dot co dot uk."

"We know that. What I don't know is why they call it a domain name and not a URL."

He couldn't be bothered to explain. "And here's the registrant, World Web Worshippers UK."

"And they are?"

"Search me."

"Search-engine me."

He continued. "Here's the registrant's agent, that's the people who host the site, and whoever it is behind the site bought the domain name through them: e-z-webbysolutions dot com. Never heard of them."

"E-z-webbysolutions sell domain names?"

"Yes and more importantly they sold the domain name izobelbrannigan dot com to World Web Worshippers UK."

"And they're our site perp?"

"Yes. Or at least a pseudonym for them."

I felt like I had a squash ball stuck in my throat. Whoever e-z-webbysolutions were, they had been contacted by the person who had made this site. They knew who it was. They had carelessly, thoughtlessly, nonchalantly registered a name for the person whose actions had dominated my recent weeks. I felt suddenly close to knowing. The screen in front blurred as if I were at the optician's and the examiner were varying the lens and focus of the light box. Ivan gave me a sympathetic smile and touched me lightly on the arm.

"Here's when they bought it," he said. It was over six months ago. "All that time, it was sitting there, waiting to be brought to life. And here"—he said, pointing at a date less than a month ago—"was when it was last updated."

"I don't understand, it was updated with new pap shots yesterday."

"This is when something to do with the domain name registrant was changed, not the site itself."

"I see." Not really.

"And look," he said. "Here are the DNS servers."

"But who is it? I don't care about the DNS servers, I want to know who's behind the site. Other than Webhead Worship UK or whatever they call themselves. Can we find out who they are? Through company registrars or whatever? You say it's the pseudonym of whoever's behind the site. Can't we find them?" Now, now, now, I wanted to scream.

"We're trying. Let's see if we can get more information out of the other address, the dot com one. I think you may be forced to give an address on those."

I shrugged. I couldn't get excited anymore. The squash ball in my throat was now even bigger. A tennis ball, perhaps.

"It's a two-stage lookup. First I've got to ask interNIC, you know, Nominet, the UK registry, in order to find out which dot com registrar it's registered with. There are hundreds of them."

I was reminded of Irene Handl, who had it explained to her how all the lighting was going to be set up by a director and had responded, "I think you've mistaken me for one of those actresses who gives a fuck."

The screen was filled with more information in dense text.

He pointed at it. "See, now I know who the dot com registrar is. I'll go there now to find out more about the registrant." He opened up what was recognizably a Web page with a convenient "who is" search box in the top left-hand corner. He became animated as he viewed more spewed ugly sans-serif text. "The registrant's the same, World Web Worshippers UK. Here's a contact, look, 'administrative contact,' one Atreides, no first name, host master at worldwebworship dot com. That must be it, that must be who they are. Do you know someone called Atreides?"

"No, I don't think so." Stupid, stupid, why didn't I know that name? Was it Turkish? It was certainly all Greek to me. I performed a "whoislookup" into my memory, but nothing was upchucked. "Sorry, I don't. Maybe it will come to me."

"But I know that name," he said. "I'm sure I know it. Atreides, Atreides," he intoned. He wrote the letters down in a circle on the white board by his desk, "S, A, I, D, T, R, E, E," striking off the letters from Atreides as he went. He looked jubilant. "There's one riddle solved, at least. That's the answer to the anagram about said tree."

"Oh yes. Amazing. But it doesn't help, does it?"

He continued to look at the screen, undeterred. "And look, our Mr. Atreides the administrative contact's got an address."

"But it's a PO box. What is a PO box anyway, other than something people use when placing personal ads? How do you get one?"

"Sorry, I know about dialog boxes, not PO boxes." His eyes continued to scan the screen. "Your 'technical contact' is Atreides again, Paul Atreides."

"Think Izobel, think," I said out loud. "Who is Paul?"

I shook my head. We looked at the screen together. There was a list of "domain servers" and a "registrar of record," neither of which meant anything to me. Paul Atreides meant nothing to me and yet I seemed to mean something to him. How could that be? The ball inside my throat must have been an inflatable one because now it had deflated. I felt flat and frustrated.

"My God," said Ivan. "I think I've got it. I think I know who

Paul Atreides is. Of course I do, how could I forget?" He inputted "google.com" to the address bar. Hadn't this been where all my problems had begun? He then typed in the words "Paul Atreides." The results came back quickly and were myriad.

"You're Googling Paul Atreides? He's a pretty popular bloke," I said when I saw the tens of thousands of sites about him. Far more than about Izobel Brannigan, that was for sure.

"Heir to the House of Atreides and savior of Arrakis, source of all Melange, the prophesied Kwisatz Haderach, superman and messiah," Ivan said.

"You what?"

"Izobel, haven't you ever read *Dune* by Frank Herbert?"

"Er, no. Isn't it a film?"

"Sacrilege, fans of the book don't like to talk about the disappointing film version. I don't know how I could have forgotten the name of Atreides. It was etched on my brain throughout ado lescence as much as Gandalf."

"It's a book like *Lord of the Rings* then?"

"Kind of. *Lord of the Rings* crossed with *Star Wars.*"

"Great. What's it about?"

"An interstellar imperium where the House of Atreides has to safeguard the source of this spice in order to protect the universe. I can't believe you haven't read it."

I smiled wanly. "Do I look like a fifteen-year-old boy? Why would I have read a sci-fi fantasy adventure book?"

"Because it's a classic," Ivan said.

"Have you ever read any of those teenage girl classics by Judy Blume or Virginia Andrews? No, I thought not. While you boys were reading about intergalactic spice racks, we girls were swapping our copies of books with stuff about sex and birth control."

"My book sounds better. Herbert wrote it in the sixties and yet was amazingly prescient about the future of the environment and the effects of globalization." He was po-faced as he spoke and I had a glimpse of the earnest adolescent he must have been.

"Well, while you boys were playing Dungeons and Dragons we were learning about the birds and the bees, so which do you think was more useful?"

Ivan laughed while I frowned. "Thing is, it doesn't help us much, does it? Arse, registering the site under a false name."

"Unless the book too is a clue to the identity," he said. "I'll reread it if you like."

"But it's not, is it?"

"No, just a pseudonym, I presume. Still, at least it's a good book and a cool superhuman slash messiah character."

"I don't care. I don't care about stupid *Dune* and stupid Paul whatsit." My voice wobbled. "I'm never going to find out who's behind the bloody site."

"Yes, we are." Again, Ivan touched my arm. "I promise. Let's see. The PO box. There must be something we can do with that."

"It's in London."

"Yes." We fell silent. Neither of us knew anything about PO boxes, clearly. One of those things you take for granted without ever really thinking any further. I never needed to, until now.

"Let's do what hasn't worked up until now," he said. "Let's look them up on the Internet."

"Ah yes, the Internet. I believe it's a craze that's taking the world by storm," I said, in best sixties radio presenter tones.

"All the groovy kids are loving it," he said in a matching male voice as he went into the Royal Mail's site. "Quick links, here we are, PO boxes."

"Hurrah."

"Cost forty-five pounds per six months, how you get one, why you get one. 'If you work from home, a PO box address can strengthen your business image.' I'll have to remember that one."

"You don't work from home."

"Yes I do. Frequently Asked Questions." He clicked on the FAQ link. "'How much does it cost? Where can I have the box? Could someone find out my home address via my PO box number?' Bingo." He clicked again. "Isn't my connection fast? I've got broadband, of course."

I stared intently. Please say yes, please say yes, I asked of the Royal Mail Web site, please tell us there's a real-life address behind any PO box. We both leaned forward and in.

"We are obliged to disclose your full postal address to anyone who asks for it. However, we will not disclose your name or telephone number," the site read.

"Eureka," we cried with one voice and leaped up and did the sort of dance performed by attention-seekers on *Top of the Pops.*

"We know where you live. We know where you live," I sang. "Nah, nah, na-na-nah." We hugged briefly and then sat down again.

"Is there a frequently asked question about how you ask the Post Office for a postal address attached to a PO box?" I asked.

We paused blankly before we both reached for the mouse to drag the cursor toward the Contact Us link we had spotted. His hand got there first, closely followed by mine, which landed on top of his in accidental hand-holding.

"Let's ring the general inquiries number," I suggested and punched it into my mobile.

"It's cheaper to use a landline, don't you know?"

I ignored him and concentrated on the options being given to me by the surprisingly un-Received Pronunciation of the recorded message. I pressed option two. It's always a bit like choosing a boyfriend—the options given never quite seem to match up exactly to your requirements but once you're on the line you think you might as well go for it.

"'Your call is in a queue and will be answered as soon as possible,'" I mimicked. "Hello," I said on at last achieving human voice-to-voice contact. "I want to find out the address for a PO box." I liked being in control. I was sick of being the appendage girl to Ivan's detective work.

The man at the other end chuckled. "But you need the sales center, not general inquiries."

"Silly me. What's the sales center number then, please?"

I rang it and was faced with another set of random options, this time mostly concerned with business reply services, whatever they were. I pressed three for the sake of pressing something.

"Is this the right number for getting the address of a PO box?"

"Yes it is," said the disdainful and disembodied voice.

I nodded at Ivan. "The PO box we're interested in is four-five-three-two-one and it's in EC One. London." I held my mobile out from my ear so that Ivan could listen in.

A pause. A bored voice. "There is no PO box of that number."

"What do you mean? We've got it registered. It must be a PO box number. We've seen it on an Internet site."

"There is no PO box of that number. Are you sure you took it down correctly?"

"Yes I'm sure." Ivan found the printout of the whois details. "Yes I'm very sure, I have the number right here in front of me."

"Then your Internet site has the number incorrectly. Or they have been given a fallacious PO box number."

"That can't be, it can't be true. Check again, please, check again."

"There is no valid PO box of that number."

"Bastard." The voice at the other end put the phone down. "I meant he's a bastard, not you, I don't know you, it's not your fault." It was too late.

"Shit." I slammed my hands on the desk, which hurt them

and caused me to exclaim once again. "They've given a false PO box number."

"They've given what looks like a false company name and false technical contact's name, so I suppose we should have expected it."

"Damn." I was exhausted. "I'm never going to find them, am I? This is hopeless. I'm going to be stalked by them for the rest of my life and I'll never know who they are. I thought you'd sort it out. I'd given up hope with Maggie's and my investigations but I believed you'd be able to do it."

"I will get it, Izobel. I promise. I'll think of something. It might be time to think of some illegal ways forward."

"Exactly. I mean, they're not legal themselves, are they?"

"I think they're completely legal, unfortunately."

"Provision of false information, invasion of privacy, misrepresentation . . ." These were the phrases Maggie would have used based on television drama. I hadn't a clue what they meant in a legal sense.

"Whatever. Don't worry, I swear I'll find out. I just need some time with my babies alone."

He called his computers his babies. I shook my head.

"Let's get something to eat."

"And drink."

I followed him out of the computer cave up the stairs to the next level. "Where are we going?"

"To my flat. I live above the shop."

"Great area to live in."

"Isn't it?"

We entered his living area and I was forced to compliment him again. It wasn't so much a flat as what lifestyle magazines would call a "space." I'd always mistrusted people who were into interiors, always thought it showed that they had no interest in their own interior life, but this was different. The space didn't make Ivan seem like a void. Quite the opposite.

He paused, evidently expecting the exclamation that must always come.

"Amazing place."

"Thanks. What do you want to drink?"

He busied himself with my gin and tonic, while I wandered around. You could wander, it was that big. It was a long, rectangular room that extended laterally across two of the street's terraced houses. It was low-ceilinged, but must have been light during the day because of the skylights. Within the space, there were areas for cooking, eating and playing. The kitchen featured a freestanding oven and stacked Le Creuset. I thought only married people had Le Creuset. Then there was an oak table big enough for ten. It was a table for entertaining, which made me think that maybe Ivan did have friends after all, unless he just held techie conventions with other spods or used it for arranging his computers in an elaborate placement. He did call them his babies, after all.

I continued scanning the room. Nothing was too slick. I hated those flats that look like they've been done up by developers and so check all the obvious design boxes: mosaic tiles in the bathroom, check; cooker by Smeg, check; big pink American fridge, check; accessories by Philippe Starck, check. This place, to use my magazine jargon again, was an eclectic mix of old and new. Everything looked like it had been lovingly chosen in a junk shop or foreign flea market. It made me think of city breaks in Madrid and Paris, weekends away in Norfolk, rooting around antiques fairs before a slap-up meal in a pub with a roaring fire. It made me think of good times.

Then there was the sitting area. Between the huge chocolate-colored velvet sofa and its equally fat burgundy corduroy companion sat an opaque fish tank. A few more mini versions of the same thing were dotted on the shelves between books (real novels, not the computer manuals I might have expected).

"Really amazing," I said. "Your flat's very"—I struggled to find an inoffensive way of expressing myself—"untechnical."

"I think because I work with computers, it's important to me to have a counterpoint to this at home. That's why everything's warm and wobbly here." He laughed. "You're such a snob, Izobel. I can tell exactly what you're thinking."

"Which is what?"

"Ivan's not such a boring techie after all. How strange, I thought his home would look like a teenage boy's bedroom, all PlayStations and pizza boxes."

"No, not at all. What's that?" I asked, pointing to the fish tank between us.

He flicked a switch and the tank lit up. I did too upon seeing it. The cloudy glass box filled with colors and movement; it looked as though flowers were billowing and blooming within it, a nature video come to life. All the colors were ones that I never thought you could replicate: the soft pink of an English rose, the shiny green of ivy, a cloudless sky that makes you happy and young.

"It's an installation," I said, not knowing what else to say faced with something so mesmerizing. "Who did it?"

"I did."

"You're an artist?"

"No, I'm a computer programmer turned systems administrator. This is just something I do because it interests me. It's a way of turning what I do at work into something else and I like bridging my two worlds."

"But it's lovely. Do you sell your work?"

"No. Like I say, it's not my work."

"But you could do. Really, I know plenty of people who'd love this. We could do incredible things with them at our launches."

"I don't want to. It's mine. I've done things for other people, but not for money, only for people who are important to me."

I wondered then what his sexual backlist was, and whether it was as dismal as mine.

I watched one of the colors pop. "How long have you been doing this?"

"Years. I was the only kid in school to do double maths, chemistry, physics and art A levels. I like to prove to myself that computers don't mean soulless."

"I really think you're mad not to do something commercially."

"Why? I'm happy and fulfilled by my day job and it would only ruin my pleasure to turn this into my source of income. It's the mistake that people make these days. They think their job is going to be creatively fulfilling when it's not. All jobs are admin, more or less, so you should go for the one that pays best and gives you the most freedom. People used to have hobbies, but now they don't have time. Do you know anyone with a hobby?"

I was about to say something about film and socializing.

"Apart from going to the cinema and meeting friends?" he interjected.

I shook my head. I didn't think George's drinking could really count as an interest, interesting though he seemed to find it.

"I think people in the media are especially sad."

"Thanks," I said.

"I mean sad in the old-fashioned sense of the word. They go into jobs like yours and television research and location-scouting because they think it will be creative and then they find out that it isn't and they'd have been better off getting a so-called boring job with regular hours so that they could fulfill this creative urge after work."

He had described my life and that of most of my friends. I went into PR because I thought it would be inspiring.

"An accountant will almost always be more interesting than a TV producer," he continued. "Because a TV producer thinks it's acceptable to talk about his work and the celebrities he's dealt with and the hilarious thing that happened in the hospitality room, while an accountant will always have to find some other topic of conversation when out with people. Why did you go into PR, Izobel?"

"Because I thought it would be interesting and because I wanted to help the world."

"Help the world?"

"I started out doing press for a charity. I thought I might go into politics. Instead I just got into office politics. I'm not sure how I arrived at where I am. You know how it is, you leave university and you don't know anything about work so you get a job that sounds like it might be interesting and then forty years later you retire and you never really made a proper choice about it."

"To paraphrase William Morris, don't do any job unless you believe it to be interesting or know it to be useful."

"And what if you can't think of a job that is either?" I asked.

"Do something really well paid."

I laughed. "You're right. People who talk about work are boring, so let's not. Let's talk about food. Shall we have some?"

"Do you want to go out?"

"There was a place just downstairs."

"No way. It's the worst food in Britain. It's like culinary time travel. The prawn cocktail is frozen prawns with ketchup and mayonnaise, the bread is sliced white and the carrots come from a tin."

"Can we stay here then? It's so lovely. Can we get a takeaway?"

"You do surprise me. I thought you wouldn't approve of takeaway food."

"Well, of course, you can get fabulous bento sushi boxes and carb-free meals based on the Zone diet these days." He looked aghast. "Joking. I want a curry and I want it now."

He ordered, we ate. Nothing too strong; his choice of creamy and mild was spot on. A cheap curry and a couple of expensive bottles of wine, it was a heavenly combination. We banned two topics of conversation: izobelbrannigan.com and work. I found out that he was brought up in the suburbs, that his parents still held each other's hands and that he had three sisters. He learned that I grew up close enough to London to yearn for it, but too far away ever to visit on my own, that it was a rainbow to me. He discovered that my parents, too, were still together, but had a disconcerting habit of communicating entirely through their springer spaniels: "I think Snickers doesn't approve of the Labour Government at all, do you, Snickers?" my father would say. "Wispa is not at all sure about genetically modified crops, but he does think it's time for supper," my mother would reply.

We were swapping childhoods. We were talking about family pets. We were confessing how insecure and unattractive we felt as teenagers. This could only mean one thing: we were on our way to a fumble.

No, no, I thought. No, we're not. I've got a boyfriend. I'm living with George. Lovely George, sexy George, fantastic-in-bed George, fashionable journalist George. I can't get off with Ivan. Ivan, techie Ivan, systems-guy Ivan, sometimes-wears-a-fleece Ivan.

Or was he artist Ivan? Ivan with the lovely flat, kind Ivan, sympathetic Ivan, handsome Ivan, piss-taking Ivan. Have you met Ivan? He's a systems administrator. No, don't like that. Have you met Ivan? He's an information consultant. Better, much better. He's a creative solutioneer. Possibly.

The angel and devil in my head scrapped. I wasn't sure which one was which though. The red wine made me think that maybe the angel wanted me to kiss Ivan. I was hypnotized by the slow blooms of his installation, the art one I mean. Flicking that switch to turn it on had been the equivalent of putting on a Barry White CD and dimming the lights.

He got up to open another bottle of wine and to make us some mint tea. Real mint tea, not bags, but leaves. It cleaned my palate, expunging the trash taste of curry and leaving my mouth icy and white. It made my mouth kissable. We chatted all the while; I wasn't sure what we were saying anymore. It wasn't important. It was just the adverts before your favorite television program, just background. The words coming out of our mouths were out of focus, our mouths themselves were sharp. He filled my bulb of a glass and his, too. He sat down beside me on the chocolate-colored sofa, looking edible himself. The sofa was so big that he wasn't anywhere near touching me. I wanted him to touch me.

"Big glass of wine," I said. So fatuous, I feared and hoped that it would destroy the moment. I put down the glass. So did he. We looked at each other. I could see his flushed cheeks. I could see mine, equally flushed, reflected in his eyes. They were dark.

I did a history of art module at university and remembered how Velazquez's brilliance lay in painting the space between people as much as the people themselves. I never quite understood what that meant, but at that moment I knew that he would be the artist to capture the hard glass ball of nothingness between our lips. That space, that distance of ten inches, was of a different density to normal air. It was more solid than we were.

It was like standing on a high board at the swimming pool. I knew that only a millisecond stood between me and it being too late to turn back. I wasn't ten inches away from kissing him, I was just a millimeter, for if I moved forward just a little bit then that would be it.

And I did and it was.

Chapter Eleven

Babe, do you want a coffee or what?" Mimi asked.

Today was the first day of probation following Tracy's verbal warning about my performance and yet I wasn't in the office. I was floating above it looking at myself operating the computer keyboard.

Snog-struck, kiss-tipsy, smooch-woozy, caress-crazy; I was all of these.

Sandpapered, sandblasted. My chin had been rubbed raw by a stubbly muzzle. I touched it. How to explain stubble burn? Why would just your chin and maybe your nose be rubbed raw, popping out in tiny red abrasions? How could something so beautiful as kissing leave so ugly a mark? George hadn't seemed to notice when I wobbled in late last night nor Mimi when I entered the office in a similar whoosh, but it scorched, I was branded by it. Could I say that I had fallen down? Or overused a new exfoliating product that had caused an extreme allergic reaction? On just my chin and nowhere else?

Stubble burn. It was more a mark of a new relationship than a packet of condoms in the pocket. Why is it that you only get stubble burn the first or second time you kiss someone? Because you kiss them so much harder and longer than you ever will do when kissing is replaced by sex? Or do you just get used to a person's skin, so that at first it's like an allergic reaction to their newness but repeated exposure takes away one person's skin's power to rip and make raw?

"Coffee would be fantastic, Mims, ta. I'm knackered."

I was tired. I was exhausted from hours of kissing, and of legs being wrapped around one another, of rubbing, of stroking. No clothes were removed, no penetration occurred. How I had wanted it to and how much I had not wanted it to.

"Morning, Tracy," I said in as gung-ho a fashion as I could muster, while cupping my chin in the manner of the by-line photo of a journalist known for his musing and thoughtful investigations. Or a silly PR girl with stubble burn.

Kissing, snogging, spit-swapping. How I'd missed that in the two years I'd been going out with George. It was the preserve of the recently met and the pre-penetrative sexual. Kissing is best when it's everything, both the journey and the point of arrival. Settled-down couples never snog anymore; they lightly kiss and hug, but they never snog for hours on sofas and get to that trance-like state that only snogging can arouse.

The kissing and the art at Ivan's had dizzied me. I had seen the clock flash on his video recorder and it had been past one. On a school night. It took me a further hour to extricate myself and find a taxi. I was drunk on so many things that I didn't care.

Perhaps I was still drunk. Then the coffee had the adverse effect of sobering me up. My hand moved from chin to forehead. What had I done?

I had coiled myself around Ivan. I was going out with George. I was living with George. I loved George. Did I want to go out with Ivan? Did I want to stop going out with George? These choices shouldn't be connected to one another, should they? Did I just want to be alone? Oh no, I didn't want to be alone, I didn't want to ever not have a body to press against, a body like Ivan's, hard and soft and without a gut that could envelop a fist such as George had.

Stop. I'm with George. Don't compare George and Ivan. Separate issues. Keep them separate.

Work. Must work. Calls to make, important press releases to draft and to send out as e-mail attachments. Attached. I was attached to George. I wished I were unattached. I wished I were attached to Ivan as I had been last night, Velcroed to one another, an almost audible ripping sound when we un-suckered ourselves.

You should never get off with people you're unsure of. Once you've got off with them you're lost, you can't make a rational decision anymore. I get drunk and get off and then find myself going out with people, spending more time alone with them than with any of my friends and yet not liking them half so much. Did I like Ivan? Or even fancy him? Could I love him? These were questions I should have asked myself before I'd sunk the wine. Now I could never know what my true answers would have been.

Ivan had fancied me for a while. He seemed quite sure of me despite the many ways in which he found me awful: my job, my shallowness, my solipsism.

I made that fatal lean forward and then our mouths met. I moved a millimeter and moved so much more. Normally lips lock clumsily and quickly in these situations, in a bid to get it out of the way, but this time it was slow and our mouths flirted with each other before unifying. Then I had pulled away; I couldn't carry on kissing because I was smiling too much. What bad design that we can't kiss and smile at the same time.

Smiling, kissing, laughing, eating, drinking. Mouths are marvelous things. Sweet words too. Like our post-first-snog conversation, the when-did-you-first-fancy-me one. He said for months, he'd noticed me in the office, he'd created spurious reasons to check out the PR O'Create systems in order to stake me. Why else should he have been spending time in the offices of one of his most impecunious clients? He'd dragged his heels about investigating the izobelbrannigan.com domain name as it was a way of drawing out being close to me. He had been horrified by the site and yet grateful for it.

He asked me how long I'd fancied him. I said for about five minutes and he looked hurt so I kissed him some more and the disparity between our crushes didn't seem to matter. I'm sure I fancied him just as much even if it hadn't been for just as long.

Could I leave it at that? At a perfect night of kissing and understanding? Maybe he's rubbish in bed. Maybe I would be rubbish in bed with him too. He could be like one of those restaurants where the starters are so much better than the mains. Maybe we'd decide to sleep with one another and he'd come too quickly. Actually I don't mind that. The alternatives are so much worse. He can't get it up and I don't laugh at him but blame myself and think it's because of my cellulite or some such irrelevancy. There is nothing more depressing than the coiled-up soft button mushroom of the impotent cock. It feels so slippery and insubstantial to the touch, the touch that's supposed to rouse it but just makes you both blush from embarrassment and frustration. You feel like every time you touch it, you diminish it still further and it retreats snail-like into its shell.

Or maybe Ivan is one of those who do manage to get it hard and then just won't come but keeps on and on, sawing away at your soreness with his blocked ducts, giving away nothing. That's only drug users though, in my experience, like dear William, who used to make me feel so bad about his lack of release and I'd be too embarrassed to tell him just to stop, to put it away.

Ivan wasn't a drug taker, as far as I knew. But then I hardly knew him.

Or maybe he's like Elliot and I'll have to talk constantly throughout in order to maintain his pleasure and bore myself with the sound of my own inanities and ensure that I never felt any joy of my own: "Oh Ivan, give it to me, oh your big hard cock, your hardware is the latest version, upgrade me to your systems, administer your love."

Or like Married Man, he'll want to spank me and have me wear scratchy panties and garters. He'll encourage me to put on a naughty nurse's outfit and then tell me I've been remiss in my duties to which the only recourse is for him to administer a love injection. He'll like it when I call him a "stud muffin" and respond by calling me his "creamy crumpet," until I feel that we're starring in our porno version of a slap-up spread in a chintzy country tea shop. And, like cream, I'll end up being whipped into shape, into what he hopes will be peaks of lust for him.

I really don't like being spanked, even lightly; why would I like the sight of a red welt across my body?

Frank, what was he like in bed? I don't remember, so long ago. Being born after 1966 meant he was condom-dexterous. He was enthusiastic, too. We laughed a lot and giggled at ourselves in the mirror and spent whole weekends eating bad student food and each other. I bet he didn't do that with Camilla.

Spanish Artist was scientific. There wasn't much in the way of tapas with Pepe, if you know what I mean, just straight in there with the chorizo.

Ivan and I had not talked about contraception yet. He hadn't pressured me for sex but had seemed content with kissing. Would we have to go for triple protection as Jonny and I had done? Rubberized both within and without.

And George, what was he like in bed? How good was George really? He was very good at convincing the world that he was a fun-loving bon viveur rather than a sybaritic louse living off his parents, me and his glory days as editor of a punk fanzine. He had conned the paper into thinking him capable of editing a whole section. He had fooled Catherine into marrying him and bearing his child. And I had believed that he loved me for me, not for the place I was offering him to live. I continued to trust that he was faithful to me, when he never had been to any other woman. Maybe he had duped me into believing he was such a hot lover. He never went down and I hadn't come in months, after all.

Ivan, I suspected dreamily, would be better than all of them. I felt my lips. They had been kissed dry. My lips were cracked, my chin rough, my eyes bagged. Yet I was sure I looked lovely.

George, my live-in lover, to use the parlance from his newspaper. We were "living in sin," yet it was I who had sinned against him. Ivan and I hadn't had sex, so did it count? But I knew I'd transgressed. I'd crept back at three in the morning and given myself the adulterer's bath—splashing water on my face and neck, drying myself between my legs, washing my mouth out with minty breath freshener and chewing gum, hoping that its sugar-free hardness would attract all the taste of Ivan into its tasteless little ball. I had lain next to George and felt smug. That was it, I hadn't felt guilty so much as smug. I had wanted sex so much at that moment, but I had not wanted it with George.

"Nice time, angel-girl?" he had asked.

"Lovely, thanks," I had said without remorse.

The phone on my desk rang.

"Izobel speaking."

"Hello, Izobel."

"Hello," I said to Ivan, both pleased and appalled. You're not supposed to ring me yet. I felt nervous.

"I was just ringing to check that you got home all right last night."

"Yes, fine, thanks. I must say it's very chic to have a black cab rank near your house. Most of us only have those really grotty minicab places with a flashing beacon outside and Formica and illegal workers inside. And then have to get into an un-MOT-ed Mercedes with a man who doesn't know where Oxford Circus is," I gabbled. "But where you live is different. It's great, the best."

"I had a nice time last night."

"It was nice."

"We should do it again."

"We should."

My mobile rang. It was Maggie; I rejected her call. "Sorry about that. Are you feeling rough today?" I asked. "I am. Gosh, I think I was really drunk last night. Steaming. Off my head."

"I wasn't."

The mobile went again, Maggie again. Its insistence was like an annoying child, poking their parent in the arm. "Sorry, Ivan, but the same person keeps ringing. Can we speak later? Ring me back."

"Fine. 'Bye then."

"'Bye."

"Hello Maggie, what do you want?" I felt guilty about the hurt note in Ivan's voice. What a cringing woman's guilt—nothing about having got off with a man who's not your boyfriend, just feeling really bad about not being more enthusiastic the next day and potentially hurting his feelings.

"You're so going to love me. In my efforts to keep my mind off all the nonspecific pregnancy anxiety, I have been working so hard on your behalf."

"Doing what?"

"Trying to find out who's behind the site, that's what."

"Oh, that." I wondered whether I should get her off the phone and call Ivan straight back. That would be craven. I shouldn't worry about being a bit cool, cool was good, cool was what I usually failed to do. Anyway, he wasn't my boyfriend, he wasn't even my potential boyfriend, I already had a boyfriend. "Great, thanks Maggie, you're a star. What have you got then?"

"Two things. For starters I've got something on our friend Pepe Gomez Gomez. I have to say, it was pretty easy. I just Googled him and then got this hilarity. I've e-mailed you the Web address to look at."

"Does it incriminate him?"

"Of doing your site? Probably not. But of being a total plonker? Yes, he is guilty of that crime. You can be judge and jury on that score."

"I look forward to it. And what's the second thing?"

"I haven't quite got it yet, but I will do. Something even better, I think. Call you back."

I couldn't phone Ivan and I couldn't do any work so I looked for Maggie's e-mail. *"Hello, you may be amused by this."* It was named "*Todas las Musas*" and the Internet address ended in ".es" to indicate a Spanish address. I could imagine her saying the name of the site in a heavily British accent reminiscent of the request for *"dos cervezas"* on a thousand package holidays.

I opened up the page as directed and found it covered in neat photos of women, equidistant from one another, like an American high-school yearbook. *Chica salvaje* read the caption beneath the photo of a girl in a dominatrix outfit, *la negra* by, unsurprisingly but politically incorrectly, a black woman, and *la inglesa* adjacent to a photo of me. I was wearing a pair of jeans and was braless in an old T-shirt, looking cheerfully toward the photographer. Pepe had never been without that Polaroid camera and I therefore looked nonchalant at being snapped in so casual a way. I might have been naked of makeup or grooming but at least I was fully dressed. I shivered as I glanced at the photo of my neighbor on the site, *la asistenta de limpieza,* who wore nothing but a pair of bright pink rubber gloves.

A photo of me? My Spanish was pretty poor, restricted as it was to filth and anatomy as practiced by my Iberian lover, but I could make out Pepe's name at the top of the page, and the words *artista* and *instalación* in the introductory text. *Todas las Musas,* of course, "All the Muses"; this was another piece of Pepe's virtual art, his attempt to turn his life into something for the world's cyber-gallery. This was all the girls he'd slept with, sorry, all his muses, all the girls he'd loved before. I looked through the arrayed photos. There were at least a hundred. How could I ever have thought that he might have been my cyber-stalker? True, online paeans were evidently a line of artistry he was interested in, but I was but one percent of his interest. And I was just "the English girl." Nothing else, not the *inglesa sexy* or *intelligente* or *bella* or *fantastica,* not even my name. At least with izobelbrannigan.com I was its star; here I was just an nth part of somebody else's life project and one that involved sleeping with as many *chicas* as possible.

In the center of the page, displayed in the largest photo of them all, was Pepe himself. His green teeth were visible even in the badly pixelated Polaroid and his eyes had that odd paleness that I remembered from looking into them. He didn't look at all Spanish. He did look foreign, but from another planet rather than merely from a country outside the British Isles. He was smiling broadly and I could not help but smile back at him. He was preposterous, but he always had been.

I laughed out loud, tiredness and drunkenness and kiss-giddiness making me almost hysterical.

"I wouldn't look at porn at work, sweets," said Mimi, glancing at the girls emblazoned on my screen.

"It's not porn, it's art," I said.

"That's what my boy calls it, but it don't change the fact that it's filth."

I laughed again. It might once have bothered me, even only the day before yesterday, that I was such an unimportant part of Pepe's grand work of art called his love life. His hubris was now merely humorous. I thought of Ivan's modestly displayed but far more beautiful pieces. He was an artist in all but name, Pepe was the reverse. I wanted to talk to Ivan about it, to tell him of the rubbish that my previous artist lover calls art. I thought he'd find it funny. On the other hand, he'd know about my past and at least one meaningless ex. Meaningless sex, meaningless men. He'd know just how dodgy they were and I didn't want him to know that, not yet. I wanted him to know only what he had so far chosen to recognize in me. There was time to reveal the flaws, the superficiality, the neurosis, even the fact that I had a boyfriend already.

I reached toward the phone to ring him; I had to speak to him, I had to make good my curtness on the phone to him. Just as I reached toward the handset, it rang again.

"So what do you think? Clever, aren't I?"

"Maggie! It's hilarious, I can't believe I didn't know about it. What a prat, all the muses indeed."

"Just think, two sites devoted to you."

"For what it's worth."

"I don't think he's your man."

"No, he never was, evidently."

"And I've managed to unearth something far more impressive in our search for site perp. You may call me clever and gorgeous, but I've only managed to go and get a list of the names of the people invited to Hot Bob's party."

I had almost forgotten about the site and our search and the party. "Oh my God. How did you get that?"

"I was brilliant. I went to the club and stuck my pregnant lady belly out and said that I needed the guest list from the night of Bob's party in order to find out a man's name. That man, I told the dippy woman at the club, needed to be found to face up to his responsibilities. At that point, I stroked pregnant lady belly in poignant way and she almost cried. They keep all the door lists in case of any trouble afterward. I explained how a young man had got me into trouble."

"But do the dates add up?"

"They almost do and how should she know exactly how pregnant I am anyway? Shall I read out the names to you, then? One of them could be our man."

I looked over to Tracy's office. "Yeah, why not." I noticed her come out of her office. "I would be grateful for your feedback on the target list. Would you like to respond to the one I e-mailed over to you earlier?" Tracy walked out of earshot. "Sorry about that. Fire away, Mags."

It was like being back at school as she read a roll call of the middle-class names that had been popular with seventies parents: Jonny, Kate, James, Edward and Charlotte. I felt my ears muffle over, lulled by hangover and Maggie's mantras. I doodled lips onto my notepad and did that schoolgirl thing where you can work out what percentage Izobel Brannigan loves Ivan Jaffy by counting up each time an L, an O, a V, an E and an S appear in your respective names. Izobel and Ivan love each other a whopping eighty-seven percent actually, that's almost the best score you can get. Was it fate? Don't be silly, I don't love Ivan. I don't even know him.

Maggie continued to read, oblivious to the fact that I only didn't love Ivan a mere thirteen percent. The names she spoke meant little or nothing to me.

"Stop," I said after Maggie had read out six dozen or so of them. The name on my notepad matched a name that she had called out. A familiar name, at last, the most familiar name to me that day. "Ivan who, did you say?"

"Ivan Jaffy. Why, do you know him?"

Know him? I knew the crease of his tongue and the stroke of his hand. "Yes, I know him."

"Could he be, you know, the one?"

I had asked myself the very same thing only that morning. How different Maggie's question was.

"Yes." I paused. "It could be him."

"Oh my God, I've got him, I found him, I found him. Forget your technical consultant, it was old-fashioned detective work that got him. Does this Ivan have technical know-how? Does he fancy you? Is he a bit creepy?"

"I suppose." Yes, yes, yes. He was all those things. Images of the truth flashed through my head: the picture from Hot Bob's party; the photo of me at the conference, hanging in the foyer right under my and Ivan's noses; the sluggishness about doing anything about finding who owned the URL; knowing too much about *Dune;* the computer nous; the crush on me; the getting close to me through the site.

And it had almost worked. I had almost slept with him last night.

"Iz, are you OK? Am I right?"

"Yes, I think you are. I think it's him."

"And what are you going to do about this tosser? Who is he anyway? Do I know him? Do you want me to deal with him?"

"I don't know, I don't know."

"Who is he?"

"He's just a techie from work."

"So he'd have the technical knowledge then. Bingo. What are you going to do about him? Do you want me around? Maybe Mick should come along too."

Artist Ivan, kisser Ivan, systems Ivan, funny Ivan.

Stalker Ivan, creepy Ivan, malevolent Ivan.

I didn't know what to do about any of them.

My landline went again and I answered it although I knew who would be calling. "Mags, I'll have to think about it. I have to go now."

"Hello, Ivan." The same phrase from an hour ago, my voice very different.

"We were saying," he said. "How we should do it again sometime."

"Maybe." This was how girls were supposed to act when with a potential boyfriend, all hard to get and elusive. Apparently drives men wild, though I wouldn't know as I'd never managed it. Until now. I didn't want to drive him wild. That had got us into trouble in the first place. "Yes, of course. Out of interest, do you know someone called . . ." I paused, what was Hot Bob's surname? "Robert. He had a thirtieth in a club about seven or eight months ago. Works in academia. An economist I think."

"Robert Ives? He's my cousin. Why, do you know him?" Listen to the eagerness with which he sought coincidence and shared experience. I almost believed him.

"I went to that party. Did you?"

"Yes I did, I was there, of course I did. Robert and I are almost the same age. We grew up together."

Hot Bob was his cousin. Made sense, they shared the same looks, though I had thought Ivan's more attractive.

"I didn't see you there. How annoying," he continued. "There's always something so bonding about bumping into work people outside work. Hang on, I wouldn't have recognised you, I don't think. It was about that time we took on this account. Did I know you then? Could we have met then? I was with my girlfriend. My then girlfriend."

I think I may have been with my now boyfriend but that was not an issue that needed to be raised anymore. Listen to lies trot from his tongue. I had loved that tongue and now I hated it.

"What a coincidence," he exclaimed.

Or not, I thought.

"Didn't you realize," I asked, "that it was the party in the photo?"

"What photo?"

Oh stop it, don't patronize me. You're not the one with all the knowledge anymore. "The photo on the site. In the first batch, there was the school one and the party one."

"No, I hadn't realized. It was pretty indistinct."

"I worked it out, I knew which party it had been taken from."

"But I hadn't even known you were at that party so why would I have made the connection?"

Connection. How he bandies round these computer-related words with ease. I would stay calm. I had to pretend that I still didn't know, that I didn't suspect. Why, I wasn't sure. Partly because it seemed so humiliating and embarrassing for both of us to accuse him of having done what I knew he had done.

"Look, Ivan, you know as well as I do that I'm on a warning from Tracy so I really had better go. Crap products to promote, horrible people to publicize, my life continues. My life goes on."

I put the phone down and felt sicker than I had ever done before. I felt the taste of vomit in my mouth. The hangover and my shock collided with one another and mated to reproduce more and more bile.

My life goes on?

"Babe, you're like a traffic light, your face keeps going from red to green and back again," observed Mimi as I tried to stand up.

"I feel like rubbish. I've got to go. Sorry. A one-day bug, some sort of virus." Still those evil computer words kept coming. "Tell Tracy for me. Tell her I looked really sick, please."

Chapter Twelve

Mimi, hello, it's me, Izobel," I said weakly. It didn't matter what your sickness sickie claim was, you always had to do the voice that made it sound like you were slipping in and out of a coma. "I can't make it into the office today. I vomited all night. I think it must be food poisoning."

If everybody who claimed to have food poisoning did have it, Britain's kitchens would have to be the most unhygienic in the world.

Despite my warning from Tracy, I couldn't face PR O'Create for a second day in a row. I didn't even care about the prospect of being sacked. Just do it, I thought. Ivan was bound to be there, skulking. I wanted to confront him. That's what all this detective work had been about, but I wasn't ready yet.

I looked at myself in the mirror. I really did look ill. It was a rare occasion when a videophone would have been of some use to the malingerer. My hair was lank and I wore an old pair of glasses and an even older pair of tracksuit bottoms. The lips that had been moistened by kissing had now dried and chapped. I had prodded my raw stubble burn so much that it had become infected and there was a little bubble of suppurating sore dripping greenish gunk continually from my chin. From sex kitten to pus galore, I said to the mirror, a feeble quip aimed at cheering myself up. It didn't work.

It was apt that I should have poisoned stubble burn from

having kissed Ivan. He had contaminated me in a way as rancid as any computer virus infecting an e-mail address book. I hated him. I wanted to squeeze my chin's festering discharge into a vial and dispatch it to his house anonymously. I wanted him to feel hunted and haunted as I had done.

And yet, I didn't. I wanted him. To be denied him at this point, the moment between kiss and sex, was too frustrating. To think of all that anticipation and to feel that kiss once again still made me tingle and dampen. I felt like I was dripping from all orifices. I disgusted myself.

My mobile was like a Post-it note with the word "Ivan" scribbled across it, stuck at every point in my world as it rang and flashed his name up three times throughout the day. Sometimes he left messages, sometimes not. He never disguised his number though, which surprised me, since anonymity appeared to be his modus operandi in other areas of his pursuit of me.

It is wonderful to be pursued, in theory, but in practice the way that pursuers choose to go about their business negates any succor an object of affection could derive from it.

I put the baseball cap on once again and went to the newsagent's. The nice man in the shop and George would be my only points of contact that day, I had already decided.

George had been good to me the night before, threatening to go round and sort Ivan out, once I had given him a carefully edited version of events.

"What did I tell you? That no good will come of technology," he said. "Who is this geek anyway? My poor darling, what's he like?"

"Like you say, a geek. Nobody, nothing."

"Creep."

"Yes, creep."

"I could expose him in the paper. What's his name?"

I paused. "Ian, his name is Ian Jones."

"Common little name for a common little man. Let me and a few colleagues onto him. Have you reported him to Tracy? Where's his office?"

"Hounslow, I think, but please don't go round. Let me talk to him, let me sort it out."

And we'd had sex that night and I thought that it would sate the desire I had worked up for Ivan but it didn't. It's like when you're at the gym, the way that the instructor says it won't work unless you're concentrating hard on pulling your stomach in or "sucking your belly button to your spine" in their anatomically disgusting phrase. Sex is the same, at least for me. If I don't engage, if I don't think about it really hard and concentrate on the muscles I'm working, it doesn't work. George, in contrast, was even more enthusiastic than normal. He didn't seem to notice that my chin was ejaculating bodily fluids, but had stroked me and called me his sexy girl and his angel-girl. All lips were dry.

That morning, I rejected George's offer of a sympathy sickie and had the flat to myself. I was the Lady of Shalott, but instead of being able only to view the world reflected through a mirror, I would look through izobelbrannigan.com. I fired up the computer in anticipation of a sign from Ivan.

I overcame the labors of passwords and connecting it up to the ancient modem. The site was now my home page, reached automatically whenever I got onto the Internet.

It was now so familiar to me in its Swedish colors that I almost didn't register it anymore. It all looked the same, I thought, and then I noticed.

There was a change.

My stomach made a yelping gurgle, but no noise came from my mouth. I started swaying.

A change had occurred, technically a very small one, emotionally a giant one.

In the middle of the page, where the introduction to Izobel had originally floated, there it was. Two words and two dates that horrified me. I touched the screen with my sweaty fingers as if the letters and numbers were in Braille. I felt blind to their true meaning.

But it was clear.

Izobel Brannigan, 1973–2003.

I fell onto my hands and knees and crawled away from the computer avoiding its range of vision, as if it could see me and were the instrument to ensure that those dates came true. My birth date and my death date? The PC monitor was a Cyclopean eye trained on me, it was a heat-seeking missile. I'm sure I even saw it move as I moved.

I curled up into a ball on my bed and covered myself in the duvet. It couldn't get me there.

*

The home phone woke me and I answered it, hoping that I'd never been so stupid as to give Ivan that number to join his armory.

"Oh, hello, Maggie."

"Why aren't you at work?"

"Couldn't face it. Didn't want to bump into him."

"You can't let him get to you like this. He's winning if you do. It's only a Web site, not a loaded gun."

I gave a wry laugh. Well, it started that way and mutated into a hysterical screech. "It is."

"Is what?"

"A loaded gun."

"What are you talking about?"

"Are you in the office? Log onto it now," I instructed. I pulled my knees into my chest as I waited for her response.

"You must go to the police," she said. "Tell them who you think it is and show it to them. Take a printout with you in case they don't have Internet connection. You never know. Tell them about Ivan and show them the dates."

"They won't do anything. I've seen the television version. They'll just say they can't do anything until he actually attacks me."

"Don't believe everything you see on television," Maggie said. "And no, you can't have that in writing."

*

I wasn't so depressed that I couldn't get dressed. Things would have to be really bad for me not to be able to theme-dress for a visit to the police station. I even put in my contact lenses. I had taken to wearing an old hiking anorak with big pockets instead of carrying a handbag, but I wanted the police to take me seriously. They must be as susceptible to theme-dressing as anyone. I tried to wodge some concealer onto the infected stubble burn but it was carried out on a wave of weeping pus. I put on a suit, my only suit, the one I had worn for the pitch in the photo on the site.

It had impressed Ivan the site-writer, who had after all described my besuited appearance at the conference as "slick." I shivered to think of it. I was trying to reconcile Ivan the artist with Ivan the sycophant whose prose style was that of *OK!* magazine without the wit.

I had never been inside a real police station before. I had expected it to look more like a doctor's waiting room, but there were no magazines for me to read or toys for kids to play with. There seemed to be a lot of pine, and it felt like a grotty Scandinavian holiday home. My rubber-soled shoes squelched across the lino floor as I read the notices that covered the walls as enthusiastically as boy band posters in a teenager's bedroom. A picture of handcuffs was emblazoned "streetwear for robbers." The public were warned not to leave their mobiles visible to thieves, but one poster later were warned more strictly still not to

make false claims of mobile phone theft. The happy smiling faces of now-missing persons were brightly color-photocopied onto posters to form a gallery of misery.

One notice told us to report crime via the Internet. I was reporting a crime on the Internet.

There was no one waiting so I stepped forward to the counter. No glass separated me from the police officers and I could see into their offices, where a helmet sat picturesquely by a computer, as if placed there by an art director.

Aren't policemen supposed to look younger every day? This one was well beyond retirement age. He was the oldest, most wizened man I'd seen outside of a retirement home. He looked like he should be an oracle of wisdom in a science-fiction film.

"I'm sorry," I said, "but have you got five minutes?" I pay my taxes, but I felt like a fraudulent time-waster. They probably had murders to deal with. But then, I shivered, mine could become a case of murder.

The old-timer looked around the empty station as if it was evident. I leaned forward, clutching the printout of the home page.

"I'd like to report what I believe to be a death threat."

He looked more interested. I unfolded my evidence. "How would I go about doing that?" I asked.

"You tell me how and where and I compile a report. Come through to the computer."

I shuddered as he ushered me through to a glass section in the corner, where he stood behind a computer and I in front. There was no getting away from them.

I stood tall as I gave him my personal details.

"About four weeks ago, this site came into being." I slammed down the A4 sheet with my hand splayed across it. "It's called izobel brannigan dot com. As I said, I'm Izobel Brannigan." He remained impassive. "This morning when I looked at it, these dates had

appeared. See, it says nineteen seventy-three to two thousand and three. It didn't do that before."

He frowned. I wasn't sure whether at me or at the site. "And?"

"I was born in nineteen seventy-three . . ."

"I see. Four weeks, you say."

"Yes."

"And these dates only appeared this morning."

"Yes." I felt as though I were reporting a leaky roof rather than my own imminent demise.

"And the address of the site is?"

"www dot izobelbrannigan dot com, my name dot com and my name dot co dot uk. It's spelled I-Z-O-B . . ." Do you even know how to log onto the Internet, Granddad?

"What is the tone of the rest of the site? Could it be perceived as threatening?"

I sighed. "No, it's flattering. A bit weird, maybe. Photos of me and stuff."

"And have you been verbally threatened or is there a more explicit threat on the site?"

"No." I was ashamed. At that moment, I almost wished that I had been, like I had wanted proof of George's infidelity rather than merely the suspicion of it.

"Are you known to us for any reason?"

"What on earth do you mean?" Nutty police botherer?

"Have you ever had call to contact the police before?"

"No, except once to report a stolen bicycle. About ten years ago."

"Do you know who is behind the site?"

Again I sighed. "Yes."

"Name?"

"Ivan Jaffy," I told him before giving Ivan's address and a description. About six foot, hair dark, eyes hazel, I said. Eyes fringed with thick eyelashes, hair that shone, a body that was hard

in all the right places, I thought. I should have been describing Ivan to my female friends in girlish excitement, not to a grumpy old policeman. "I think it's him."

"Think?"

"I am almost certain, but he hasn't confessed to it yet. Actually, I haven't confronted him yet."

"Have you any proof?"

"Not exactly, but all the clues add up and he's got a motive."

"Which is?"

"He admits to being sexually attracted to the site protagonist."

"And do you think he has a motive to"—Officer Aged paused—"attempt to make true the statement introduced to the site as of this morning?"

I heard that medics now wore their stethoscopes slung around their necks and rode on the stretchers in a way that they never did before *ER.* I wondered whether police officers walked in synchronization around the beat and talked of things going "pear-shaped" in deference to actors playing police officers. This policeman looked to be more *Dixon of Dock Green* than *NYPD Blue.*

"I don't think so, no. I don't think he'd want to do something so," I stuttered, "terminal. But I think he wants to frighten me. Maybe to hurt or harm me in some way. He knows that I know he's behind it. I discovered likely proof yesterday and sort of accused him."

"And that may have provoked him?"

"I don't know. That's what I'm here for. Can't you tell me?"

"Not for me to say, I'm just making a crime report."

"What will you do with it then?"

"Send it upstairs to CID. Criminal Investigation Department. I'm just a station officer so I don't have opinions. I leave that to them."

"So what will they do? How long will they take with it?"

"Couldn't tell you. Like I say, I don't have the thoughts, just the fingers." He waggled them above the keyboard in a way that reminded me of the gesture that boys from the grammar had used to indicate that they'd "fingered" a girl.

"I'm not asking for your opinion, just wondering if you could give me a guess about what they'll do with the information you've so kindly collated."

"You'll have to ask one of the boys." He emphasized the last word. "Oi, guv, can you answer this lady's questions?" he asked a young plain-clothed man who had appeared on the other side of the hatch.

The man nodded. Male-pattern baldness and adult acne, always an unlucky combination. Officer Krupke began explaining my predicament to the young upstart, who was looking at me lasciviously, his lips as shiny and slimy as the wet-look gel in what remained of his hair.

"There's an e-mail that says she might die in the year two thousand and three. But she doesn't know who it's from and the rest of the e-mail site is quite nice about her."

"It's a Web site," I corrected, "in my honor but created anonymously, which now implies that my life's dates are nineteen seventy-three to two thousand and three."

Youngster seemed to be computing this information intensely. "You don't look thirty," he concluded and switched into a more professional mode.

"How long would CID take over investigating this and what would you normally do about it?"

"There would be an assessment of the matter overall—for example the tone of everything else on the site, a check through our records to see if the suspect's got previous, a check on you to see if you've been threatened before."

I shook my head.

"Then we'd run a threat assessment."

"How long would that take?"

"Could be today. Could be next week. We prioritize. Depending on the result of the threat assessment, we ask our IT experts to try to find out who designed or updates the Web site. Maybe confiscate the suspect's hardware for examination."

"That would be good. Then you could arrest him."

Kid cop giggled. "As you can imagine, our IT experts are very busy with matters pertaining to global child pornography."

"Of course."

"And until the threats became more specific, we could only issue a warning."

"Fine, thank you." I was desperate to dab my chin. "Thank you for your time."

I scored some powerful and probably prescription-only antibiotic cream on the way home. I think the pharmacist felt sorry for me on seeing the fountainhead on my face. This gave me something to do these days off work, as I could dab my chin with chemicals in between trying to nibble on dry toast and turning the pages of the magazines I had bought.

I went into a bookshop, too, and found a copy of *Dune.* It had strange snakelike pods across the cover and the recommendation of having won a "Nebula Award." It looked to me like a seventies prog rock concept album cover and I knew even as I bought it that I would not be reading it that afternoon.

I was in a state of nothingness. I couldn't go out as Ivan would be watching out for me. I couldn't eat, which was a rare state of affairs. I could make a dash for the gym, I supposed, or read some edifying literature, but daytime television and pulpy magazines were my limit.

Everything came back to the site. I looked at the photos in magazines of stars walking down Manhattan streets in their celebrity casual wear and was reminded of the ones of me (albeit without that studied insouciance). How did they feel, I wondered. Sometimes they smiled at the paparazzo, usually only the minor celebrities, to collude with their stalker, to say, I know you're there and I don't mind. This goes two ways. What was it like to walk down Bond Street and feel yourself papped and snapped? I ought to know.

I had been snapped. I was breaking.

The slim magazines with exclamation marks in the titles continued their candyflossed hold on me. They all had covers with a recently married couple cooing about the joys of marriage. "Why being a wife is my greatest role," proclaimed one actress; "I never knew true love until we had our baby," said another of life with her dorkish-looking husband and preposterously named child. Another couple were being married on a beach, with the white dress of an English country do incongruously superimposed onto a Caribbean resort terrace. Some stupid cow of an actress who probably blow-jobbed her way to the top was saying that the professional acclaim meant nothing to her, she preferred to cook up some pasta and hang out with her husband. "Starry parties and a cupboard full of awards just aren't our thing. Give me a pair of jeans and a free weekend to go hiking with my fella."

Being George's girlfriend wasn't my greatest role. I did the George-Grand-loves-Izobel-Brannigan schoolgirl game on a page of the magazine, though I already knew how it turned out. One L, two Os, no V, three Es, no S in our names that leaves a score of 12030, reduce to 3233, 556, until it came down to two figures, 23. He loved me twenty-three percent. Twenty-three percent was a less than mediocre score. It was almost as bad as it got. Eighty-seven percent was much higher. George and Ivan.

I did some more maths, thinking about those two and the others, Pepe, Jonny, Elliot, Frank, William *et* Alan. I'd kissed a number of men and boys, slept with that number minus ten and gone out with that number minus five. These were the mathematics of my sexual past, but would there be a final figure in the calculation? Had I ever thought that the final figure would be a portly and family-burdened one? When I was with George, did I ever think he was my future, or even my present? He had always had a sense of the past about him, not only in the way he dressed and spoke, but in my relationship with him, one where I was always unknowingly thinking ahead to the day when he would be my ex-boyfriend. He had just been the old bloke I had met at a launch and our fling had segued sexually into my one and only living-together relationship. He was never supposed to be the one.

I had laughed so much with George. He made life fun. We had laughed and drunk and partied and screwed. He was ten years older than me but he made me feel ten years younger. I had stayed up all night and all day too. But life wasn't fun anymore, we couldn't be irresponsible.

"Please, George," I said to him on the phone. "Please come straight home from work today."

He almost managed it as well, arriving back at about seven. He once explained to me that although he knew he could have a drink when he got home or met me across town, the drink straight after work with colleagues was always more immediate and always more enticing. I was glad to see him, nonetheless.

I held onto him like a koala to a tree. His overweight belly offered me ballast against the site's threat and the police's indifference. Beneath the soft overhang of his gut, I felt his cock harden.

"There, there, darling girl." He stroked my hair. "To what do I owe this? Are you feeling a little bit horny from a day at home, honey?" As if playing Twister, he reached behind me, shuffling me along slightly in the process, to grab a gulp of his drink and to light a cigarette. I continued to bury my head in his chest as he smoked and drank around me, and then he switched on the news. He was really so very good at multitasking. Having finished his cigarette, he prized us apart and put his hand up my T-shirt. I pulled away.

"No." Too forcefully.

He looked puzzled and sat back on the sofa, still watching the news. "I thought that's what you wanted, with all that clinginess."

Not now. "I wanted you to hold me." He beckoned me back and into the crook of his arm and held me against him. "I think I've got a death threat against me."

He pulled back. "A what?"

"I think somebody, Ian maybe, has threatened to kill me."

"What, he phoned you? Just pull the plug out on the phone, we don't need the landline. In fact, why don't we stop paying the bills? We've both got work mobiles. Or has he been around? Let me at him." He leaped up and expanded his chest.

"No, no. It's on the site."

He sighed. "Oh, the site." Bored voice. "What does it say?"

"Izobel Brannigan, nineteen seventy-three to two thousand and three."

"And?"

"And nothing. Izobel Brannigan born nineteen seventy-three and presumably dies two thousand and three."

"Presumably."

"Yes, presumably. Well, what else do you think it means?"

"Look, some little creep hasn't got the guts to chat you up properly and so creates a site. When you don't react to it in the way he wants you to, he puts something on it to scare you. This is a man who doesn't believe in action. He didn't act on fancying you so he's hardly going to act on a murderous threat, is he?"

"I suppose so."

"I know so. It's nothing."

"The police wouldn't agree with you. They're taking it very seriously indeed. The whole of the CID department are running a threat assessment on it as we speak and will act on it immediately. There was even talk of a permanent police presence, actually."

*

Later, I asked, "Is there anything I could do that would make you want to kill me or yourself?"

"Of course not, sausage-girl. I might want another drink though."

"What about Catherine, did you ever feel so passionately about her?"

"I frequently wanted to kill her, yes, irritating little bitch. Especially during the divorce case."

"And you'd kill yourself if anything were to happen to Grace?"

"Yes. Children are different, they always come first. How often do I have to tell you that, poppet?"

And how often did I think, well, if Grace comes first why did you cheat on your wife and ensure that your daughter therefore came from a home not so much broken as shattered?

"I'm tired and I'm bored of feeling tired," I said. "Thank God for the spa weekend. It couldn't be better timed. Thank you, George." I would go and I would forget Ivan and the site and escape it all in a fug of aromatherapy flavors. George's and my ailing and sagging relationship would be made taut and well-oiled by the spa's health-giving properties.

"Yes, well, I had wanted to talk to you about that." He went to the kitchen to refill his glass, while leaving a trail of ash in his wake. "I'm afraid, poppet, that it's a bit of a no-go."

"Did they pull the plug on it? That is so unprofessional! Which agency was it anyway?"

"They didn't exactly pull the plug on it."

"What then?"

"Grace's eczema has come back and the doctor said getting out to the country would do it good."

"You're taking Grace? It's hardly the country anyway. I thought that was the whole point of this place, that it was the country for those who don't really like the country in all its smelly, manure-spread reality. I can't believe you're taking Grace."

"She is a child, she is my child."

"You could take us both. Surely we could get a family room. She's not exactly going to be enjoying shiatsu massage, is she? Oh God, don't tell me, Catherine's already taking her for beauty treatments. She did tell me my nails needed shaping one time."

"I don't think it's possible. Grace is clearly stressed at the moment so she probably needs time with just me."

"Just you?"

I saw him pause for a second. "Don't tell me, not Catherine as well? You and Grace and Catherine in a 'family room' because you're such a perfect family, aren't you. Jesus, George, my life's being threatened and you're just fucking off without me and with your bloody ex-wife."

He was cold. "That woman is the mother of my child. My child. You just never get it, do you, Izobel, that Grace takes precedence over you. You're not the center of the universe, just that bloody site. You're not being threatened, that's all in your head. Grace's eczema, on the other hand, is real. And if you don't think you take second place to a five-year—"

"She's six."

"To a little girl, my little girl, then I don't think we've got much of a future. Why don't you try Ian Hounslow? Maybe he'll put up with you."

"Maybe I will, he can't be any worse than you."

"Fine, if you like stalkers."

*

We lay in bed, me wearing a pair of pants, as a not-so-subtle signal. They were very much emergency knickers too. "George, do you love me at all?"

He sighed, "Of course, I do. What a silly question."

"But how do I know? Can you prove it?"

"I don't have to prove it, though there is a way," he said, attempting to ping the elastic of my knickers, not realizing that it had already gone.

"But all you do is say you love me. And you say that to lots of people. One of your 'I love yous' is worth a lira, while one of a normal person's is worth a pound. There are two thousand of yours to one of everybody else's. There's a different exchange rate."

"Darling, why don't we all just use euros?"

"I'd still like you to do something, a gesture."

"What, like stalk you? Create a creepy crappy Web site about you? Propose to you on daytime television or take out a Valentine in the papers? Spend all our money on French restaurants and jewelry? A dozen red roses? For Christ's sake, you have become so common in your pursuit of reassurance. Stalking isn't love. Clichéd gestures aren't love. Your friend Ian should try living with you, he'd soon stop adoring you. Why don't you ask him to move in with you if you're so keen on sappy soppy sods. Maybe he'll make good his threat, because I tell you, you're killing me with boredom."

He was right, of course, love isn't obsessive or infatuated or crushed. But I wasn't sure love was convenience, sex and a place to live, either. My parents loved me, but they loved Wispa and Snickers too. My friends loved me, but I irritated them and they did me. We were pleased for each other's achievements but better in disappointments. Ivan said he fancied me, which had potential, but his love was twisted. George snored beside me and I felt my whole body flush. I looked at the copy of *Dune* by the bed. All that "Atreides, who could that be?" when he'd been the one to put in that stupid crossword clue and register the administrative contact in the name of the book's hero. Stupid cult sci-fi novel, anyway, just the sort of book I don't read, exactly as stupid, nerdy, geeky Ivan is just the sort of man I don't go for.

I go for men like George, don't I?

Chapter Thirteen

The next day I decided to go home. When does your parents' house cease being called 'home'? I suppose when you're no longer leaving boxes of old clothes there and escaping to it when being a grown-up gets too tiring. I'd need to stop being stroppy like a teenager on entering its walls and to start helping with the washing-up for it to no longer be my "home." My sister has children of her own and a house with more than one toilet and with its own eat-in kitchen and a car in the drive. I don't think she calls our parents' house "home" any longer and she's transcended the description "the children" that includes my brother and me.

It was Friday at least, so I only had one more day of ringing Mimi and putting on that voice of sickness again.

"You poor thing," she had said. "You sound terrible."

"I feel terrible," I had croaked.

"Do you want to talk to Tracy? She's been asking after you. No offense, babes, but I don't think she believes you."

"No, no," I said, as if each word would be my last. "Just tell her I'm really bad."

After only two days off work I had already slipped into not wearing underwear, and not in a sexy way but accompanied by tracksuit bottoms, and not noticing that the weekend was almost upon us. I topped off the look with some shades and a bobble hat.

The look was not so much celebrity going incognito as mad woman with rusting shopping cart.

I bought my ticket at the station and made my way to the appropriately named "suburban platforms." I liked the dogs Wispa and Snickers anyway; they were my biggest fans, well, had been until Ivan had made his appearance and his tribute site.

They'd worry about me, my parents, when they saw me. I caught sight of my reflection in the mirror outside the photo booth, onto which someone had drawn a beard and glasses in marker pen at about head height. Bearded was better than the wan reality.

I had disappointed my parents. My mother wanted for me all the dreams she had held for herself and that were now only partially realized by the Creative Writing evening classes. She had given me a unique name in the belief that I would live up to it. I wasn't even proving adept at the grandchildren-churning stakes as at least my sister had been. They had been so proud of me. I'd won the English prize at school and was solid academically. They thought I'd become a barrister or newspaper editor or politician. But then, so did I.

I supposed I ought to ring them first. I pulled up H for Home on my mobile and spoke to my father, who was now in semi-retirement and, as a consequence, approaching semi-dotage.

"Hello, it's Izobel."

"And how is my youngest unwed daughter?"

"Fine. Is Mum there?"

"I'm afraid she's just popped out." He knew I always wanted to speak to Mum, and not to him, and was as resigned to the fact as other middle-aged fathers across the country. We had a desultory conversation anyway.

"What are you up to this weekend?" I asked.

"Busy, busy. We're going to see that new film about women on

Saturday night and are having lunch with the Jacobs on Sunday."

"The Jacobs?"

"Yes, I expect we'll hear all about Jonny's latest adventures. I'm sure you could come along, too, they'd love to hear about your job, I'm sure."

He didn't sound very keen for me to do so. There was a window, just after all three of us had left home in our early twenties, when my parents' life was so empty that my mother would ring every Wednesday and ask "Are we seeing you this weekend, then?" and then on hearing the negative response say, "Oh, that is a shame. Your father will be so disappointed," as if it had always been a given that I'd be there for every Sunday lunch. Soon, they and their friends realized that we were never coming home, not for good anyway, not until the messy divorces and the redundancies kicked in, and so they remade their own lives with a disconcerting degree of efficiency. My old bedroom had recently been turned into an office, or "snug" as my mother called it, with broadband connection and an aggressively powerful PC. My brother's room was their gym.

"No, I wasn't thinking of coming back. I just wondered, that's all. I've got a hundred things to do in London." I couldn't face being lumpen adult daughter in front of their friends and answering their questions about public relations and not being asked questions about my marital status. Especially not by Jonny's mum and dad. "How are Wispa and Snickers?" I asked.

"A bit worried about the United Nations, actually," my father replied. They had never disappointed Mum and Dad, especially not now Snickers had a new trick. They alone had fulfilled their puppyish potential.

I went home and slouched, wondering how long I could survive on cereal. It couldn't be any less nourishing than the diet of daytime TV that I also snacked upon. I ate my Frosties dry, in great handfuls. I couldn't tell if I was gaining or losing weight. That's the joy of elasticized waistbands. As I stood in front of the mirror, I pulled my tracksuit bottoms down and stuck my stomach out over them and put my hands on my back. I really could look pregnant when I did that.

I wondered what it must be like to be pregnant. It's a strange parallel universe where everything that has been bad is now good. Where a round sticky-out stomach is to be celebrated and touched; where you must eat lots but drink nothing; where smocks are a fashion item; where women stare at your body on the street, but men ignore you.

It must be great to be pregnant. Lucky Maggie. She had everything sorted.

I pulled my trackie bottoms up and held my stomach normally. I wasn't pregnant. I didn't even want to be so, at least not with George. I tried to think about what life with George as the father to my children would be like. They'd have stupid thirties country-house names like Ralph and Rollo and Hermione. Little Ralph would be a plucky little chap, stoical, who liked to look after Mummy because Daddy wasn't so good at it, and wore shorts even in winter. Ralph, George and I would be stuck in my same old flat, unable to move out as the mortgage was getting bigger rather than smaller. Grace would sneer at it and us.

I shivered as I thought of Christmas future, with George and Ralph. "Will Daddy have the falling-down sickness again tonight?" the little nipper would ask. "Yes, poor Daddy's very sick and we must be brave for him," I'd reply and then he'd inquire why there were no presents under the Christmas tree this year.

I made an effort to end this daymare. I doubted George could fertilize anymore anyway; his swimmers would be lounging round on lilos, drinking martinis rather than doing the front crawl anywhere near my ovaries.

Ivan's wouldn't. His sperm would be twisted and double-crossing. Why had he written the death date? I could almost have forgiven him the rest of the site, I could almost have thought of it as an elaborate Valentine. But not the death date. Why, Ivan, I longed to ask him.

I hadn't heard anything from the police, but then I hadn't expected to. So I was just stuck there, suspended, snacking on food and trash TV, waiting for a sign that life would change once again.

As usual, I switched on my PC and clicked on the Explorer button to bring up my site. The sound of the modem ringing the connection was the modern equivalent of chalk scratching on a blackboard, whiiirrr-eeee, bee-bo. I grimaced. It verified the username and password and yet the familiar page did not fill the screen. I refreshed izobelbrannigan.com in a way that I could not Izobel Brannigan dot woman, but the site was as listless as I was. Ivan was clearly experiencing server problems again. Or maybe he was adding a whole new batch of photos, all with the same theme, me badly dressed nipping out from here to the newsagent's to buy the evening paper.

There was a message from him on my mobile.

"Izobel, listen, I know you think I'm behind the site, but I'm not. I can't prove it to you, but I wish you'd believe me. There must have been hundreds of people at that party. That I was one of them doesn't mean anything. Please phone me so we can at least talk about this."

"Don't give me that," I said out loud to my mobile. "What about everything else? That you fancied me for months, that you admitted coming to the office on false pretenses, your creepy computer set-up at home? Hey, what about that?" But I hadn't said these things to Ivan, not yet. I was going to confront him, I just didn't know when or how.

I wanted to ask him why the site was down again. He wasn't

the best advert for his own server capacity. I wanted to ask him what new horrors he was planning. What if he had taken photos of us kissing? Of our mouths meeting, of my legs and arms wrapped around his, our limbs as twisted as his mind? "George," I practiced saying, "it's not how it looks."

I blushed, although I was quite alone. What if I had slept with Ivan? He could have had photos of me naked, of me licking him, or him stroking my breasts and the tops of my thighs and touching me everywhere, penetrating me, making me come.

Phew, I thought. That would have been horrific.

I checked the site again. I am still down, I am still broken.

*

I went back to the site at midday. I could see the logo forming slowly on the page and I knew that it was back. Despite my fears that kissing pictures were planned and my lurid thoughts about the things that Ivan and I never did, the site looked much the same, including the death date. I leaned in but that didn't make any difference. I watched the ticker tick until a new message from Ivan appeared.

"We're sorry for izobelbrannigan being down for a few hours. Our servers were disabled by a dramatic surge in the number of users logging onto the site. We believe this spike in traffic was caused by unexpected press coverage."

Press interest was the holy grail of my profession, but I didn't like the idea of my life and site being bared to strangers.

I rang Maggie. "You get all the papers at work, don't you?"

"Officially, yes. They all get filched first thing, though."

"Apparently there's been some press interest in the site. Could you have a look and see if you can see anything for me?"

"I'm just about to go into a meeting, but I'll try to check later. Is that OK?"

How inconvenient of her. What meeting could possibly be more important than my site?

I thought about ringing Ivan and asking him what he meant by "press coverage." I did hope it was a broadsheet rather than a tabloid. If he had taken pictures of us tussling, then it could be the *Star.* I shivered. Saucy sexpot Izobel's site shows sizzling sex. However, in the great scheme of Internet titillation, I reckoned that some fully dressed shots of me kissing Ivan were unlikely to get the punters drooling.

A broadsheet would be better. There might be an article about the rise of blogging or self-promotion on the Net. I might be like that Turkish man, what was his name, Mahir, who became an international star through his use of the phrase "I kiss you!!!!" and his desire to take foto-camera of nice nude models.

I went into my e-mail account and messaged mail@izobel brannigan.com. Aka Ivan.

Subject: press interest

What on earth are you on? What press coverage? Tell me now, Ivan.

I paused and deleted the word "Ivan." And added:

The police know about the 1973–2003 business.

Send.

Ten minutes later, a message marked *re: press interest* came back to me. It was a short missive, only containing the name of a middlebrow tabloid. The middlebrow tabloid that kept George in vodka and tonics.

I put on my baseball cap and slunk out of the flat to the newsagent's. Having your newsagent greet you like a friend seemed shaming. Other than George, he was the only person I had seen the day before.

"You don't usually buy that one," he said on handing me the change from the purchase of George's newspaper.

I felt like I could have been buying porn. "I know, I don't usually. It's not for me, I mean, there's an article in here that I'd like to read. But no, generally, not my cup of tea at all." We looked complicit in our disapproval of George's employers.

I waited until I got home and opened it up. I had lied; a terrible part of me enjoyed reading the articles about celebrities being too fat or too thin, the which-bikini-for-which-body features and the stories about murderous divorcees. I skipped them all that day, though, as I searched for something about izobelbrannigan.com. Nothing, nothing, nothing, until I got to the section in the middle, called the women's bit, as if all the news and politics preceding it had been nothing for them to worry their pretty little heads over.

MY GIRLFRIEND THE INTERNET STAR shouted the headline on a full-page article, illustrated with screen grabs from the girlfriend in question's Web site. "If another man is after your beloved you can always fight it out, right?" said the introduction. "Not if he anonymously uses the Internet to woo her, finds George Grand." George's name was in bold letters, accompanied by a photo of him where he looked more Second World War Ministry of Home Affairs correspondent than ever.

I skimmed George's piece, but not so fast that I couldn't judge it very ill-written. In it, he recounted how he'd found a site on the Internet devoted to his girlfriend and his dilemma as to whether to tell her or not. He wrote of how unnerving it was to find that your girlfriend has become Web-famous and that strangers were offering up proposals to her, both sexual and marital. He attempted to garner sympathy by painting himself the old fuddy-duddy who knows he can't compete with these young things with their technology and wacky ways. Why, he can't even work out how to text-message yet, the old curmudgeon that he is.

I shook my head. Even the site seemed to contain more truth than this piffle. I was pilloried in print and online. I half expected to turn on the radio and hear a panel discussing me or find myself the subject of a television investigation by a consumer affairs program.

George went on to interview others whose lives were dominated by Internet presence: a porn star's boyfriend, the partner of a boy band star and the new lover of the girl whose e-mail about blow jobs had ripped through the nation's in-trays.

"I can't help but wonder," he wrote, "whether it doesn't add a little frisson into a relationship and whether every jaded couple should have an Internet site devoted to one or the other. It certainly seems to be working for my beloved and me. Not that I'm suggesting, of course, that the girlfriend could have created the site with this intention herself . . ."

The calumny of this statement was further compounded by the fact that careless copyediting ensured I was referred to in this last sentence as "girlfiend."

Then in italics at the bottom of the article:

George Grand's girlfriend's site can be found at www.isobel brannigan.com.

Hence the spike in page impressions as noted by Ivan on the site.

I once went into my primary school and removed my coat only to find that I had forgotten to put my skirt on that day, just my thick woolen tights. That was embarrassing. Ten years later, I got my period when staying at Frank's parents' house, actually in their marital bed, which we'd annexed in their absence, and left it looking like something from a medieval wedding night. That was humiliating. At about that time, I was a member of the chorus of wailing women in a musical version of *Chronicle of a Death Foretold* at university that was wrongly interpreted by the audience as a satirical comedy. I still blush at the memory.

But nothing, none of these things, could come close to the mortification I felt at the thought of hundreds of thousands of tabloid readers logging onto my site and assuming it had been created by me. I bloated with discomfort at the idea of strangers reading about how I rocked my world and how I liked to keep my shopping basket to ten items or less. What would they make of the pap shot of me pulling my knickers out from where they had crept up my bottom? Or picking my nose? Thank God the message boards hadn't been introduced to the site yet.

I felt my face sieve with sweat.

It was as if George had taken my most horribly soiled pair of pants, perhaps with some sort of thrushlike discharge upon them or period-stained, and pinned them to the noticeboard at work with a plaque identifying them as mine. No, worse, he was flying them as a flag over a central London landmark. Everybody would be laughing at me.

I looked at the site as if a stranger, one of the strangers now examining it. I must look like an egotist with no shame, the sort of person who praises themselves yet at the same time abases themselves with their actions. I was like the very worst sort of reality TV contestant, enduring any humiliation to get myself noticed, showing off my shortcomings.

And PR O'Create got all the papers and this was one of the most read. I thought of Tracy slamming the article down as further damnation of me and proof that I was behind the site.

I e-mailed the site.

Please take the site down, please, please, I can't stand it being looked at by all these people. If you do care about Izobel Brannigan at all please take it down.

Then I rang George, hoping to get to him before he went out for lunch. Too late. I tried his mobile.

"You fucking fuck-off fuckhead fucker," I said articulately.

"Sorry darling, I can't hear you," he shouted through the noise of a fashionable London restaurant on a Friday lunchtime. I felt estranged from office life so quickly, the ebullience of the end of the week. "It sounded like a random selection of expletives."

"You fucker," I said again. "How could you do this to me?"

"Do what?"

"The fucking article, that's what. I'm so humiliated, it's so embarrassing."

"Oh, that. I thought that's what you wanted me to do. I don't know, sweetheart, I can't get it right. You said I didn't pay it enough attention and then when I bring it to the world's attention, you make a fuss. You can't buy that sort of publicity. You should know that."

"I don't want that sort of publicity," I wailed. "All those people looking at my site. I feel so exposed."

"But darling, haven't you always wanted to be famous? Isn't that what everyone wants?"

It was true; I had practiced my Oscar acceptance speech in the mirror, I had always walked down the street as if about to be papped, I did write my biography in my head.

"No, not famous," I said. "Renowned. I'd like to be respected and not as some loon who creates a site about themselves. You've abased me."

"Not my fault, is it? I mean, I didn't create the site. As you're so fond of reminding me."

I thought I could hear his chums chortling in the background at the neuroticism of the "girlfiend," only increasing my ire. "Come home now, come home immediately. We have to discuss this at once. You are in big trouble, George, I am fucking furious."

"Ooo, I'm scared. What shall I do? Have delicious meal with funny, clever colleagues or come home to dry toast and a mad bint who's ranting at me? Ooo, I don't know, what a tough decision. You know what, I think I'll stay here if that's OK."

"It's not OK. You fucking fucker, come home at once, fuckhead," I shouted but realized I was shouting into a mobile that had been cut off. I felt my whole body tingle and tense with impotent fury. There were so many levels to the anger I felt toward George. It had subtexts and interpretations. There was the normal, everyday, why aren't you more reliable and why do you never come back when you say you're going to? anger. Then there was the betrayal. This was more like the pointing hysteria that I feel when I suspect him of having been unfaithful, ditto the anxiety that my humiliation is public. Then there was a new fury, a blacker and bigger one than any of the others, one that was telling me: this is it.

I rang him again, but his mobile was switched off.

I rang Ivan.

"Izobel, I'm so pleased . . ."

"Take down the site."

"But I can't . . ."

"Take down the site, now, or I will tell the police something that will make them take you down."

"Izobel, wait . . ."

I rang George again and left a message. "George, if you don't come home right this instant, you'll be sorry. I'm giving you ten minutes to call me back."

Ten minutes passed and site didn't come down and George didn't get back to me. That's it, I thought. Another message. "Seriously George, you are going to regret it."

I quickly showered and wore non-slob clothes for the first time since visiting the police. I only seem to wear my sports clothes when there's no chance of me doing anything more strenuous than switching over TV channels. I wore a sharp little skirt, the one George liked me best in, and expensive shoes. I took a taxi to the restaurant where George lunches every Friday. He and his friends were very keen to damn the rest of the world as boring, but no one was as entrenched in their customs as they were.

I stood outside its large plate-glass windows for a second. It was designed as a goldfish bowl, to allow ordinary people to look in at the fashionable diners. I could see George with four males and one female, all with their mouths agape to imbibe or cackle or snipe. His hair was still swept back and his suit impeccable, but as he guffawed his mouth opened to reveal its cargo of carpaccio.

His body was falling apart as his suits would never do. The whites of his eyes were the color of a fashionable National Trust paint, way off-white, string-colored, jaundiced, shot. His body was apple-shaped, while his teeth suggested they never went near fruit. He had always looked as though he belonged in an old film. But now he just looked old.

"Hello, all. Hello, George," I said.

"Hello, darling," he replied. "What a pleasure that you've come to join us."

None of them attempted to make space for me to sit down. I knew they referred to me as that "little PR girl," never as Izobel. Today they all murmured greetings toward "Internet girl."

"Actually, I haven't." My resolve almost crumbled. "George, can you leave with me now? It's important that we talk."

"We can talk here, can't we, chaps? I'm sure if you've got anything worth sharing, you can share it with the whole class."

"No, please, come away with me. We need to talk in private. About the article and the site and us."

He didn't stand up, but made a tiny move with his back so that it was turned from me. I felt my anger mutate and take on a whole new shape, but I tried to remain calm. I wasn't going to be the "hysterical little PR girl." I crouched down and spoke into his ear.

"George, if you don't come away with me now and talk about this, it's over."

He leaned away to catch some piece of gossip about the managing editor.

"George, have you heard me?"

Nothing.

"That's it. I'm going home and removing every single one of your possessions and putting them into the bike shed. Then I am changing the locks of the front door and you are never entering my home, or me for that matter, again. I mean it."

He finally turned to me and raised one of his elegant eyebrows. "Yes, darling."

*

At last, I had a purpose. Finding the site perp had been a goal, but one that had always seemed beyond my control. This one was firmly within it.

The newsagent gave me the cardboard boxes and sold me the extra-strong rubbish bags knowingly. The locksmith nodded at me as if he knew, too, as the fourth emergency service to domestic disagreement. I changed all the locks except the one for the storage shed to the side of the Victorian conversion in which we, or I, lived. We had no bicycles or surf gear or strollers as our neighbors had in theirs. We had no other life or hobbies.

I reckoned I had at least six hours before he came home. That would be enough.

I started in the kitchen. His chattels had not included all the upmarket Le Creuset and food processors of his wedding list, Catherine had got those in the settlement, but the bric-a-brac that had preceded the order and elegance considered worthy of married couples. A saucepan with pasta shapes clinging to its base like barnacles to a hull, a couple of now-sticky nonstick pans and a set of cast-off cutlery from his parents.

I filled one box and marked it "George Grand: kitchenware."

The sitting room took longer, containing as it did the only thing worth anything outside of his wardrobe. The expensive stereo had wires connecting to amplifiers and speakers that coiled across the room. I'd always wanted a neat, self-contained little number anyway, but this machine had been worth thousands.

Why hadn't we "ex-libris"-ed the CDs? I kept all the ones that I had given him. I was always buying him little presents on the way home, but I piled the Leonard Cohen, Bob Dylan, Neil Young and hip-hop into the box with their player. There was another box of vinyl that was never played and probably never would be again.

The books were easy, since most of his were still in piles stacked at the base of the shelves. The ones that duplicated my books were little indications of the sort of tomes bought by everyone over the last decades: Delia Smith, Ian McEwan, Donna Tartt.

I paused over the first edition Evelyn Waugh I had given him for his last birthday. I threw it in; I could afford to be generous, I thought, though that was an emotion I had long since given away.

In TV dramas they make packing up somebody's life look easy. It's always just a question of sweeping a wardrobe's worth of garments into a big, flat, fat suitcase and snapping it shut. Throughout the flat George's clothes had left a trail that I tried to follow. I dived into the dirty-laundry basket, picked pants off the clotheshorse, attacked the drawers that he'd annexed from my chest and stuffed the whole lot into bin liners.

I dragged the five boxes of junk, eleven cartons of books and six bags of clothes into the lockup. It was damp, I noticed, and I worried about the cashmere–wool of his winter coat and the lush cloth of his suits. I forced myself not to fret over them and to treat them with the disdain with which he had treated me.

At last, it was done. I waited.

George returned at 10 p.m. Early, you might think, but it had allowed a nine-hour bender, a working day's worth of drinking.

A jangle of keys, expletives sounding. I hid myself in a corner of the living room with the lights off. The doorbell started ringing, to be joined in its symphony by my mobile, followed by the landline. Percussion came in the form of coins being thrown at the sitting-room window, which was raised ground floor.

A voice came through on the answerphone. "You bitch, let me in. Let me into my house."

So tempting to pick up, but I resisted. The mobile phone message was similar but with increased antagonism.

The coins being thrown at the window were replaced with stones. George was only good at throwing away other people's money, not his own.

"For fuck's sake, let's at least talk," the answerphone told me. "Two years, you're going to let go like this. Where's all my stuff? I know you're there."

I couldn't bear it any longer and picked up. That was always my problem: I never knew when it was more powerful to keep quiet. I wrote too much on postcards and said too much on first dates.

"So now you want to talk, do you? It was a different story with your little friends this lunchtime, wasn't it? Well, it's too late," I said into the mouthpiece, though we were only ten meters and a pane of glass apart.

"Darling, sweetheart, be reasonable," he slurred.

"I tried to be earlier on. I told you what would happen if we didn't talk."

"But darling, I was at work."

"Well, maybe work can give you a place to live."

"This is my place to live."

"I don't see anything of yours as evidence."

"My things, my stereo, my suits, they're all in there."

"Wrong. All your stuff is in the shed. You can keep it there for a fortnight, but then I take it to the charity shop."

"You can't do this. It's my home. I'll sue you."

"Fuck off, George. You've never contributed anything to here.

I could sue you for all the money you owe me and the bills you never paid."

"I'm sorry that I had to pay maintenance to my ex-wife and my child. I gave you all I could."

"No, you spent all that on fags and booze."

"You never could understand my responsibilities as a father."

"That's where you're wrong, George. I know, you see, that your parents paid the maintenance and Grace's school fees. I know you lied about that, you deliberately made me think you paid out half your salary every month, but it all went on your own debts and your habits."

He paused. "But darling, I love you so much, you're so special to me."

Not enough.

"I never loved anyone as much as you. Only Grace."

Too late.

He started pounding on the front door of the house. His voice was so loud that the words in my earpiece were echoed by those coming from outside.

"Where am I supposed to go?"

"To your bloody spa weekend with bloody Catherine and Grace. And then maybe she can take you in so you can be a family again." I said "family" in the sort of sneering voice which George would use to utter the word when it preceded "film" or "fun."

"You stupid mad bitch," I heard in stereo. "You can't forgive me for not being your stalker. Go to your Ian, your creep, your stalker, if that's what you want. Or if you want stalking, I'll stalk you." I heard him hitting the window. He must have been leaning across the railings from the front door. "See, you like it. You love it. I'm stalking you."

"You never thought me worth stalking, George."

At the same time as he gave up on trying to break in, he gave up on me.

"Well, you're fucking not, Izobel." He spat out my name. "You're just a PR girl with a pretty face. Nothing more. You're nothing special."

"I was never your number one," I said. Damn it, don't cry.

"And you'll never be anyone's. You're not worth stalking. You're a B-list person, Izobel Brannigan."

I went to bed with earplugs in.

Chapter Fourteen

"Mags, sorry, it's me, can I come round?"

She had sounded sleepy. I had waited until 9:15 to call her. Once upon a time you never phoned anyone before midday on a Saturday, but these days my friends got up early to go to the gym or leave London for the weekend.

"What's wrong? Is it something to do with the site? Have you been threatened again?" She sounded mildly exasperated.

"No, it's nothing to do with the site. Something unrelated." I paused. The good thing about splitting up with your live-in boyfriend of over two years is that it counts as a proper reason to go waking people up from their lie-ins. The end of an affair has been legitimized by women's magazines and pop music as the loftiest cause of depression. Especially in your thirties. "George and I are over."

"What, you've split up? What happened?"

"I chucked him and I chucked him out." I felt a surge of pride. I had turned George out of the house. I had bundled his possessions together in a great gesture of dramatic female empowerment. I hadn't waited until he dumped me or until I'd found a replacement. I was chucking him to be single.

God, single, hadn't been that for a while. Frantic organizing of trips to art galleries on Sundays, not having an automatic person to go on holiday with, having to go for expensive massages in lieu of free human touch at home, overdressing for parties, coming home disappointed.

I wasn't much good at being single. I used up the most creative part of my brain daydreaming about the next person and how special they'd be. They never were.

"Oh Iz, you brave girl. Do you want to come round and talk about it?"

"Yes, please," I sniffed, not at sadness of the end of a past shared with George, but at a future shared with no one.

Mick was dispatched to buy expensive croissants, while Maggie made me tea.

"I saw the article he wrote," she said. "It was an absolute disgrace and full of lies. Plus it was so badly written. I thought he was supposed to be such a scribe. You should sue. Have you definitely split up?"

"Yes."

"You won't get back together? You promise."

I nodded.

"Because this is the bit when I tell you what I really thought of you and George and then you go and get back together with him and our friendship is stuffed."

"I won't get back together with him." As I said it, I knew my words to be true.

"And it's not just me. It's what everyone, me, Mick, Frank and the rest thought of him. We once held a summit meeting to work out a way of splitting you up."

I groaned. "How humiliating. I'm so embarrassed. Frank? Camilla wasn't there, was she? Please tell me she didn't put her oar in. Did it ever occur to you that you should talk to me about it rather than each other?"

"That's what I'm doing now."

I lay back on the sofa with my head covered in a cushion.

"Here goes," she said. "I, we, think he's boorish and boring, he's a snob and a slob. It really annoys me how he always talks about stuff being the new stuff, the new black and the new rock and roll all the time. He treats you like shit and you're worth so much more than him. He uses you in order to have a place to live in and it's not going anywhere. His daughter's vile."

"That's harsh, she's only six."

"But so knowing. Of course, the fact that she told me that her mother would die if her arse got as saggy as mine does not in any way endear her to me."

"She said that I looked like a cleaner in my Birkenstocks."

"Quite apt, given the way you have to run around after her." Maggie took a glug of tea. "He brings out the very worst in you, your insecurity, your obsession with appearances and glamour and silly parties and your concern for what's in and what's out."

"Thanks."

"I'm not criticizing you. I'm trying to tell you how much more you are than that. You're clever and principled and profound, but you wouldn't know it when you're with him."

"Or without him."

"You can, you can. It's just a bit buried." With that I entombed myself still further behind the cushion. "And he drinks too much."

"You think he's a functioning alcoholic?"

"No."

"Well, that's something to be relieved about."

"I think he's a dysfunctional alcoholic. And you've got a codependent relationship with him in which you enable his drinking."

"You read too much pop psychology."

"I don't need to define codependency for you as you define it yourself with the way you act. You pay the bills, you give him somewhere to live, you cover for him at work. Have you ever rung his office for him and told them he's ill?"

"Yes, but . . ."

"Classic enabling behavior. All you're doing is allowing him to spend all his money on drink and fags."

"And Grace," I lied.

"And Grace. But wouldn't she be better off if her father wasn't an alcoholic, the alcoholic you're helping him to be? Poor thing can't choose her father. You can choose your boyfriend and you're much better off without him."

"Oh." I peeked out from under the cushion. "You've really got to hope I don't get back with him after all that."

"No, Iz, you've really got to hope you don't get back with him. He's a twat. And you know it."

My eyes welled up but I suppressed tears with much exaggerated exhaling, blowing air out heavily like a parent making a pantomime show of filling a balloon in front of their birthday child. I did that thing of waving my hand in front of my face as if fanning myself on a hot day, attempting to blow away the tears. I couldn't cry over George. I was the strong one, I had chucked him, hadn't I?

Too late. I cried. Not cinematically in deference to the way Maggie lives her life, but with messy, snotty, simultaneous liquid pouring from eyes and nose.

Maggie rubbed my back as if I were vomiting rather than crying.

"Life's so shit," I wept. "Life's so shit for me."

"It's not, it won't be. It's going to be all right."

"Yes, it is. I've split up with my boyfriend and there's a site with a death threat to me. And the only man I've fancied in months is the man behind it."

"What? You fancy this Ivan guy?" He was not yet Ivan to her, only "this Ivan guy," the systems bloke. I suppose he never would be familiar to her now. "You didn't tell me that."

"I snogged him."

"Oh, Iz. I'm sorry. Do you like him?"

"Did like him. Yes, I really did like him. Even though he was a techie and stuff, he was lovely to me. He's got the kindest face with huge eyes and really thick lashes. He has a long, straight nose, I'm a sucker for noses. And his body was perfect, slim but no six-pack. You know how six-packs are so disgusting as they make you wonder what agonies of boredom they're prepared to put themselves through doing stomach crunches. And his flat is amazing and he does this art, which is the most beautiful thing I've ever seen, but he's modest about it. He's funny too, he's serious but he doesn't take himself seriously and certainly not me. He took the piss out of me and I felt like I could be better by being with him. But what do I care? Now I find out he's a git too. And you know what?" I didn't wait for her reply. "I've found out that every man I've ever been out with has been a git. Well, not William, but that's not because he's not a git, because he is, but because I haven't caught up with him yet and it would only be a waste of git time. I didn't find out that any one of them was responsible for the site, apart from Ivan, but I did find out that they were all gits. Except, perhaps, Married Man, and him being married and sleeping with me pretty much means he has to be a git too, or at least that's what his wife and her friends would conclude should they ever find out."

I put the pillow on my stomach, aping Maggie's stance on the opposite sofa, except her bulge wasn't a cushion.

"I don't think you're quite right. Frank's OK. But I understand."

"No, you don't. How could you? You've been happily trotting along with Mick all this time and he's lovely. You've never gone to a party on your own and left with a stranger, you've never had the feeling of yet another relationship going wrong and wondering whether you're ever going to have a normal one. You don't have to frantically fill your Saturday nights and put on a performance should you find yourself out with a couple. You don't have to parade your dire love life for the amusement of others. You don't have to worry about everybody forgetting about your birthday. You don't understand."

"I think I can empathize. And anyway, it's not all been an episode of *Little House on the Prairie* with Mick, you know. I've had my doubts. I have them all the time. His silences drive me mad. I wonder if I want him to be the father of my child or the partner to me. I've fancied men at work, and I've flirted with them too. And I think Mick has, with women I mean. I have fantasies about George Clooney. That's how much of a frustrated thirty-something cliché of a woman I am."

"But your fantasies and flirtations are just a sideline. When you're single, they're all you've got." I continued to cry, yet even then I knew that I would feel good about ending it with George someday soon. I would enter the brief optimistic phase, of having fun with other single female friends and obsessing over heels and beauty treatments, of relishing the expectancy and excitement of being in that on-the-pull, every-day-is-like-Christmas-Eve time. When I knew, even then in my period of mourning, that life with George had been a permanent February. I wailed some more at the boredom of being miserable and the mourning of all the time I had wasted.

"Iz, you're supposed to be a feminist. Surely there's more to you than having a boyfriend?"

"Yes, I know, of course you're right, but everybody defines you as single, the single thirty-something woman. It never used to be like that, but when we hit twenty-seven suddenly whether you had a boyfriend became significant. It was a lifestyle choice and we were no longer the same, those with and those without, different species, lining up on different sides, like boys and girls at a school disco."

"Everybody? Your site doesn't, does it? It never mentions George or any of your exes. It talks about your job, your studies, your day-to-day habits, and it says you're great, irrespective of your love life."

I wailed some more. "The site. That site has taken away my life. I never would have split up with George if it hadn't been for it. It's like a voodoo doll of me and any information on it is like sticking a pin in to produce awful consequences in my real life. I sometimes feel that izobelbrannigan dot com is more 3D than Izobel Brannigan, that it leads and I follow. I feel like the site has robbed me of my identity; I'm an aborigine thinking his soul will be stolen by having his photograph taken. Mags, you've no idea what it's like, I don't have an identity anymore. You're so lucky to have your own."

"Identity?" Maggie stood up quickly and then looked dizzy so sat down again. "You're talking to me of identity?"

"Yes," I said grumpily.

"Izobel, I'm pregnant."

"Exactly, you're lucky, you know what you're doing in life and who you are and your life has taken shape." I looked at her profile with its wonderful curves, the pregnant belly and the arching back. "You don't have to worry about which way your life is going anymore."

"Haven't you thought for a second what it does to your identity to be pregnant?"

I was about to mutter something about identity consolidation, but looked at her and shook my head.

"It's shattered it. And that's just being pregnant. God knows what it will be like after the baby's born. Having a pregnant belly is like being the girl with massive tits, people talk to it and not to you. Nobody looks me in the eye anymore. All anybody talks about is the bloody baby. Even my body's not mine now, as everyone else seems to think they know more about what it's going through than I do, you should feel that, you shouldn't feel that, my friend says morning sickness is psychosomatic, blah blah blah.

I am dispossessed of my own body. I've got a sitting tenant in there, a squatter with far more rights than the landlord, and every time I put food or drink into my mouth I am supposed to ask myself: "Is this the very best I can be giving my baby?" I found a Web site that accused women who have the occasional glass of wine while pregnant of being child abusers. How do you think that feels? I'm a child abuser. Nobody asks me about me anymore, just when's it due, is it a boy or a girl, what names are you thinking of, are you moving out of your flat, what kind of car are you getting, have you read *Contented Little Baby*?"

"I don't think I just ask you about the baby," I protested.

"No, but that could be because you're so preoccupied with yourself that you haven't asked me about anything at all. I don't know how you can lie there and talk to me of losing your identity. You're still Izobel. I'm Maggie pregnant woman and soon I'll be Maggie mother. It's bad enough at the moment, but friends tell me that when you're pregnant you at least feel celebrated and special, then when you're schlepping a stroller round dingy London streets you feel very unspecial indeed. I don't know if Mick and I will ever have sex again. Once the baby's born, his life can go on and mine will be irrevocably changed. Up until now it hasn't made any difference that he's male and I'm female, but now it's everything. I don't know if I'll ever have a career again, let alone any money. Or what my body will be like. I'll have saggy tits and belly and, you know, bits. A woman I know put a Tampax in six months after giving birth and it fell out."

I winced.

"Only women will talk to me now, not men. I am no longer sexually desirable."

"There are those porn magazines devoted to pregnant women."

Maggie snorted and walked into the kitchen area and put the kettle on again.

"Sorry, Mags."

"Forget it."

I hadn't known it would be possible to feel worse than I already had done, but I was tripping into whole new potholes of remorse.

"I don't need pity," she said.

"No, but you'd like some support. And that's completely reasonable of you." I wanted to cry but knew I wasn't allowed to anymore. The site could caption me at that moment with "Izobel's a selfish solipsistic cow who completely ignores the needs of her best friend!" I needed to say something, anything, to absolve myself. "It's the site, it's distracted me . . ."

"It's not since the site, Izobel. You used to be such a brilliant listener. You loved listening and your advice was better than anybody's. You had a sense of people, the people generally—politics and the outside world—and then the people close to you. You cared about stuff. It's not the site that changed you, it's everything, your job and George. I wish you could do something that would make you like you were."

I did too. I wanted to go back to being the girl with principles and optimism. I used to think I was great. I *was* great. I once was worth creating a cyber-paean to, but somewhere along the decade the pappy press releases and bad boyfriends eroded that girl.

"You're right," I said. "And you're not just pregnant lady, you're an absolutely brilliant friend. I only wish I could apply the same good judgment and discretion to my choice of boyfriends as to my choice of friends. I couldn't be luckier with you."

She shrugged.

"And I wish I could be as good a friend to you as you are to me. I really am sorry."

"It's all right."

But I knew it wasn't really.

*

I spent the rest of Saturday on my own, with only the site for company. It had not changed; the death date remained and with it my unease. My new life of exhibitions, seasons at the National Film Theatre and parties could not begin until they or I had been removed.

I rang the police apologetically. "I don't suppose you've had time to get a report from CID asessing a threat made on a Web site."

Blankness from the other end, then transferring me up to CID. They were laughing at me, I'm sure. "Silly bint reckons we'll be onto this within a couple of days. Doesn't she know we've got murders to solve?" "Reckons she's more important than an abused kid, Sarge." Chuckle, chuckle, especially from greasy-look hair, greasy-look face young copper. A different voice came onto the phone.

"Hello, Miss Brannigan. We are taking the matter seriously and it will be dealt with very soon. We'll contact you when a decision has been reached. Thank you for your patience."

I wasn't patient. I thought about Maggie and George and Ivan in equal measure, though all were dwarfed by the amount of time I still spent thinking about myself. The site didn't say anything about my relationships with others and it was as if, by ignoring them, the site had caused them to putrefy into nonexistence. Nothing outside of the site had the chance of life.

I thought about Grace, too, and this added another crust of guilt and misery to my mood. I should have been a better common-law stepmother to her. She was only six and I had treated her like a manipulative ex-girlfriend rather than a damaged little girl. I might have made a difference, but it was too late now.

I called Maggie, Ivan called me and I waited for George to call, but he did not. There was a text message. *Bitch.* That's all it said. Text messages are the preserve of the newly in love, so that they can write billets-doux of abbreviated words, *yr lvly, I wnt 2 b wv u.* And then text messages play no part in relationships until the end, when the spoken word cannot be trusted to express the bitterness, when people no longer pick up their phone for fear of the eruption of bile.

Two years of life with George and that's all I get. One word. At least, I thought, it was fully spelled out.

There was a place where words were plentiful: izobelbrannigan .com. It provided me with Saturday succor. I closed the curtains on reading the new additions to the site.

There, ticking along across the bottom of the page, were a dozen messages from my "adoring public."

"Following the article in a national newspaper, messages from her fans have been pouring in for Izobel. Here are just a few of them," announced my narrator.

"Izobel is fit," wrote fourteen-year-old GarethGreat, "where does she live?" "I like the dress she's wearing at the supermarket. What shop is it from? Does she have a favorite designer?" asked Jenny5000. Wolfie said that the site should have more pictures of me in a bikini, while JGG demanded a live Web chat with me, possibly naked. RealGrrl wanted to know if I ever agreed to meet people through the site.

"But not everyone's a fan . . ." it went on to explain. Here we go, I thought. "What a terrible testament to hubris that somebody should think a nonentity worthy of a testament. How characteristic of our age of the celebrity for the sake of celebrity. Who was this Izobel Brannigan anyway?" I shuddered at the "was" jeremy_jones used; he alone had interpreted the dates as I had. The rest of his criticism seemed a more predictable response from the stick-in-the-mud readers of George's paper. "The elevation of nobodies to fallacious somebodies has to stop," Jeremy concluded with almost an audible harrumph. "I think she's unattractive," wrote a rather less articulate fan.

I continued to watch as the messages trickled past. They were, on the whole, trite, but all suspiciously lacked spelling mistakes or abbreviations. I didn't believe them. I wasn't fit or well-dressed or hubristic, and I couldn't believe that they wouldn't use the strangulated slang of instant messaging.

The site didn't seem to know I was single, either. Did Ivan care? Maggie was right; the site had never been much interested in my love life, when that was all that my friends and I had ever discussed. I felt a misplaced benevolence toward it again, despite the malevolence with which it reciprocated. While Izobel Brannigan had wasted the decade in pursuit of parties and men who were better in the telling than the doing, her alter ego izobel brannigan.com was vibrant, world-rocking and independent. She was the superhero to my flawed everywoman.

I began to cry. About Maggie, about the site and about George. Or not George himself, but the prospect of being alone and the humiliation of having screwed up yet again. I felt an overwhelming impatience to get this bit out of the way, the sadness at the end of yet another relationship, and get onto the next stage. There was a finite amount of tears I had to shed on the way to feeling better. I imagined a big measuring jug or an outsize cardboard thermometer shape like they have on TV charity appeals. This would fill with my tears and when we reached a pint, I'd feel better again. I wanted to fast-forward to that time, skip the scenes, but with clarity, like on a DVD, when I would be over both George and Ivan and when Maggie would have forgiven me.

Another text came through. I wondered what one word's worth of insult would be etched onto my mobile screen this time.

When you feel like it, please phone me, Ivan.

Words spelled out in full and everything. For a crazy, creepy stalker he was very sweet. I had nothing to miss, and yet I missed him.

Chapter Fifteen

Izobel, please, it's me again. I hate this. I'm not the one behind the site.

If you pick up the phone we can at least talk about this. It's not even about the other night anymore, it's about clearing my name and explaining that I'm not cyber-weirdo.

Why? Why would I have created this site about you? I didn't even know you then. I might do now. Oh, that's come out wrong. You know what I mean. You're so aggravating.

The last of Ivan's messages had a point. It was clearly presumptuous to believe yourself to be so freak-sexy that a man you barely knew was busy creating cyber-paeans to your loveliness. But somebody had to have done it and I wanted to know why. I would find out why.

Sunday saw a surge in spirits as I lathered myself up into a frothing frenzy of self-righteousness by scrubbing the flat. A murderer donning rubber gloves and cleaning the scene of the crime could not have expunged George's presence as thoroughly as I did. I dug around in the bathroom sink to remove short dark hairs; I used his expensive facial scrub on the oven; I threw away the bottle of vodka from the freezer and the beers from the fridge; I changed the message on the answerphone from "we" to "I." And that was it. We had no children to fight over nor possessions of any worth. Our mutual ties were dissolved by bleach and Flash liquid.

Just at the point when the flat had reached a zenith of clean and my body a nadir of filth, the doorbell rang. I trotted toward it and then stopped to think who it might be. I presumed George was on his spa weekend, that his desolation at being dumped by me had not impeded the journey to Gloucestershire with Catherine, so it would not be him. Ivan? It could be Ivan, of course, bored with harassing me by text message and now here in person. I slunk toward the door and used my raggedy nails to pull back the letter box flap and look out onto the street. My eyes were just above the crotch level of the visitor and I could see that it was male with a reasonably well-filled pair of gray cords. I pressed my face further to the letter box. It was like some terrible, smutty late-night game show where the female contestants have to try to identify their boyfriends by looking at their groins alone. I could not tell who this was, though I didn't recognize the crotch as belonging to George. He thought cords were for geography teachers.

The crotch crouched and a pair of dimly familiar blue eyes met mine, only inches away on the other side of the door. I sprang back into the hallway, propelled by embarrassment and shock.

"Izobel, does Izobel live here?"

"Who is it?"

"It's an old friend of hers. William."

"William?" I opened the door in curiosity and finally got a full view of the person on the doorstep, rather than the game-of-consequences part vistas I had previously had of bits of his body. He was wearing a neat button-down shirt and a crew-necked sweater, while his hair was almost crew-cut. He looked very different from the long- and lank-haired ex-boyfriend I remembered. He looked like a nice young man who worked in marketing, except for the fact that he was aggressively chewing gum.

At the same time he looked me up and down. He smiled slightly at the beginning of this journey, when looking at my head, and I remembered that I was wearing an old pair of knickers to keep my hair off my face. I pulled them off and stuffed them into my pocket. My disheveled appearance was in contrast to his immaculate turnout, though it had always been the other way round.

"Hello Izobel. You look the same."

"And you look so different."

"I am very different," he said.

What, no longer a drifting rich kid, trustafarian with a penchant for ever harder drugs, I wanted to ask, but instead came out with the question: "Do you want a cup of tea?"

"That's exactly what I want."

I ushered him in, only then wondering at the wisdom of letting in a man who, even when we'd been together, I'd known to be weird. I thought of the death dates on the site for a second, but letting him in seemed less embarrassing than leaving him on the street. I thought that would be a characteristic way for me to go, done in by my fear of social unease.

"Your flat's nice," he said. It was true, I thought on looking round. It now looked chic and minimalist, uncluttered by George's presence and possessions.

"You've never been here before, then?"

"No, you were living in that house with those girls. And at mine mostly."

"Of course."

"How long have you lived here?"

Less time than since last we met, I thought. I hadn't seen him for about six or seven years. After Frank, with some overlap with Jonny, but before Pepe, Married Man, Elliot and George. And here you are, after George. And after the site, what was he doing here?

"A while now. Time passes."

"It does, but every day we learn something new."

"I wish. I feel like every day I just forget something I had once learned."

He looked earnest. He always used to be a giggler, but that was perhaps because he was mostly stoned or on something harder. He could spend hours watching his video of cane toads or old children's television programs. "Do you mind?" he said on getting out a packet of cigarettes.

I was surprised. He seemed too clean-cut for nicotine. I had toyed with the idea of making my flat nonsmoking now George had gone, but I got out an ashtray, into which he put his piece of chewing gum, wrapped in the clear cellophane of the cigarette packet. I fought an urge to whip it away and empty it immediately. Even George didn't leave bits of gum lying around.

"The NA doesn't have a policy on nicotine, caffeine and sugar," he said on putting three heaped teaspoons into his cup.

"NA?"

"Narcotics Anonymous. I've been clean for almost a year," he added proudly.

"Great. I didn't know you were a drug addict, actually. I mean, I knew you were a bit of a stoner and there was the coke. But a junkie?"

"That was the first step in curing myself, admitting that I had a drug problem."

"Well done," I said and I meant it. With the money he had, the company he kept and the indolence he maintained, that must have been hard. I couldn't see George ever admitting to a drink problem and seeking help. For a start, he might have to become as earnest and squarely dressed as this figure before me. William looked like a priest in home clothes.

There was a silence while I thought about the coincidence of having had relationships with a junkie and an alcoholic. Then I wondered what the hell William was doing here. Spending awkward moments with ex-boyfriends had become so natural to me that I had forgotten that this time it was he who had sought me out and not the other way round. I now understood how unnerving it must have been for the others.

"It's great to see you, William, but to what do I owe this pleasure?"

He twitched and I was reminded of the old William, the druggie one. He'd been much more sexy then, it pained me to think. Our time together had been a mixture of high glamour and low life. He lived in a house that had the exterior of a pastel-colored mews house in an expensive part of London and the interior of a student crack den. We'd gone to Glastonbury and slept in a sludge-filled tent, but we got there by helicopter. He was a vegetarian whose mother organized a home delivery of a box full of costly organic vegetables in season. We'd stay up smoking all night, but we would almost never have sex.

"I was at my training course. I'm going to man the NA helpline once a week. You can only do that when you're at least five months clean. I'm not a sponsor yet, you've got to be clean for longer for that."

"Great, but why are you here?"

"It was nearby so I thought I'd pop round. I remembered you lived here."

The William I had known had never remembered anything, nor had he ever known I had lived here at all. I had never told him. We had not ended badly but I had loved that house of his so very much that I felt its loss too keenly to ever go back to visit. I began to feel uncomfortable.

"Do you still use your computer much? You played a lot of games on it and stuff," I asked.

He shook his head. "That's another addiction. I got hooked on the Internet and all the games so Wise Al, he's my sponsor, he said I should give that up too. After the drugs, I was spending fourteen-hour stretches at my computer so I was replacing one drug with another, you see, instead of achieving a sense of a power beyond the addictions I had around me."

"So you never use the Internet now?"

"Never. Al says I'll slip back into all my old habits if I do."

"What were you doing on the Net anyway?"

"Games that you play across networks with other addicts and the porn, of course."

"Porn? But you never, well, I never thought of you as being an aggressively sexual person."

"Exactly."

"I suppose."

I didn't know whether to believe him. Did it matter, since I knew Ivan was behind the site? I realized then that I didn't know anymore, that I wasn't sure I had ever really known it was Ivan. I feared it might be him and I feared it might not. I supposed I should be asking William leading questions and telling him a falsehood to incriminate him, but at that moment I felt very tired of the whole business.

Another pause. "You're probably wondering what I'm doing here."

"Well, yes. I did ask."

"I'm trying to make amends for harm I may have done."

"Big Al told you to do that, did he?"

"Wise Al, yes he did advise me to, as well as the power beyond myself. For me to really break free of the past, I have to right any wrongs that I have done in the darkness of my addictions."

"You didn't harm me. Really, any mess I'm in is entirely my own, thanks."

"I bumped into your friend Frank recently. It was him who told me where you lived so I guess that's why I'm here."

"I see."

"He told me other stuff about you."

"Like what?"

"The fact that you weren't moving on and that your boyfriend was an addict. I feel that I may have started off a chain of codependency in your life and I wanted to help you break it. There are support groups for people like you, too, you know, partners of addicts."

"Mumbo-jumbo, codependency. Next you'll tell me that I'm an enabler."

"You are."

"Thought so. Anyway, I'm not with George anymore. I dumped him and I'm leaving my job, too." Was I? "I am moving on." Yes, I was, I thought at that moment.

"Cool, Izobel, it looks like you're beginning to have your own spiritual awakening. Would you like a sponsor?"

"No, I wouldn't. Thanks."

"We could work through some of the issues, the ones that we developed while we were together, go through the past together. I want to make amends, Izobel."

He wasn't the author of the site, of that I was certain, but he sure was creepy. He always used to be weird, with that high-pitched laugh and that occasional rage against his father, but this beatific calm was even weirder.

"But you can't. I mean, you've nothing to make amends for. And it's pointless going back to the past to sort out the future. It doesn't solve anything. I thought it did, I thought the past held all the answers, but it doesn't, I know that now. You're not going to sort things out by talking to me, but by talking to Brown Al and thinking about what you want to do in the future. The past is only helpful up to a point. I've been looking at the past and now I'm done with it and I want to get on with the rest of my life."

He nodded slowly and repeatedly.

I shrugged. "So I guess I ought to get on with the future right now," I said and stood up to usher him out.

*

I got up early on Monday morning and washed the weekend out of my hair. I decided to go into the office. Apart from anything else, more than three days off work and I'd need a doctor's note. I wasn't sure whether I ever wanted to write one of PR O'Create's press releases again, nor did I think I wanted to see Ivan. I shivered at the thought, God forbid, but I had to go in.

"Babes, you're back," shouted Mimi. "Loved your bloke's article about the Web site."

"A word in my office," greeted Tracy.

"Why don't you return our calls? I've called you three days in a row," barked Camilla on my voice mail.

"If you're back give me a call," pleaded Ivan by the same medium.

"Sorry about the other day," Maggie told me on my mobile. "Must be the hormones. Such a fantastic thing to blame all crabbiness on, I wish I'd thought of it sooner."

"No, I'm sorry, I really am. You've nothing to apologize for and I've no hormones to blame. I've been a stupid cow lately."

"Forget it. Listen, I've been thinking, have you done anything about William? We'd forgotten about him, hadn't we? And he's such a likely candidate to be site perp."

"Funny you should mention him. Sometime I'll tell you all about William, but let's not talk about the site."

"But I want to. It keeps my mind active."

"But we've got our man, haven't we? It's Ivan." Again, I tried to convince myself.

"I'm not sure."

"You've never met him."

"More's the pity, he sounds lovely."

"For a creepy techie stalker."

"I don't know. It's a bit circumstantial: he happened to be at Hot Bob's party. It's not exactly incriminating."

"And he's admitted that he fancied me for months and used to stalk these offices, knows how to work a computer and can create a site in minutes. Anyway, enough about the site, though. How are you doing, Maggie? Are you well? How are your last few days in the office going? What do you think about the single currency?"

She laughed. "I'm pregnant so I have instincts now. And my instincts are telling me it's not Ivan. And don't forget my leaving thing on Wednesday night. I need all the support I can get from you lot; my friends are the civvies to the troops that I work with. I'm sure they make these events deliberately mortifying in order to ensure that nobody ever leaves their jobs. You hadn't forgotten, had you?"

"Of course I hadn't forgotten." Of course I had. "Can't wait to meet all your colleagues at last. Anyone eligible? Joke, by the way, am so not on the pull. Yet."

"Yeah, right."

It had been a terrible effort to drag myself into the office that morning. I didn't feel strong enough to dress up and face a jostling party full of people who lived their lives with all the drama of their profession. But there was no way that I could shirk Maggie's party. Death threat or no death threat. I felt mildly disgruntled for a moment that Maggie should feel that a cyber death date was not a valid enough excuse for nonattendance. I looked at my office computer screen in its sleek flatness. I imagined a hand coming out of it and grabbing me by the throat. I had seen too many horror films.

*

I spent the morning looking toward the door of our open-plan office and looking busy should Tracy pass by my desk. There was no sign of Ivan.

"You're skating on thin ice," she had told me in our five-minute meeting. "There's no room for deadweight at PR O'Create," she continued. "It's time to pull your socks up." That original mind had made us one of the best PR firms in the game.

"I don't think any of my clients would complain."

"That's where you've got completely the wrong end of the stick, Izobel."

"Who?"

"Camilla Jenkinson."

"What?"

"I met her at a launch on Thursday, she's fabulous, and she mentioned that you hadn't been very forthcoming with a PR proposal for their fascinating-sounding venture, OnLove. Internet dating, it's going to be so big. Wouldn't use it myself, mind you."

"But, she's not paying anything. We haven't been hired by her and I didn't want to do work on it as it was just a favor, she's a friend, well a friend of a friend, and I didn't want to use up company resources on that."

"It's called a pitch, Izobel. It's how we win business. Well, maybe not how you do. I've always been the pitch queen."

The pitch bitch, I thought, but muttered, "All right, I'll have something for them by tomorrow."

"By today. I invited her into the office by way of an apology. She'll be here at one thirty."

"But that doesn't give me any time . . ."

"She can only come in at lunchtime. Some people work for a living. Anyway you should have thought of that when you decided not to grace us with your presence for all of last week."

"It was two and a half days. And I was ill . . ."

With a wave of her French-manicured hand, I was dismissed. A prophetic gesture, I thought. So what, I also thought, sack me. The idea of leaving PR O'Create, of leaving PR in general, had germinated and was now growing at the rate of bamboo. Maggie was right. I had not only been diminished by my choice of men. Working in this office for six years had wizened me too. If I could chuck George, I could chuck my job, couldn't I? I'd supported him for two years and now it was time to support myself.

On returning to my desk, I found an A4 brown envelope. "Who left this?" I asked Mimi.

"Technical bloke. One who mends our e-mails."

"He was here? He came in person?"

"Yeah. When you were in with her maj. He's all right, isn't he?"

I had missed him by only moments. I ripped the envelope open and out fell a sheet of paper. I stared at it and realized that it was the blurry mess of an enhanced photograph. I held it upside down at first and then turned it round and began to make it out. It was indistinct and over-pixelated; the false colors of the printer threatened to overwhelm its content. I put my head to one side and made out the bright flash in the center of the page, and then down from that a body, legs and a pair of feet.

There was a note, from Ivan. "This is a blowup of the photo on the site of you and a man coming out the pub. I've enlarged one corner of it." He had nice loopy handwriting. "The photographer was reflected in the window and this is the detail I've cropped." But the face is obscured. "Yes, I know, there's a flash obscuring the head," his note continued. I stared again. How amazing, it was a photo of site perp; this shadowy silhouette actually provided evidence that a physical presence had stood near me and taken a photo; it was not a phantom. Ivan's note concluded: "Can't you remember anything about that day? Didn't you see anyone close enough to take a photo?"

I didn't recognize the figure. Nor could I recall anything suspicious about that evening, though I would have been drunk at this point. "I'm sorry, Ivan, I don't remember," I muttered out loud. You'd have thought if it had been someone I knew, I'd have recognized them. How stupid, stupid, stupid. Think. Nothing. It could have been Ivan; I hadn't really known him at the time the photo was taken, or had I? Was it after I had enlisted him? I didn't know. I stared at the figure, which looked as amorphous as the Loch Ness monster in one of those faked-up images that purport to show her.

There was a Post-it note with an arrow pointing to the photographer's head, with the strange halo effect created by the flash, and Ivan's writing continued. "They're wearing a hoodie. I don't own any hooded tops, honest."

I didn't like hooded tops. If men knew how much shuffling down dark streets wearing hoodies unnerved women, I wondered whether they'd do it. Or maybe that was the point of them. It seemed appropriate for the stalker to be wearing one, given that it was the garb favored by murderous joggers in made-for-TV movies. At that moment, the phone rang.

"Oh, it's you," I said to Ivan. My heart was beating so hard that I felt my head was pulsating too, as if I'd just climbed a very steep mountain.

"Please don't hang up. I've been feeling so awful."

"So you should." Tracy walked past and raised her eyebrows at me.

"Knowing that you must have been feeling bad about those dates. Why would anybody write such a thing?"

"You tell me."

"Come on, Izobel. I know you doubt that it's me. I can hear it. You can tell it's not me in the photo. That's why I sent it to you. Look at it again, surely you must remember something about that night, seeing someone close to you. It's a very bright flash, after all. And you'd know if it had been me."

"Everything else says it's you."

"Nothing says it's me."

I was wavering. "Why did you write the death dates?"

"I didn't. And, anyway, they're not there anymore."

"What?" I opened the site on my computer and to hell with Tracy thinking that I was working on my "home page."

He was right, the death dates were gone, with no explanation or acknowledgment. The phone handset shook against my ear. "So what?" I asked. "You put them there in the first place. How should I know what it means that you've taken them down?"

"You are infuriating."

"And you're a creep."

"What can I do to change your mind?"

"Bring me proof that it's not you."

"What about the photo?"

"Not enough." On my part, this conversation was bordering on banter, on flirtation.

"Please, Izobel."

"Find out who else it could be. Get me some conclusive proof." I put the phone down. I was being the hard-hearted harridan that I've always failed to be on meeting a new man. Those horrible dating manuals were right—it worked a treat.

I stared at the site. It was good, wasn't it, that the death dates were down, though I realized then that I would never get the police interested in the site without them. I felt relief and a small smidgen of disappointment.

*

Frank wanted to have lunch with me and I wanted to have lunch with someone unconnected to the office. We met at a sandwich bar, where our choice of sustenance lay in congealing piles of shiny egg salad and coronation chicken that had just celebrated its golden jubilee. I looked around before we sat down and he looked at me doing so.

"What's your problem, Izobel?"

"What? Nothing." The death dates had gone, I reminded myself, the threat had gone.

"I'm sorry to hear about you and George," he said as we bit into our overstuffed granary rolls.

"No, you're not."

"No, you're right, I'm not."

"You thought he was a tosser. You all did."

"He was."

"You're talking about my boyfriend of two years. Anyway, I feel fine about it, I really do. I'm over him already. Though slightly surprised that you and your girlfriend know about it when it only happened on Friday afternoon."

"Maggie."

"I guessed."

He did head-cocked-on-side sympathetic look, so exaggerated that I thought he must have cricked his neck. "I'm sure you'll find someone."

"Maybe, whatever, maybe I won't. Doesn't matter. I'd rather be on my own than with someone who all my friends thought was unworthy and might drive a wedge between us."

"Have you thought about Internet dating?"

"Piss off."

"What's so wrong with the idea? Do you think it's beneath you?"

"No, of course not, I'm just not interested in meeting anyone new. Least not yet. Nor am I particularly interested in your girlfriend's site."

"Internet dating is going to lead to a massive sociological shift in our perception of meeting life partners. History will look back at the second half of the twentieth century and the first decade of the twenty-first as an anomalous epoch when people thought they could meet their mates by random means. In previous generations we had matchmakers and small communities, now we will have people like Camilla and global networks."

"Yeah, yeah." I raised an eyebrow at him. "I'm sorry Frank, not to have got Camilla's venture any publicity and I'm sorry she thinks I've been remiss and I'm sorry that she told my boss how crap I'd been. Now she's coming in at half one, that's why we had to have lunch early."

"With the others I suppose."

"Tweedledum and Tweedledee, yes, I should expect so." We smiled at one another. "I've drawn up a detailed publicity plan for them." I had dug out an old plan for a new moisturizer we'd PR-ed a couple of months before and had just done Find/Replace on any keywords, exchanging "skin care" for "love online" and "wrinkles" for "loneliness." Fortunately all the stuff about "advanced technology helping people to become the best that they can be" fitted both products.

"I wouldn't worry about it," he said. "She can be quite a bully sometimes."

"Assertive, I'd say. Which is a good thing."

He made patterns in the cocoa powder of his cappuccino. "Do you ever wonder what our lives would be like if we'd stayed together?"

I remembered what I had liked about Frank. He asked girly questions. "Yes, lots. But it never would have happened. We were never the sort of people who were going to last with the person we met in first term. Worse, we might have stayed together throughout our twenties and then split up, leaving ourselves completely unprepared for dating in the age of e-mail and the mobile telephone. Why, do you think about what it would be like to be with your college sweetheart?"

"Yes, I do." He sighed. "It wouldn't have been disastrous. A woman at work, professor of anthropological history, told me that the best thing you can do career-wise is settle young. That way you don't use up valuable energy in chasing and getting together and then getting over it."

"She's right. Look at Maggie and Mick." I stroked the remnants of my pustulant chin and felt the merest quiver between my thighs as I thought of the last time I had come into work after a random caress. "I waste so much of my office time on my crappy relationships. Worrying about George and wondering who his successor might be."

"Is that why you took three days off last week?"

I paused. "Yes, I was psyching myself up to split up with George. I'd been fretting about doing it for a while."

"You never said."

"I can be quite enigmatic, you know."

"Of course." His head was now so to one side that his eye almost met his shoulder.

"Honestly, I'm great, I'm fabulous about it now."

"Did you ever find out who was behind your Web libel thing?"

"No, no. It wasn't important. It just gave Maggie and me a distraction from my bad job and her good pregnancy."

He looked thoughtful again.

"Frank, are you OK?"

"Fine, fine."

"There's nothing wrong between you and Camilla, is there?"

"No, no. Quite the contrary."

*

"So good of you to see us at last," said Camilla. "Kind of lucky coincidence that I should have met Tracy on Thursday."

"Indeed."

"She is so lovely. You are lucky to have a female boss. And so young, too."

I ushered Camilla, Becksy and Alice into a meeting room, papers in hand. I had jazzed up the tired old publicity plan that I had created for OnLove by adding their logo and ours, printing it out in color and binding it in black plastic spirals. That usually proved disproportionately impressive.

I could see why Camilla and Tracy might have liked each other on first meeting. They both had ironed hair, straight backs and rigid good taste. Camilla was brighter than Tracy, Frank wouldn't go out with a girl with no culture, but they were hewn from the same piece of granite.

"So, how's the Internet dating going?"

"Great. It's hard when we're all working on other jobs, but we're raising the money to get toward its launch. A little publicity wouldn't go amiss though." Camilla laughed.

"And that's where I come in. Here's an initial plan, with certain guarantees. And the projected costs and comeback are outlined on the last sheet. I've suggested two models: one with a monthly retainer and then additional costs per campaign based on results, the other a higher fee but all-inclusive and with fixed guarantees." I handed them their packs, which were thickened by a couple of brightly colored cover sheets with words and phrases like "love," "communication," "through the keyboard" and "why online?" floating around in an oversize font.

"Good, very good," said Camilla, on not having read any of the content. "I like it. I'm impressed, Izobel. So, when do we start? I'm available for interview."

"Have you looked at the costs? There's a budget on the last page."

"Costs? I thought you were doing this as a friend. I don't think Frank will be very impressed by your attitude, especially since I gather from him that you might need our matchmaking services now that you're a bit of a lonely heart yourself."

"I don't think that will be necessary, thank you, Camilla."

"And Tracy said—"

"Tracy would not approve of giving our services and resources for free. Look, I've done this plan for you and I'm very happy to advise, but any further active work will require you hiring me on a professional basis with the negotiated costs as outlined in the proposal or some sort of revenue share."

"OK," she said. "Thank you, Izobel." There was no sarcasm in her voice, just acknowledgment. I liked the new me. "Izobel takes no nonsense from demanding clients and gives as good as she gets." That's what the caption to this meeting would have read.

"See you day after tomorrow, I guess," I said to Camilla.

"Yes, Maggie's thing. Where is it again? Frank can't find the e-mail."

"Blakeney's, it's a new bar near here. Don't know what it's like."

"Should be fun. I think we'll go straight after work."

"Me, too."

Alice spoke next. "Are you coming to the reunion?" Camilla and I both turned to her. "The school one, next month. Didn't you read about it in the e-mail newsletter?"

"No," we said with one voice, to which Camilla added, "I so don't read the school newsletter."

"Neither do I," I said.

"Nor me," said Becksy, "I never do."

"Alice, you've really got to get a life. Get a hobby or something."

"I've got lots of hobbies, actually, Camilla," Alice said.

I looked at her and thought of Ivan. He had his art. I could believe Alice had a hobby, something geeky at a guess. Camilla, Becksy and I were the ones without interests, but I'm sure we believed ourselves to be the most interesting. I would get a hobby, I decided.

*

When I next checked the site, a couple of hours later, there was a new pap photo. It hadn't taken long for it to respond to the fact that my life once again consisted of more than going out to get a pint of milk at the newsagent's. The photo showed Frank and me at the fuel-polluted outdoor table of the café where we had lunched. I was gesticulating wildly with a piece of chicken clearly visible on the side of my mouth and he was listening intently. We looked happy, it was sunny and we seemed to be interested in what the other had to say. It wasn't how I remembered the event that had taken place such a short while ago.

I always feel a poignant jealousy when I look at other people's photo albums. Their lives seem a perpetual round of holidays, parties and weddings. But then, of course, they never take photos of themselves slumped in front of the television or cleaning the oven.

The site was my own photo album and yet I envied the life it portrayed. I wanted to be site Izobel Brannigan, a woman who "grabs an alfresco bite with a handsome friend" before heading back to her glamorous job in PR. Real Izobel Brannigan just had salmonella chicken, an opaque conversation and a job that was deadening.

Chapter Sixteen

Tuesday: get up, check site, avoid Tracy and Ivan, await phone call from George, hear nothing.

Wednesday: much the same, though the site sported an extra photo of me staring into window of fancy boutique with the caption "Izobel loves to mix designer and vintage for a romantic look that's truly hers." I'd gone to shop in my Tuesday lunch break because I was looking for something to wear to Maggie's leaving party. I had a theory, never disproved, that if you wanted to pull you wore a light-colored top. Not necessarily white, just pale blue or green or any pastel. In the pitch-black morass of women decked in darkness, the girl in the light-colored top would always have men around her, as if programmed like thunderflies congregating on a yellow car.

I think pale colors make your breasts look perkier, too.

The boutique was beautiful and expensive, but I had lost the will to shop. This was like losing my lifeblood, it made me feel like a Lothario without his lustfulness or George deciding he didn't much like the taste of alcohol. Nothing was as it should be anymore. Clothes had always been both my ballast and my millstone. They gave me comfort and confidence and yet were part of the shallowness that meant I was excited by meeting the daughters of famous men and liked the thought of others envying me my glamour.

I had ignored the siren call of the aquamarine, diaphanous fitted shirt in the shop and was wearing a black dress that day. All girls love to wear black dresses, indulging in their communal crush on Audrey Hepburn. That day I was dressing for women, for me, and not for men; I didn't need a pulling top as that was the last thing I wanted to do. I would remain alone, I vowed, for at least half the length of time I'd been with George. A year of living celibately.

*

"I heard about you and George," said a well-meaning acquaintance, head to one side.

"No, it's great. It's fine, really I'm fine."

"You're being so brave. It must be so difficult splitting up with someone in your thirties."

I suppose Maggie's party marked the beginning of a new era for it was the first time I'd been out since George and I had split up. I looked around the bar for escape. It was an old men's boozer that had been stripped and kitsched up, like an octogenarian displaying her crepey embonpoint in a Vivienne Westwood corset. It was the bastard child of a fifties diner and the Palace of Versailles, where swags of brocade curtain did battle with an old Space Invaders game and antique mirrors mottled our reflections. What was I doing there? I knocked back my overpriced drink. I could at least get drunk.

"Excuse me, I need to go to the loo." There it was cool and deliciously lonely. I came out only when somebody started pounding on the door. I did the panicked walk of someone coming into a party and not knowing to whom I was going to talk, who'd want to talk to me, did I know anyone. Salvation came in the form of Frank and Camilla at the bar.

"Hello, people." Kisses all round. They seemed ill at ease, as if I had just interrupted an argument. I started talking breathlessly to diffuse whatever tension I had inadvertently stumbled upon, making a mental note to talk to Maggie about Frank's odd conversation with me at lunch on Monday. "Look at all these people. Maggie's obviously really popular at work. I'd hate to have a party with all my work colleagues and my real friends, would be such a strange mix. Don't think it would be good at all. What do you think?"

They were both staring intently at me, not even exchanging the briefest of glances with each other. I thought I saw Frank grimace.

"Izobel, what would you like to drink?" I turned to the voice at my shoulder.

"You remember Molly, don't you?" said Frank. "Another from the old alma mater."

"Of course, hello, Molly, I didn't know you knew Maggie." Frank muttered something under his breath. "I'll have a gin and tonic, thanks. What's that, Frank?"

"Nothing."

We were soon joined by Alice and Becksy, who, with Molly, formed a little trinity of blonde cloning clustered around Camilla. Frank and I moved closer together, propelled by the Stepford unity that confronted us. Camilla took a small step in our direction and I could feel that a social evolutionary scale was forming at the bar with Molly, Becksy and Alice forming the prehistoric amoebas of our lineup. Nobody was talking so it was up to me to burble.

"What are your work colleagues like, Frank? Well, there's that Robert who had his thirtieth for starters, I know him." Frank and Camilla did at last look at each other and almost smiled at the mention of his name.

"I hear you know him by a different name," said Frank. "He's Hot Bob to you, isn't he, Izobel?"

I ignored the superiority of the coupled man. "And Camilla, you're still with the management consultancy, aren't you?"

"Part-time," she said. "They're fabulous people. So dynamic. I love them."

"You'll miss them if OnLove takes off. Still, you'll have colleagues there, I suppose. I wonder whether you'll socialize with them?"

"I'm sure you won't be able to escape them," said Frank.

"Frank, please." Camilla forced a smile.

"It's true."

"We'll talk about it later."

"I love my workies," said Molly.

"I love my old ones and my new ones even more," said Becky. "It's so cool working and playing with a big gang."

"We should go and pay our tributes to Maggie," I said and off we shuffled like conjoined contestants in a twelve legged race. We loitered around Maggie, who was being feted by a succession of colleagues.

"When's it due, exactly?" asked one.

"Do you know if it's a boy or a girl?"

"What names have you thought of?

"When's it due?"

"I like Cormac for a boy and Iris for a girl, like the writers. Have you thought of those names?"

"What about Alfie, that's a sweet name for a boy."

"Or for a girl."

"Short for what? Alfreda?"

"What's your due date?"

Maggie caught my eye and announced, "It's due in a month's time, we don't know the sex and we're waiting to see what he or she looks like before thinking up names." She then whispered to me, "I feel like I should get a T-shirt printed."

"Is it weird to be stopping work for six months?" I asked, mindful not to ask anything about the now-unmentionable baby.

"Very. And very wonderful too. Isn't that awful of me."

"Not at all. I swear we get broody not because we want a baby but because we want time off work."

"Probably not time off though, is it, but at least I have got a whole five weeks of daytime TV and sitting on my fat arse allowing myself to bloom."

"Why are you leaving so early?"

"I couldn't go on; I can't sleep and I'm so tired. And everyone keeps saying how sad that if I go on maternity leave this long before due date I'll have over a month less with the baby, or 'baby' as the health workers rather yukkily call it, but I'm rather thrilled by that prospect."

"Bliss."

"I will go back to work though. I'm not going to be, what's it called now, a full-time homemaker."

"A stay-at-home mum. Ouch, Frank, that's my foot you're stamping on."

"Is it? Sorry," he said without apology. "I wanted to talk to Maggie too, you're monopolizing her. When did you say it was due?"

"Next month, though they say first babies are often late," replied Maggie.

"Is it a boy or a girl?"

"I don't know."

"I think it's a girl," said Camilla. "Because of the way you're carrying it."

"That's tantamount to calling me a big, fat cow who's bloated all over my body, Camilla. You're always supposed to guess it's a boy." Maggie sighed. "Where's Hot Bob? I asked you to bring him, Frank. I thought that would cheer you up, Iz."

Frank sniggered.

"No way. I'm not out there yet. Please God, tell me you haven't really invited him." I turned. "Oh, hello Robert, how are you?" I looked down with embarrassment.

"Blinging." Above his feet clad in old-school trainers were hairy shins and combat shorts, topped with a chain around his neck and a joint in his hand. And, I noticed, a hooded top. It was hot out, but really there was no excuse for shorts in an urban area. Frank was dressed similarly. In the same way that primary schoolteachers and childminders get infantilized by their charges, so university lecturers are made studentlike by theirs. It was embarrassing how down with the kids they tried to be, with violent rap on their CD players and trainers on their feet.

"I know your cousin Ivan. He works with me." They did look alike, but Robert was Ivan gone wrong, like when you see siblings of film stars or supermodels and they always just seem to be compiled from all the leftover imperfections. Ivan's voice may have been too high, but Robert's was positively squeaky. Ivan's nose was straight and his hair thick; his cousin's nose was slightly snub and his hair coiffed and gelled into a silly but fashionable mullet. Ivan's body was slim but slightly squidgy, so not to look like he was boring enough to do all the stomach crunches necessary for a six-pack, while Robert had muscles bursting out of a tight cap-sleeved T-shirt.

"You're kidding me. For real?" he replied.

"Yes, really. He's the systems administrator for the company where I work."

"Ivan's all that."

"Yes, he seems really competent. Very efficient, knows his stuff."

Hot Bob was jigging to the imaginary rap track in his head. "Do you want some bone?"

"I'm sorry," I said. "Do I what?"

Hot Bob giggled and pointed to the joint in his hand, before toking deeply on it.

"No, I'm all right thanks."

"You chilling."

"Yes, I suppose so. Excuse me, just going to the . . ." I gestured toward the loos and Hot Bob gave me a wink, which either suggested that he thought that I was going in there to take something stronger than a joint, or that I might be inviting him in there with me. I scooted fast across the room and locked myself into the ladies.' I was not ready for bad conversations with faked-up interest, especially not with Robert. I think we only thought him hot from the safety of our own relationships. The only thing smoking about him were the embers of his poorly rolled joint.

I found it difficult to believe that he shared genes with Ivan.

"Maggie." I grabbed her on my way out. "Sorry to talk about myself for a change, but how could you have invited Hot Bob for me? He's a prat. Thinks he's in South Central LA rather than West Central London."

She giggled. "Is he awful? I am sorry. I think he's rather handsome, in a boy band kind of a way."

"Not a patch on his cousin Ivan, the bastard. Thanks anyway, but I don't think I'm quite ready to be Hot Bob's honey. Speaking of stickiness, what's with Frank and Camilla? They seemed a bit weird with one another."

"They did, like they'd been discussing something and then I saw Frank rather hilariously visibly groan at the invasion of the schoolgirl hordes."

"Those girls are ubiquitous, aren't they?"

"I heard him say something like 'I'm going out with you, not your schoolmates.' "

"Really? Juicy. I wonder if he means any one of them in particular."

"Or he could mean you, you were at that school too, weren't you? That's it, he's still in love with you."

"Yeah, right. Though we did have a weird lunch together. He was a bit funny and kept on wanting to talk about what would have happened if we'd stayed together and hinting that things weren't perfect between Camilla and him."

"I'm right, he is still into you. That would make him site man, wouldn't it? That would be so great, you two going out with one another again. The childhood sweethearts who grew up enough to realize that they'd never find anyone sweeter. I love it. University didn't teach them that they were in love with each other . . ."

"Never going to happen."

"Hello," said Alice or Becksy, appearing from nowhere once more. It was Alice, I divined, the smaller one. Maggie escaped to talk to more of her public and I suddenly felt very tired.

"How are you?"

"Really well, thanks."

"And the Internet dating thingie?"

"Really brilliant."

"Great. I've got to go," I told her. "I was ill last week."

"Yes, Camilla told me."

"You seem to hang out with each other a lot."

"Sort of."

"Have you been friends since school then? I only have one friend from school."

"No, we haven't, not really. I had to go to a different place at sixth form, so we hadn't seen each other in ages."

"I see."

"Then I read on Friends Reunited that she was a management consultant so I got in touch with her about OnLove."

"So you really do believe that important partnerships can be created through the Internet?"

"Oh yes. And though this started out as a business partnership, I suppose we're friends now too."

I saw that I could be there for a long time. "Like I say I was ill, so can't really stay," I said, knocking back the gin and tonic. "Nice to see you again."

"Thanks." I saw her melt back and disappear into the crowd, while I escaped with an apology to Maggie and a quick "when's it due and have you thought about names" conversation with Mick.

*

Thursday: same site, same sort of day at the office. No hangover from Maggie's party, that was the advantage of having had such an awful time. I didn't want to be out there, back in the place where parties were significant, especially if out there involved men like Hot Bob.

I had expected photos from the party or me emerging from the party but there were none to distract me from another busy day of PR. I already felt the loss of Maggie the e-mailing friend, as she settled into her new life of daytime television. I didn't want a baby, not yet, but how I envied her the six months of maternity leave. Maybe I should just have a baby for that reason alone, though it didn't seem a very good reason to bring a child into the world. Couldn't be any worse than Maggie's argument that she'd needed to get pregnant in order to finally give up smoking.

It had sunk to this level. Contemplating having a baby just to get out of coming to work for a few months. There must be easier ways of leaving PR O'Create. I could leave right now if I wanted to. I had a high-interest account that I'd kept secret from George, even when he was about to get sued by his divorce lawyers for not having paid his fees. I could use that money to retrain or live off. And hadn't Tracy hinted that there would be redundancies in the company? Please, please make me redundant with my six years of service.

Even if I didn't get made redundant, I didn't need to stay there, did I? I mean, I was Izobel Brannigan who rocks her world. I wasn't even causing this office to tremble. Every educated office worker has a fantasy about the manual job they wish they were doing. I quite wanted to be a hairdresser, or if not that a waitress. All the women I knew daydreamed about chucking in their office jobs and becoming a waitress, while most men I knew seemed to want to become cycle couriers. Both would free the mind and slim the thighs.

I looked toward Tracy's office and fantasized about sticking her stupid job. Now that I no longer had to support George, I'd need less money. And I could always sort out the spare room in my flat and let it out. That would cover the mortgage.

I began to plan my very own publicity campaign. What were my strengths and qualities? What interested me? What was I good at? What did I want out of a career? I began to whittle away and scribble and type and Google prospective courses on the Internet. Ideas were beginning to form for the first time in months or even years. I could see a different future.

Chapter Seventeen

Friday: different. The site was different and therefore so was my life. That was the order of things these days.

I had waited until 10 in the morning before taking a peek at my virtual reflection. The array of pap shots was the same as was the old text about me "cutting a swath" that had replaced the vanished death dates. It didn't know that I'd soon be cutting out the PR industry from my life. It didn't know everything about me. I was in control.

But the ticker was different. I almost didn't notice at first amid the usual bumf about much-vaunted but never-delivered new sections of the site, the promised message boards and e-mail alerts. The words leaned limply across my screen like items on an ancient conveyor belt.

Then not words, characters: Chinese characters. My head leaned forward in interest.

They danced where the Latin alphabet had merely moved, but were soon replaced by an English translation.

That means "good morning and good wishes, people" in Chinese script. Izobel is an enthusiastic student of Mandarin, though she's not been attending her classes lately!

True, I hadn't been to a class for ages. What? I'm not learning Chinese and I don't have six toes on one foot and I don't breed chinchillas. I looked at the frowning girl in myriad photos on the site. That woman doesn't know how to speak Chinese, but somebody thinks she does: Frank.

I had told Frank on the phone when I'd tried to investigate the possibility that he might be the site perp. It was a month or so ago, the day that I went into George's office and rummaged through his e-mail in-box. It was a rubbish lie, but it was definitely Frank to whom I had told it. I knew that because he'd brought it up again when we'd been out in the pub, that time after seeing Elliot; he'd said I'd be able to order our food at the Chinese restaurant and I'd had to make some excuse about it being Sichuan.

Frank. All that "how would our life have been together," those strange looks, those sentences half started. Surely not him. Frank, who had been so indignant and yet so incurious when I had told him there were things about me on the Internet. He never even inquired what site I meant when I had asked him if he'd been writing the things himself.

Frank. Let it please not be my first love, my first serious boyfriend and the only one who's remained my friend. Frank, not Ivan, let it please be Frank. Let it please be neither.

Ivan. Did I tell him about the Chinese lessons? No, when would I have done, it's not true. Could he have overheard a conversation with Maggie? He can tell Tracy about my Internet usage; can he read my e-mails? Yes, of course he can.

I did a search on my e-mail in- and out-boxes. "Chinese." Nothing. Not that way, Ivan did not find out that way. Perhaps he never knew about my nonexistent Chinese lessons. Frank knew.

But Frank was in two of the pictures on the site. How had he taken the one of him and me having lunch? He had an accomplice. He must have paid someone to make the site so he'd pay someone to take photos too. That would explain why I never recognized the photographer. Poor Camilla, if she knew what her boyfriend was up to. Perhaps she'd need the services of her OnLove Internet dating after all.

It wasn't Ivan. I felt a sensation that I had not experienced in over a week. I bubbled with that intangible, often frustrated, blurred emotion of having something to look forward to: a party, a hot date, a financial windfall, a delicious meal.

It couldn't be Ivan. He was not behind the site, surely? Ivan was innocent. I looked around, expecting, hoping to see him arrive in the office at that moment. All I saw was Tracy, who glanced at my screen as she walked past.

Frank—it couldn't be Frank, could it? He seemed so normal. Though he had not looked entirely happy with Camilla when we had lunched. And hadn't he said something about her being a bully? Not a comment you'd make about your girlfriend if you were truly contented. Of course, the arguments at Maggie's party on Wednesday night, the "I'm not in love with someone from your school." Me and I didn't know it. Maybe Camilla does know.

I had always had a soft spot for Frank, we'd stayed close, but I had no idea that he felt this way about me. Frank is in love with me. I would never have thought it, but he is. He's besotted with me. I rock his world. Poor Frank, how awful that he is trying to get his academic treatises published and yet has such a terrible prose style. I'd never have thought that.

And I never would have guessed that he wanted us to be together. That would explain why he was so furious when I defined him as an ex-boyfriend of mine. Frank wishes we had never split up and he hates his bullying and bullish girlfriend. He was always ruder than he needed to have been about George. Something about his vitriol went beyond a platonic friend's concern. Frank had been in love with me, that I had known all those years as we had spent whole weekends in bed together, pinging condoms at each other and plotting our future, but Frank still in love with me? I supposed you never got over your teenage loves, nor, it seemed, your teenage prose style.

Frank was undergoing the long dark night of the soul. I'd read about such things, people having third-life crises instead of midlife ones. He'd gone bonkers. Academia must do that to you; trying to be a media don must be very wearing.

Poor Frank.

Poor Ivan, that I had doubted him so. Innocent Ivan.

Evil Frank, the misery he had caused me. The death dates. The bastard.

Ivan versus Frank. I knew who I wanted to win.

My phone went.

"I'm innocent and I've got proof!" said that now-familiar voice, a slightly squeakier one than is strictly attractive on a man.

"Ivan," I shrieked in a voice so high that only bats could hear it. "Ivan," in a lower tone. I had been rocklike with Ivan, but now I was fluttery. He was no longer the enemy, but a boy I had kissed and now fancied and was engaged in the awkwardness of telephone calls with. "Yes, I know." Innocent Ivan. "Well, at least I think I know. I assume so."

"How do you know?"

"The Chinese thing."

"What are you talking about? What Chinese thing?"

"On the site. What are you talking about? How else are you innocent?"

"I've found the postcode of whoever registered the site. We know where they live, well, more or less; it's got to be one of about twenty houses with that postcode. And it's not my house."

"What? How?"

"I'll explain when I see you. I can see you, can't I?"

"Yes," I cried. "I suppose so," I said.

"What do you mean, 'I suppose so'? Won't your hectic schedule of fashion launches and restaurant openings allow it? Got a hot date with a media type?"

"Ha, ha. I said I suppose so because I still don't know whether I can trust you."

He sighed.

"This postcode," I asked. "Is it in London?"

"Yes."

I felt the phone receiver tremble against my ear. "Where?"

"West Fourteen. Shepherd's Bush."

"Oh," I said.

Frank didn't live in Shepherd's Bush.

"How do we know it's not a fake one?"

"We don't, but there's only one way to find out. Are you free at lunchtime?" he asked.

"Yes, I am." I was badly dressed and hadn't washed my hair that morning. If only dry shampoo actually worked but instead it makes you look like you're wearing a dandruffy old wig. Could I at least wash my fringe in the sink and then fluff it up in the hand dryer? "Yes, let's meet then, Ivan. Thank you. For everything."

*

I nipped out midmorning and bought a wildly expensive chiffon top that was just on the right side of see-through: a glimpse of the curves below rather than girl band member about to go solo. It was an appropriate compromise between dressy and casual, perfect for a lunchtime first date slash investigative showdown and a wonderful sage color. I supposed I should be saving my money for potential unemployment, but I had that binge-before-a-diet feeling.

I looked in the mirror and made a pouty face as I admired it. The office toilet's liquid soap had done a reasonable job on my hair, rendering it no longer greasy, when it actually changes color.

I knew how I wanted to look for Ivan but I wasn't sure how I was to behave or what we were to do. We had the postcode, or what we assumed was the postcode, who knew whether it wasn't just another red herring or false clue.

*

Ivan arrived at my offices punctually, ready for lunch. I looked through to the foyer where he stood and reveled in the seconds that I had to examine him. How could I have ever thought him unattractive? Staring at him then, he seemed embarrassingly handsome, out-of-my-league handsome, film-star handsome. If we went out together, jealous girls would think us a mismatch and consider him fair game as I didn't deserve him. Girls did that. I had done that. They get angry when they see ugly old men with gorgeous young women, but they are even more offended should they see a plain girl with an exceptional male.

I felt his looks almost smite my eyes. I searched his face for imperfection, but instead saw that long, straight aquiline nose, that thick shiny hair, that mouth; I wanted to kiss that mouth. I appraised the broad shoulders and slim body where I had been used to seeing George's slim shoulders and broad body. He was IT-boy indeed.

I shook my head and stood up tall. He wasn't innocent yet. I had to try to remember that. I wasn't sure that I fancied him. I had to stop just getting off with people and then working out whether we were compatible afterward. He was systems administrator man to whom I had never given a second glance, after all; my mind was just addled by kisses, sites and splits. I couldn't fall for a techie, I had to remember that. I hadn't slept with him yet. I was enjoying being single, wasn't I, I didn't want to meet anybody else right now.

He turned to me and grinned. We did a sort of break-dance around one another as we worked out what greeting to offer. We settled on kissing each other's cheeks, a compromise we had not made before. Before it was all or nothing. We giggled awkwardly. He wore aftershave, another unfamiliarity. I had doused myself in perfume. I had put on lipstick, blotted so thoroughly with tissue paper that it almost didn't exist, but left a stain upon my lips that only I could be aware of.

"Nice top," he said.

"Thanks," I said. We stared at each other and made our way to a restaurant with a terrace. It was one of those rare London days where things go right without trying. The sun was shining and yet we got a table outside. The waiters were efficient and our beers cold. The site and the office receded. We stared at one another again.

"Tell me how you got the postcode. And why I should believe you," I said.

"And what's this Chinese thing you're on about?"

"I asked first."

"All right." He drew breath and I felt one of Ivan's explanations coming on. Oh dear. "I had to lie."

"You lied? You who have a code of professional conduct, who won't do anything remotely illegal?"

"Yes, I lied and I gave false information. There, are you proud of yourself? I couldn't see any other way of disabusing you of the ridiculous idea that I might be behind the site."

I blushed.

"As if," he said and I reddened some more. "Don't flatter yourself."

I mumbled something that approached an apology.

"I kept on looking at all the information we had gathered and hoping to find some sort of clue. I even went through every line of code to see if there was anything more embedded there."

"Was there?"

"Only the occasional 'Izobel rocks' and other such nonsense, along with more references to *Dune.* Nothing scandalous or useful. There was nothing else for me to go on, except what we'd gathered already, which was some false names, a false PO box number and the names of a couple of domain name registrars."

"Remind me."

"Registrars—the companies that register the domain names and URLs of the sites."

"Not the person from *Dune*?"

"No, that's the registrant."

"Of course." I remembered now why I could find him so irritating.

"There was no point pursuing the registrar in the States, but I reckoned that the two-bit company that had registered the co dot uk name in this country might be a little more open."

"How did you know they were two-bit?"

"I'd never heard of them and their own company Web site looked like it had been done by a myopic teenager in his bedroom. It was rubbish."

"Not like izobelbrannigan dot com," I boasted.

"Indeed." He had finished his beer already and ordered another. "From directory inquiries," he continued, "I managed to get a telephone number for e-z-webbysolutions . . ."

"The registrars," I commented, flaunting the word.

"Yes, the registrars of the izobelbrannigan dot co dot uk domain name, the British one. So I rang them up and it was my good fortune to talk to a girl in customer services who was both bored and stupid."

"As is often the case."

"But unusually, I wanted someone bored and stupid. I said to her that I was the registrant for the domain name izobelbrannigan dot co dot uk and that I was furious that they had been giving out my address to junk mail companies. She of course says, 'But we don't give addresses of our customers out to third parties.'"

"Reading this off an answers-to-frequently-asked-questions list she's got in front of her," I said.

"Exactly."

"So?"

"I get really angry, really apoplectic. It was quite easy, I just thought about how pissed off I was that you should have accused me of making the damned site and I found myself to be enraged."

"Sorry about that. Then what?"

"'Well,' I say to bored stupid girl, 'if you don't give out addresses, then why have I received mountains of junk mail since registering the domain name with you?'"

"But she'd just say how can you prove it's them giving out your details and not a credit card company or some other list. You can't pin it on them."

"Which is exactly what she did say. But then I said, 'I know it must be your company because I made a mistake in the post-code I gave you and this mistake has been replicated in all the junk mail I've received ever since. Ergo, it must be you that's making money out of creating mailing lists.'"

"Cunning. But also a long shot."

"I know. This wasn't the first route I tried taking to try to find out who registered the site. I did call the company in the States, I tried the Post Office again . . ."

I smiled. "So what happened when you told stupid bored woman about the mistake in the postcode?"

"Of course she said, 'What's the postcode you gave us,' to which I said, 'You tell me the one you've got,' and this ping-ponged for a while until I eventually bullied, or bored, her into submission. She cracked just to get me off the phone. I was demanding to speak to her manager by this point as well as throwing some crap at her about privacy laws and data protection. Just as I was about to give up she told me the postcode that they held for the domain name izobel-brannigan dot co dot uk and I scribbled it down."

I looked at the postcode. A letter, two numbers, another number and two letters, six characters that could answer the question that had dominated my life for the last month and a half. "Thank you."

"That's all right. Do you believe me now?"

I did, I believed him utterly. I doubted that I had ever doubted him. Yet I also believed that we would never find out who was really behind the site. And I couldn't shake off that residual anger I had felt toward him when I thought he was the perp. "How do we know that it's not a false postcode?" I asked.

"It's a real postcode all right, but whether it's our site person's real postcode is another matter."

"And they didn't give you an address? How can you tell what exact address this is other than somewhere in W Fourteen?"

"Izobel, will you never learn the power of the Internet?"

"I know it all too well."

"The Post Office has a site and if you input the postcode, it will give you the address, or should I say addresses, that correspond to it. Unlike America or the Continent, where the zip code covers a huge area, British postcodes are absurdly specific. A letter will arrive if you just put the house number and the postcode on the envelope. You don't even need to put the town or name or anything. It's amazing really."

"Indeed. So what's the address of this one then?"

"It gives us only about fifteen buildings on one street, some single-occupancy, others divided into flats."

"Quite a lot of people then," I said ungratefully. "At least thirty or so."

"True." He pulled out a printed page from the Internet with

a page of the London *A to Z* on it, with one section of a street highlighted in pink. "Does this mean anything to you? Do you know anyone who lives around there?"

I shook my head. "Sorry."

"And the photo I sent you didn't mean anything?"

"No." I shook my head. "Hooded top, not a lot else. Could be Frank."

"Who's Frank?"

"He's taken over from you as our most likely candidate. He's an ex of mine who wears a hoodie and I told him I was learning Chinese. And I know he remembered that fact as he made some sarky comment about me being fluent in Mandarin later." I knocked back my beer to catch up with Ivan. "But I'm not learning Chinese. Then today there was this stuff on the site about how I'm a keen student of Chinese."

"I saw that. I was impressed."

"But I'm not learning it."

"Too busy reading *Hello!* and *Heat*?"

"Yes, as a matter of fact. And researching some courses I'm thinking of doing."

"So that's it, this ex of yours must be guilty as nobody else thinks you're a Mandarin speaker. Or," he exclaimed, "he's in league with whoever is behind the site."

"There's a team of them?"

"Could be." We were silenced by the image of a factory full of Izobel obsessives.

"Or, he happened to mention that I speak Chinese to the site perp. He just *knows* the site perp rather than *is* site perp."

"Only one way to find out. Why don't we confront your boyfriend?"

"Ex. I'm not sure. He doesn't live at the address you've got. And it just seems so unlikely."

"And yet when I turn out to have been at the same party as you months ago, that's damning evidence?"

I was about to point out that he was also a geek who admitted to having followed me around the office for months, but refrained. "I've learned from that mistake, Ivan, and I am loath to jump to conclusions just because everything seems to add up. This time we've got to be sure. I don't want to blow it. Let's see what happens if we go to West Fourteen first."

"So let's go after work tonight. Westward ho."

"Who are you calling a ho?" We laughed disproportionately at my feeble quip. "But we can't. Not after work."

"Why not? Got a hot date?"

"No. What do we know about the site perp?"

"That they're not me, that they're weird, that they take photos of you . . ."

"And when do they take those photos of me?"

"I don't know. Whenever."

"No, not whenever, that's just it. Let's think about this. There are photos of me at the supermarket on a Saturday, there are ones in the evening after work and ones at lunchtime. But there aren't any during the day, there are none of me heading out to meetings, none of me during that three days I had off last week."

"And your point being?"

"I think site perp's got a job. A proper job. He doesn't stalk me full-time, just outside office hours. He's a boring nine-to-fiver just like the rest of us."

"Not like me. I work flexible hours. What about your friend Frank?"

I thought. "He's flexible too. Has a certain number of hours teaching and then the rest of the time is in the library and can do what he wants. But then I don't think he's taken the photographs as he's in a couple of them."

"So the photographer has a nine-to-five job, but not the perpetrator, this Frank character?"

My head hurt. "Unless it's not Frank at all."

"Make up your mind, Izobel."

"Look, I'm sure the person who follows me has a regular job. In which case, we can't go after work as then they could follow us following them and we wouldn't have the benefit of surprising them, would we?"

"So?"

"We have to go now. After lunch. That way we've got an afternoon to check out all the addresses and try to pick up some clues, see if any of the names on the doorbells mean anything to me. And then we can wait for them to get back from their normal job at six."

"Presuming they come straight home."

"I'm guessing site photographer doesn't have a lot else to do. Their only hobby seems to be following me and once they see that I'm not in the office, then hopefully they'll come straight home."

"And we just leave this Frank character alone."

"For the moment, yes."

"You seem to be treating him a lot more generously than you did me."

"I'm so sorry, Ivan." We looked at each other properly. I stared at his mouth. I wanted to kiss him and I wanted to find out who was behind the site. But I wanted to find out who was behind the site first. The site's mystery was George-era, the site solved could be Ivan-era. My love life was all too bound up with izobelbrannigan.com to be able to move on with Ivan. I looked around. "The photographer's probably watching us now."

"And what would the caption to this be?"

I pulled a face. "Izobel enjoys beer and conversation with an unknown man. Exclamation mark."

"Come on, you can do better than that," he said. He stroked his chin and I stroked mine, giving silent thanks to the antibiotics that had cleared up my infected stubble burn. I felt a twitching between my thighs and cursed my weakness. Mustn't get distracted.

"We should go," I said. "Are you free this afternoon? I could go back to the office in case we're being trailed and then nip out the back way to the Underground. To schlep over to Shepherd's Bush. Schlepherd's Bush as it were."

"I'm free, but you're not. As my own boss, I'm often generously giving myself time off. But you work a nine-to-five, remember? Even if it is in PR. And even if it is a Friday afternoon."

"Sod that. This is more important."

"Come on, Izobel, you can't just bunk off work. You'll get in trouble." He grimaced.

"What? You know something, don't you?" I asked.

"I so shouldn't tell you this."

"You've got to."

"Tracy's been asking me if she can get a reduction on our costs if there are less employees at PR O'Create. And she was also asking me if I'd ever been involved with a dismissal based on an employee spending too much time on non-work-related Internet sites."

"Shit."

"And you can be sacked for that, you know. However, I told her that all her employees spend time on non-work-related Internet sites so it was going to be difficult to prove in the case of just one. Not to mention all the time she spends on home-furnishing sites and cheap designer outlets."

I giggled. "Can I have that in writing?"

"Now that would be unprofessional."

"But so useful if she wants to sack me on the grounds of using the Internet on non-work-related business."

"I don't think she's going to sack you. I don't know, but she'd have to give you a verbal warning . . ."

"Has done."

"And then a written one and endless assessments. And that would take months and I got the impression she wanted to get rid of this employee more efficiently. She doesn't like you."

"I don't like her. Do you think she feels threatened by me?"

"Maybe. I reckon you might be at risk of being made redundant with a payoff. She did talk about having to reduce headcount, having lost a couple of accounts."

I smiled. "And you think me bunking off work may make this a more likely prospect?"

"I'm afraid so."

"Let's do it."

Chapter Eighteen

A Friday afternoon off work, the thrilling joy of it. Even as I sat in the gloom of public transport, I gave off little telepathic V-signs toward Tracy.

Ivan strap-hung over me as we burrowed westward on the Underground. He'd given up his seat to a grateful old lady. If it was done for my benefit, it worked. I compared him favorably to the discourteous George. We smiled at each other occasionally, but mostly studied the adverts for cheap car insurance and air con systems.

The train seemed to stop between every station. It would lurch us into one another and then pull us apart. It was a very long journey.

"Who do you think we're going to find?"

"Don't know. Do you think we will find someone?"

"Don't know."

By the time we arrived, I was enervated by anticipation, both for what we might find and for Ivan. We slunk up the escalator into the mass of people around the area that was incongruously known as the Green.

"Flats round here are really expensive," I said, loking round at the fast-food chicken joints and twenty-four-hour bagel shop.

"Prices in London really are ridiculous."

"Absolutely ridiculous. I feel so sorry for first-time buyers."

Our ruminations on the capital's favorite topic continued as Ivan led the way to a row of buildings in a section of a street in a corner of Shepherd's Bush. I'd never noticed how empty residential areas were on a working day. Chichi bits of London were always inexplicably full at three in the afternoon and you wondered how all these people had the time and the money to be lounging round hip bars in the middle of the day. Unemployment signified extremes of wealth and poverty depending on where you found the people lounging. An area like this, one that lay at the suburban fringes of fashion, was as empty as the faces of those left there. It had the air of a Continental city in August, with the few remaining inhabitants wishing they were somewhere else.

"It's half past three," I said.

"And?"

"I reckon we've got at least two hours before we need to start hiding somewhere to avoid him coming back. If he does come back." I looked at the house numbers and at the street opposite. "In that restaurant," I said, pointing to the sort of generic French bistro only found in local neighborhoods and sitcoms.

"Perfect. Let's go investigate."

At number twelve, the first house in our area, "Johnston" was out to work, as was "Smith" in the basement. "Jerry and Dave" were similarly unavailable for comment. I rang the doorbell to the middle flat of the next building. We had no luck with the simply named "Flat One," nor with "The Goons" on the ground floor. I rang the doorbell of the middle flat.

"Hello, I'm from a market research company." I winced and Ivan winked at me. "And we're doing a survey about routines of those not working regular office hours." I could hear a baby crying in the background. "Would you mind answering a few questions?" She buzzed us in. Ivan and I looked at each other in surprise, but darted into the communal hallway. We rifled through the junk mail and curry house flyers that blocked our path, to find out the names of the other inhabitants, but still none of the names meant anything to me.

A woman in jeans and a crisp shirt answered the door. Her top was White-Out white, a fact made surprising by the small baby snuggled up to it. Ivan passed me his envelope folder and I got out a piece of paper and angled it away from our respondent so she couldn't see that it was empty of questions.

Her name was Serena Whittaker, she was twenty-eight and she lived with her husband in flat three, number fourteen, a flat filled with expensive things made by indigenous peoples and sold in West London boutiques. Her cream sofa was as yet unsoiled by her three-month-old baby.

"Question one," I said brightly. "Why are you at home on a normal working day?"

She glanced at the baby.

"Sorry, stupid question, we just have to ask it. Do you enjoy stepping out of the nine-to-five routine that most of your peers undertake?"

"You'd think, wouldn't you?" She put the baby down on a brightly colored activity center. "I spent so many hours in the office wishing I wasn't there, but each of those hours feels like a day being stuck here. I really thought it would be fun being at home with a baby." She laughed. "I thought it would be like a holiday. But do you remember the school holidays and how boring they were?" I thought back to my blissful discovery then that reading made time pass quicker than you guessed it did and nodded.

"I force myself not to look at the kitchen clock," she continued. "And then I guess what time it is and it's about half past nine and I thought it would be at least eleven. I battle with the Underground to have lunch with friends, just so that some of their office efficiency might rub off on me. I ring them up in their offices and they talk to me for three minutes before saying 'I mustn't keep you,' and hanging up. The bit between six and seven, that's the worst, waiting for Tom to come back and then he says how was your day and I have to say it was exactly like the day before and he's done lots of interesting things and sometimes he has to go out in the evening, work stuff he says, and I am so bored and so sick of the television. I bet you think Radio Four is really good, don't you?"

"The *Today Programme* . . ." I muttered.

"Exactly, it's good before work and it's good after work but the rest of the time it's so boring and I'm so bored listening to it and watching rubbish on television. They must assume that anyone not in a 'proper' job is a halfwit."

I now understood why she had so recklessly let us into her home.

"It's not like I'm not busy. I'm boring busy. I'm really busy, emptying the washing machine, filling the washing machine, emptying the baby, filling the baby. But I'm so bloody bored, I've started talking to the neighbors."

"Really?" Ivan and I said with one voice.

"Worse than that, I watch them." She pointed at the bay window of the house opposite. "That man, he's weird."

"Yes?"

"He cleans the house all day, all those knickknacks, dusting, airing, old-fashioned things like that."

"Does he have a computer?" I asked, to which Ivan shook his head and made a face in return.

"Can't see it."

"What about your neighbors on this side of the street?" Ivan asked. "Do you have any contact with them?"

"A bit. They're almost all people like me but without the baby, you poll people would call them young professionals. Going out, careers, having fun, friends coming round with bottles of wine from that off-license. They're not around during the day."

"Why did you stop me asking her more about the weirdo man opposite?" I hissed at Ivan as we left.

"Because he's not in the right postcode, he's on the wrong side of the street."

"Oh," I said.

"And it's half past four and we've managed to do a mere two out of the twenty houses on the list." I must have looked chastened. "But nice move with the market research line."

"And we found out that most of the people who live around here are young people with jobs, which fits site perp profile."

"Which we would never have guessed by the area," he said, looking at the latte bar and deli stuffed with ready-made meals.

He needn't have worried about getting through the next eighteen houses in time. We peered through basement windows and we knocked and we rang. We got one bloke who claimed to have the flu, an old woman who said, "I've been expecting you," and some posh stoner students in number twenty-two. Other than that, our bell-ringing was unanswered. Serena Whittaker was right—residential London's a lonely place between the hours of eight in the morning and six in the evening. Its daytime inhabitants feel themselves to be a separate species from their commuting colleagues.

We retired to the bistro with our notes and dimmed enthusiasm.

"What have we got?" I asked Ivan.

He spread out his notes—scraps of addresses, names from pieces of junk mail, the Excel spreadsheet. He had nice handwriting, I noticed again, more feminine that I would have expected.

"Not a lot."

I sighed. "This is a wild-goose chase. We're never going to find them. Who's to say that it's not a false postcode anyway?"

"Come on, Izobel, don't be defeatist. We'll sit here and we'll see everyone coming back from work and we'll catch them, won't we?"

I shrugged.

"So," he said brightly. "What did you get up to last week?"

I went a bit mad, started wearing an anorak and tracksuit bottoms, gave your name to the police, didn't wash my hair for four days, converted my boyfriend from live-in to live-out, hated you passionately and my biggest achievement was filing the hard soles of my feet.

"Oh, you know, was a bit ill so didn't go to work. Food poisoning or something. Not a lot."

"I didn't have a brilliant time either, stewing away, thinking about you thinking I could be behind the site. And my week had begun so well."

I looked away from the street for a second to look at him. "Mine, too." I glanced back to the houses. It was difficult to have a meaningful conversation while having to remain vigilant, like trying to declare yourself to someone who's got a football match on in the background. The street, however, was boring. Ivan's face seemed infinitely interesting.

I continued to force myself to look at the houses. Only one person had returned to their home, a middle-aged woman with a dog. As I stared out of the window, Ivan held my hand and started stroking between my fingers, nuzzling the joint and then bringing his finger up to my tips. It was most distracting.

"That's nice," I said, with bland understatement.

"You should feel what I can do to feet."

I knew that the foot-filing would pay off. It had been like grating Parmesan, but now they were soft and ready to be stroked. I was ready to be stroked. My body was ready to be stroked.

"I'm sorry about everything, Ivan."

"Don't be. Actually, do be. You're awful, Izobel, you assumed I must be dodgy because I work with computers."

"It wasn't that, really. Well, a bit. I was snooty about it, but I'm not now. I've changed. Everything's different. I don't want to work in PR anymore and I . . ." I paused and looked out of the window, wondering how far to declare myself. I stopped and watched the only figure in the street. "Oh my God!"

"It's not that good," he said, but continued to rub the soft breasts of the palm of my hand.

"No." I snatched my hand away. "I know that person. I know them."

Chapter Nineteen

I had never recognized her before. She still had that air of insignificance. I wouldn't have noticed her then had I not been forcing myself to notice everyone who walked past. I still almost couldn't place her, having only been able to recognize her previously by her proximity to her shinier friends. Until now I had never seen her alone.

She seemed to make a deliberate effort to blend into the background, but on this occasion it only made her stand out more as she wore a heavy brown coat, while the rest of London's flesh flashed in spaghetti straps and shorts.

"Who is it?" Ivan asked as I continued to stare out of the window, not even thinking to disguise myself with dark glasses. I pressed my nose toward the glass, leaving breath marks upon it.

"Alice, it's Alice."

"Who?"

"Exactly. Alice, she's just this girl."

"Which girl?"

"This girl."

"You don't think she can have anything to do with the site, do you?"

I stood up and made my way to the door, watching her all the while as she walked into number twelve. Smith in the basement, of course, Alice Smith, she'd given me her business card the first time we had met with Camilla. She was still working full-time as a programmer in a software company round the corner from my office while they set up OnLove. I heard Ivan talk to the waiter and pay for our coffees and I couldn't focus on his question. I turned to look at him quizzically. "I don't know."

I didn't.

I stared at number twelve. It was a spindly redbrick building that looked as though it had always been divided into separate dwellings. It was the sort of place where strange loners had digs in the 1950s, cooking disgusting food on one-ring gas cookers. It once would have had a slum landlord, but now it would feature beige-painted walls and oatmeal-colored carpets. It was the sort of place anybody could live in and everybody would. Every second building on the street had an estate agent's sign outside. This was a place that people passed through anonymously. People like Alice.

"Shall we go?" I said to Ivan.

"Wait, let's make a plan. Do you think she's got anything to do with the site? How are we going to approach this? Believe me, you can't just go around making accusations. And anyway, she's a girl."

I ignored him and crossed the road and rang the bell to the basement, which had its own entrance. A hand inside twitched the drawn curtain to my right, but there was no answer. The windows were open but guarded with latticed bars. I put my hand in and drew back the curtain.

"Alice," I shouted. I felt calm. "Hello, it's Izobel, Izobel Brannigan. I just saw you on the street. What a coincidence that you should live here and that we should just be having a coffee across the road. Do you want one?" Behind the curtains the room was dark, while the street pinged with the pyrotechnic sunlight. The interior began to get clearer as my sight adjusted, while Ivan became more bleached out behind me. I pulled the curtain back further to admit more light as I peered in, before hearing a voice at the door.

"Hello," said Alice. "What a coincidence."

"Coffee?" I said as I came face to partial face with her through the small crack in the door that she had conceded.

"I'm just on my way out, actually."

"That's a shame. Oh well, let's have a quick chat inside then, shall we?" I pushed the door and she pushed back. It was a tussle that I was determined to win, while at the same time we both had to pretend that we weren't competing at all, as if an arm wrestle had segued out of merely shaking hands. I forced my way in, with Ivan following.

"Nice flat," I said on coming into the sitting room. It wasn't, particularly. It was a set decorator's version of a typical young middle-class flat: the lampshade was a Habitat paper ball, the carpet burlap, the low coffee table from Ikea. Along one side was a galley kitchen, which was empty but for a packet of supermarket own-brand cornflakes. Like her face, Alice's dwelling had almost no character or distinguishing features. It was an unliving room. "Have you lived here long?"

"A year or so." She stood in one corner of it. Although it was low-ceilinged, she was diminishing all the while. Beside her was a monstrous computer, along with a scanner, color printer, speakers and the biggest flat monitor I'd ever seen.

"You haven't met Ivan, have you? Ivan, this is Alice. Alice, this is Ivan." He crossed the room and they shook hands.

"I want one of these," he said, pointing at the computer screen.

"I got it in the States. Same price in dollars as it would have been in pounds here."

"Fabulous," I said. "Can you show us what a page of the Internet looks like on it? We'd like that, wouldn't we, Ivan?"

"It's not working. My processor's bust at the moment."

"Really? Don't you need it for your work, though?"

"No, I do all my work in the office."

"What do you need such a powerful computer at home for then?" I asked.

"Stuff."

"What sort of stuff?"

"OnLove stuff, developing that."

"So you do need it for work."

She moved protectively in front of the desk, revealing the wall and bookshelf behind her. There hung a framed print of the Doisneau kiss and a cinema poster for *The Italian Job.* There were no knickknacks in the flat, no birthday-present vases or pebbles from foreign beaches. There were no photos, either, no blowups of me going about my daily business as I might have suspected of site perp. I walked a couple of paces toward her and she moved to cover the computer completely. I scanned the shelves, where all the manuals and books were ordered so that their heights and spines matched their neighbors and became smaller in a series of subtle gradations, like children in a well-organized school photo. This pattern was broken by a snapshot, unframed, curled up at the edges on the third shelf down. It was the photo of me with Frank and Maggie, the one taken at Hot Bob's party, and it nestled by a full set of the novels in the *Dune* series.

I stared. Of course her living in this street was an indication that she might be the one, but a clue that I had chosen not to truly believe. She was such a nonentity, a negative presence. It could not be that I had been made to feel a somebody by such a nobody. I felt an odd sensation of disappointment.

"Look," I said. "It's me." She moved to block it, only confirming her guilt. "Where did you get that photo from?"

"Camilla didn't want it."

That didn't surprise me.

I looked at Ivan, who gave me a smile. That was all I needed. "Alice, we know what you've done."

"What do you mean? Why are you here?"

We're here to accuse you of creating a Web site in my honor, you random person I was once at school with and hadn't seen for thirteen years, if I'd ever seen you in the first place. I couldn't say it. I couldn't quite believe it. "We know you registered a domain name. The registrant confirmed it."

"Registrar," corrected Ivan.

"Piss off." I felt fury froth within me. At Alice, but I channeled it toward Ivan. "The registrar confirmed that you bought," I paused, "Izobelbrannigan dot co dot uk. And there's dot com too. They gave us your name and address."

"That's impossible. That's not true, they don't give away names and addresses. They don't even have them," she replied quietly, while edging toward the door. I moved toward it while Ivan stayed by the computer, making her piggy in the middle. "I don't know what you're talking about."

"Yes, you do." I still couldn't accuse her directly. It was embarrassing, that's what it was, it felt too socially inappropriate to have to say it. "Do you want me to spell it out?"

"What?"

"Come on Alice, all the evidence is there. That photo, and you'd have easily found the one on the school site. You said the other day that you're signed up to the school Web site e-mail letter or something."

"So?"

"Those were the first two photos on the site. You could have got the other photo from the foyer of my office and you know how to program sites, you were a bit of an admirer of mine at school. Shit, you were there, you were there when Frank said that snidey thing about me being able to speak Chinese. You knew that."

"I expect lots of people know you speak Chinese."

"But I don't. Ha. It was a lie to catch him out. But I've caught you out instead."

She sat down calmly. "I really don't have any idea what you're talking about."

"Izobel," said Ivan. "Are you sure? Why would she?"

"I've just said why it's her."

"You've explained how it could be her, but not why. Why did she do it?"

I shook my head. "I don't know, but I'm going to find out."

"And Izobel, she's a girl."

At that moment, I was sure that I saw her stick out her chest at him. She was small, but had an unexpectedly fine embonpoint. It was a tiny puffing movement, but enough. I flew at her and pinned her arms back on the sofa while sitting on her, like I used to do to my little brother so that my sister could fart in his face.

"You stupid fucking cow. Don't you have any idea what you've done to me?"

"No," she said, looking me straight in the eye. Her face was too close to mine and I leaped back.

"Ivan, keep an eye on her, don't let her move."

"OK," he said to me. "Sorry," he said to her.

I went to the kitchen area and opened the fridge. It was the usual single dweller's void, a jar of pesto, a couple of yogurts and some milk. I found a can of cola lurking. That would do.

"Right," I said on returning to the sitting room. I pulled the gargantuan computer processor out from under the desk and tipped it up so that the underbelly spewed out its wires. I pulled out its intestines and held the can high above its target. "If you don't start telling me why you created izobelbrannigan dot com, the computer gets it."

She remained silent.

"Fair enough," I said and opened the can, letting some of its caffeinated stickiness spurt out. I started tipping it.

"Stop," shouted Ivan and Alice with one voice. "Have you any idea how much one of those is worth?" he added.

I continued until a little dribble began to form on the can and then ooze its way toward impregnation.

"All right, all right. It's me," said Alice. "Please stop."

I had been sure of it, I had been convinced that she was behind the site, but I still felt my legs buckle at her admission. My face flushed as if I had been slapped across both cheeks. I didn't want it to be her. She wasn't supposed to be the one. "But why?"

She exhaled, as if more relieved about her computer than embarrassed about what she had been accused of. I held my weapon above her beloved once again and repeated: "Why?"

"Why not?"

"Not good enough, Alice."

"I made a site, so what?" She was kicking her feet together and looking at them like a bolshie teenager accused of smoking.

"So what?" I repeated. "It's weird, that's what."

"Why?"

"Why?" This was getting repetitive. "Because it's creepy and weird and not normal. You must be obsessed with me or something."

"Not really. Elizabethans wrote sonnets, artists paint pictures, photographers take photos, I create sites about people I admire."

"Sorry? Why do you do that?"

"It's what I do, it's my hobby. Don't you have a hobby, Izobel? I thought you learned Chinese, but you don't, do you? People like you and Camilla don't do hobbies, do you? You've got nothing like my family of sites."

"Sites?" I asked, with almost a trace of disgruntlement. "Sites plural?"

She did that whinnying giggle that I remembered from our first meeting. "Yes, you're not the only person."

"Good," I said. "Thank God for that."

"Like who else?" asked Ivan.

"Tim Berners-Lee . . ."

"He sort of invented the Internet," explained Ivan to me.

"George Clooney . . ."

"But aren't you, aren't you, I mean, not interested in men?" Alice and I united in a disparaging look thrown in his direction.

"Ada Lovelace," she continued. "She was a nineteenth-century mathematician who wrote the first computer program. Who else? Mrs. Bredwin . . ."

"Our old maths teacher." It was my turn to patronize Ivan. "Does she know about it? Has she seen it?" Alice shrugged. "What does she think about having a site devoted to her? Have you thought about that?"

"I expect she'd be flattered. Weren't you?"

"No."

"Not even a little bit?" She was growing in confidence. I wanted to slap her down again. "Isn't your life better for it?"

"No, it's not. I've felt hounded and I'm about to get sacked from my job and my," I paused, "my life's just not the same."

"Isn't it better? I mean, you've got rid of that drunken boyfriend of yours."

If I could have gone any redder, I would have done at this moment.

Ivan looked at us both. "Boyfriend?"

"Ex-boyfriend."

"He was horrible. Always drunk, wasn't he, Izobel?" said Alice.

"Me splitting up with George had absolutely nothing to do with the site. And fuck off, how dare you comment to me about my life when the only reason you know anything about it is because you've been following me. You disgust me. Don't you dare claim responsibility for anything I've done."

"Bit of a coincidence though, that you should chuck him now."

"Did you chuck him for me?" asked Ivan.

"Shut up. Shut up, both of you, I chucked him for myself."

"Really?" said Alice.

"You can shut the fuck up!" I wanted to shove her, to grab her hair and pull it out of her head, I wanted some sort of physical contact because words alone could not express the strange mixture of fury and curiosity. I felt a tingling anger prick my skin and my fists clench so hard that the skin was stretched taut. "Why?" I wailed. "You didn't even know me when you started it. How can you claim to admire me?"

"You were so cool at school."

"That was a long time ago. I didn't know you."

"I remember it so well. I thought you were amazing. You wore a black polo neck and funny secondhand clothes and always had on a Walkman and I'd ask you what album you were playing and it was always something really obscure while everybody else was listening to Michael Jackson."

"I was cool, wasn't I?"

"Amazing. You stood for the Greens in that mock election. I mean, I'd never even heard of the environment until you did that. I used to try to find you every day in assembly to see what you were wearing and doing and then copy you at weekends. Didn't you ever see me on home clothes day?"

"No."

"I wore stuff that you did, like velvet trousers and men's jackets and fifties shoes. I don't dress like that anymore."

"Sounds horrible," added Ivan.

"But it wasn't. It was so brilliant," she said to him. "Izobel was just so different to all the other girls and she wrote poetry and recommended Sylvia Plath to me."

"I did?"

"I heard you talking about *The Bell Jar* to one of your friends."

Ivan was shaking his head. "Izobel, this is all very sweet but why the site?"

"Yes, why then, why did you create a site a few months ago?"

"I started working on OnLove with Camilla and she was talking about Frank's friends and I recognized your name. Then I was looking through her photos and I saw the one of you and Frank and Maggie and it gave me the idea."

It grated on me that she should even dare to use Maggie's name. She doesn't know her, she's not her friend.

"What, and you saw a photo of me and you thought, 'Oh, I know, I'm going to start stalking her'?"

"Camilla told me what you were up to these days and I remembered how brilliant you'd been."

"Thanks."

Ivan rolled his eyes. "So you created a site?"

"Yes," she said simply. "I thought I'd make it and then I'd contact you and I might show you it and we'd become friends like I always thought we would and hang out with each other. Maybe we'd update the site together."

"You created it before we met up again?"

"Yes, I created a site about the Izobel who I remembered. Then I met you, when Camilla and I came into your office."

"And?"

"And you weren't the person I remembered. You were still pretty and funny and stuff, but you hadn't become what I thought you would. You were less than that."

"What the hell do you mean?"

"You hadn't become extraordinary."

"Great, thanks, so why continue the site?"

"Then it changed. Rather than being a tribute to you, I thought I'd help you to become extraordinary."

"You what?"

"I thought I'd help you fulfill your potential. To become that person that I thought you'd be."

"I still don't understand. How is freaking me out and becoming my stalker going to help me?"

"I thought if someone admired you then you might start admiring yourself. And the public too, the ones who wrote stuff about you and which I put on the site. Your public."

"They were real? The 'Izobel's fit and unattractive'? I thought you made them up."

"No, they were real. Some found izobelbrannigan after the article George wrote, which wasn't very accurate by the way, others by just general Googling. There are bloggers who write up every site on bulletin boards. I do that too, so I just took their comments and those that were e-mailed and put them on the site. With a few spelling corrections, of course, what with you having won the English prize at school. I wanted Izobel's fans to be grammatically correct. I knew they wouldn't help you if they weren't."

"Help me what?"

"Celebrate yourself."

"What, like if you made me into a sort of celebrity then I'd become my own biggest fan?"

"Exactly." She was so calm now, while I felt flustered.

"For Christ's sake," interjected Ivan. "Don't listen to this crap, Izobel. Look, she's clearly a lesbian with a dangerous obsession."

"No I'm not."

"No," I said. "I don't think she is."

"But she was in love with you at school."

"No, she wasn't, she admired me. It's different when you're at school." Alice and I looked at each other in rare concurrence. "Was your school an all-boys' one?" He shook his head. "When you're at school, you see the same people all day every day and it's like an office and you end up obsessing over people you wouldn't do in normal circumstances. I mean, haven't you ever obsessed over someone completely inappropriate at work?" He raised an eyebrow. "At school, you don't know quite who you are yet and you don't have exposure to boys but you do have older girls . . ."

"Sapphic school frolics kind of thing?"

"No. With teenage girls it's not about sex at all. Even the crushes you have on pop stars aren't particularly sexual. You fancy really pretty girl-boys who you want to look like rather than get off with . . ."

"And with the girls at school, the girls two or three years above you, it's that you want to be them rather than be with them." Ivan and I turned to Alice with a start.

"And still do?" he asked.

She shook her head. I leaned against the wall and then found myself slithering down it in exhaustion. "Then why?"

"I wanted you to be you."

"Oh right," he said. "And just how was putting those death dates going to help Izobel become Izobel?"

"They weren't death dates," she said. "They were section dates. I was going to start a new section for two thousand and three onward."

"I don't believe you," said Ivan.

I thought back to the day I discovered them. "It was after I got off with Ivan, wasn't it? You were jealous."

"Exactly, she's a lesbian."

"No, she was jealous of me, not of you. She fancies you. You fancy Ivan."

"No I don't. Of course I don't." As if being accused of fancying a boy was worse than people thinking you were some weirdo cyber-stalker. "I just thought that things weren't going very quickly. That things weren't changing in your life despite all my best efforts. So I upped the ante."

"By threatening to kill me."

"Hardly, I just planted an idea in your head. And it worked, didn't it? You're happy to blow off work in PR and you dumped that George."

"Who is this George?" asked Ivan.

"He's the one in the photo outside the pub," she said. "Balding."

"What, the old man?" They looked at me pityingly.

"Piss off, both of you. If you're so concerned with my happiness, why did you carry on with the site after I e-mailed you asking you to stop?"

Alice shrugged.

"Don't you shrug at me."

"I was going to stop when I was ready."

"I see, it's all about control, isn't it? What sort of a sad and empty life do you lead that you should have to create and control your friends online?"

"It's what I do," she repeated. "I do most things online, including chatting to friends and helping them to change their lives for the better."

"Weirdo. Why don't you hang out with your real ones more?"

She drooped.

"Oh, don't tell me you're lonely. You've got Camilla. And the other ones. Why don't you create a bloody site about them? Why isn't there a camillajenkinson dot com?"

"She's not you."

"Well, at least have a normal friendship with her instead of an abnormal one with me."

"She doesn't like me."

"Rubbish, you're always hanging out."

"She's just working with me as I'm so brilliant at programming. The others only put up with me because Camilla does. She never wants to see me outside work unless it's to talk about Internet dating and making lots of money."

"But I've seen you together—at Mick's birthday in the pub, at Maggie's party and stuff."

"I followed you to that bookshop and then the pub after work and then pretended to bump into her. And I heard you and Camilla talking about Maggie's so I went along. She'd invited Becksy and Molly along, but not me."

I thought back to that night and how I had come upon her with Camilla and Frank. "What does Frank think of you?"

"Your friend Frank doesn't like me or any of Camilla's friends much. They've been arguing about us for ages and then they had a row in front of me. Camilla said that he had to be nice to her school friends if he loved her and anyway she had to be nice to me because of OnLove and he said it was creepy how I kept turning up places."

Of course; I thought back to the atmosphere between Frank and his girlfriend and their overheard remarks. "He said he wasn't going out with one of Camilla's school friends, but he was going out with her."

"Yes, they argue about it all the time. But don't worry, I think they're going to get married anyway."

"Married?"

"Yes, he's proposed and they were just about to announce it at that party but then they had the argument."

I always thought I'd mind the moment when Frank said he was marrying somebody else, but I didn't. "Not quite the little home-wrecker this time then."

"But aren't you glad about your and George's home being wrecked? Don't tell me your life isn't better because of me and the site."

Something about her smugness and her self-belief and everything about the fact that she was right filled me with fury that turned itself into energy. "That's it. That is fucking it." And then I started screaming. It wasn't as if I really felt I wanted to scream, more that I was wondering what I would do if this was happening to me and screaming seemed to be what I or a good actress would do. I couldn't feel what I wanted to do, only try to think what I wanted to do in such an instance. It was as if I were autistic and had to teach myself human reaction, the whole situation being so far from one that I had programmed instincts for.

After thirty seconds of yodeling I stopped and looked at the horrified faces of Alice and Ivan. "I feel better now." I did. The weight of curiosity had at last been lifted. I was disappointed that it was Alice, but I would have been more disappointed had it been Ivan, or even Frank. "You're going to say you're sorry."

"Sorry," she mumbled.

"No." I was so assertive I thrilled myself. I poked her in the chest. "You are going to say sorry like you mean it and you're going to make some effort to understand why you should be sorry."

"Sorry," she said again.

"And why are you sorry, Alice?"

"Because I made you feel uncomfortable."

"You freaked me out. You tried to control my life when you had no right to do so. You tried to steal me away from myself. This is not some inoffensive little hobby, Alice, it's manipulation and you mustn't ever think otherwise. Don't you ever dare think you've improved me or my life. Don't you claim credit. It's my life, my doing. Do you understand?"

She bowed her head and looked at her feet. She was tiny, as was everything about her. How could I not have noticed how small the photographer was in the photo that Ivan had blown up? I hadn't realized the scale of it. How stupid we had all been, Ivan, Maggie and me. We had looked for someone important, when only someone insignificant would have wanted to do this and would have got away with it.

"But I forgive you."

Ivan looked at me and raised his eyebrows.

"I forgive you on two conditions." Alice had reverted back to grumpy adolescent mode and I had a glimpse of what she must have been like as an odd little fourth-former, trying to become me. "You must stop the site, you must get rid of it." I paused. "But first you must save it for me, is that possible?"

"Burn it onto a CD," she said.

"That means copy it," said Ivan helpfully.

"Right, yes, you must burn it onto a CD and then you must destroy the site. You can't keep your own copy." She looked up. "No, really, you can't. It's not yours to keep. It's my life. And secondly, you must give me the URLs, izobelbrannigan dot com and izobelbrannigan dot co dot uk. They're mine, they belong to me and I need them now."

She muttered.

"What's that?" I was beginning to enjoy myself.

"You can have the URLs I bought."

"They're not yours to be so generous with, they're mine. Always have been. And if I ever find out that you've been following me or taking photos of me again, then I shall make sure you regret it." How, I wasn't sure.

She lifted her head up. "All right." I almost felt sorry for her and then I remembered the raw angry curiosity that had driven me for the last months and the way I had wanted to scratch myself until I bled just to give me something else to fret over. I thought of George and of my job. And then I thought of Ivan.

I looked round at her as we left. She was switching on her computer.

"I don't understand," Ivan said to me as we came out onto the street that now chugged with returning commuters and their self-important busyness. It had become a different place to the one it had been before we had entered number twelve. "Is that it?"

"Yes, I suppose it is." I was a bride after a wedding or an actor after the last night; the project was now over and I felt empty. I wanted to lie down.

"But why? Don't you think she should be punished a bit more? You were a lot angrier with me when you felt I might be behind it. And, I mean, you split up with your boyfriend over this, didn't you? The oldest boyfriend in Christendom."

"George, yes. My inappropriately named boyfriend, my ex. That's the most annoying thing—she's right. She is the flipping angel from *It's a Wonderful Life.* I shouldn't be with George and I shouldn't be in my crappy job. I had potential and now I have nothing. That's why I want to own the URL, because I'm going to need it, when I'm doing my own thing. Which I will do."

"And that is?"

"I've been thinking about what I'm good at and how I can use my qualities."

"What are you good at, then?"

"I'm good at, well I was, no, I am good at listening to other people. I'm academic, I can learn fast and I'm quick at thinking through problems. I can give useful advice when I think about it hard enough. And I want to help people, I really do."

"And feed the starving children of the world?"

"Don't make fun of me."

"I'm not, Izobel. Really, I'm not. Tell me about your plans."

"OK. I'm good at PR too. I'm used to having to try to sell rubbish products, so now I could try to sell people the best version of themselves. And weirdly, this business with Alice has made me think too. If I could help people to become celebrities in their own lives, then their self-esteem would go sky-high."

"You're going to make Web sites about people?"

"No. Well, I might do. I don't know. I'll use whatever tools there are, but for a good basis I'm going to do a psychotherapy or psychodynamic counseling course. I've been looking into them and you need a degree but it doesn't have to be science-based. I can do one part-time and it will only take me about four years or so."

Ivan laughed. "Four years?"

"Yes." I shrugged. "I can temp throughout and, after all, I'm only thirty. I've got the rest of my professional life ahead of me so what's a few years' retraining? Besides, it will be so great to use my brain again. Just think how amazing it might be to help people change the way I have. That stupid Alice has made me feel like my own star now. I'm not going to keep bloody Tracy happy and I'm not going to sleep with self-obsessed media types. Artists my arse, they're all piss artists."

"My, my, could swath-cutting Soho-working media-man-hunting Izobel Brannigan actually sleep with . . ." He paused, uncharacteristically lacking in sarcasm.

"A techie? Could I sleep with a techie?" We smiled at one another, mouths-shut shy smiles, the sort that photograph badly. "I'm sorry, Ivan, for doubting you. You've been brilliant over all this. I should never have accused you being the site person."

"That's all right. It wasn't that unlikely. I think Alice and I may be your biggest fans. I think you're amazing and if I was a little bit weirder and a little more inventive then I could have been behind the site. What was it she said, pretty and funny and stuff, you are those things."

"I am, aren't I? Well, I think so, I hope so."

"You're more like izobelbrannigan dot com than you realize."

I stood looking at him and purely out of habit stepped outside myself to create the paparazzi shot of us moving toward one another, still figures, mouths meeting, while people jostled past us to get home, like some bad pop video that attempts to express otherness through the contrast.

Chapter Twenty

It's so big and hard. This bed I mean." We giggled.

Ivan's bed was indeed comfortable, but I had not slept all night and now we ate stale toast and Marmite with long-delayed hunger at dawn. I hadn't even ever liked Marmite before. I kissed his fingers and they tasted salty with savory spread and me. It was light outside and I felt it suffuse me with Vitamin D and joy. I was exhausted and elated, desperate to sleep and yet so unwilling. Why would I want to sleep when euphemistically sleeping with Ivan was all that I ever wanted to do? We had tried to switch ourselves off but in doing so we only turned each other on. His skin was much darker than mine and as our limbs entangled we looked like a pornographic Benetton advert.

It was the sweet, perfect moment of excitement, when all is well, when the relationship is all present and future, and both those things are wonderful. If I could jump through the forthcoming scenes what would I see? That Ivan's niceness and enthusiasm add up to a seductive ploy that would fade as soon as the girl reciprocated? Or me trying to persuade him to follow art not technology because it sounded better, introducing him as an artist much to his annoyance? Him being boorish or me being bored? Him talking about technology too much and my old snobberies returning to reject him? He read and loved sci-fi novels, after all. I should probably give them a try myself.

I knew so little about him. His friends could be leery and leechy, his family clingy or combative, his work oppressive.

And yet then, I could only see the scenes jumping from holidays to weekends spent in bed to introducing him proudly to my friends. I could only see photo-album scenes, the ones you see in other people's collections that make you jealous of their lives. My, was he handsome.

"More tea?" he asked.

"Hot tea, hot toast . . ." I replied. It wasn't hot sex, it was warm, suffused with smiles and giggles and enthusiasm. How did I ever have sex with a straight face? Straight-faced sex was vile, it was like tea without sugar to Ivan and me.

We were right in the heart of the city yet the world seemed far away. The world, what was going on out there? I hadn't had my mobile on since I had escaped the office and taken flight to Shepherd's Bush. I rummaged around in my bag and found my phone and switched it on. I shuddered as it told me that we were not alone. Three missed calls and a text message. Damn it. I had been with the only person I might want to call me. I called the voice mail number. Just two messages, the first sent at fifteen hundred hours and twenty-three.

"Izobel, it's Tracy. We don't run a policy of everyone pissing off early on Fridays, especially not those already on probation. And especially when we're having to make expenditure cuts. Which you'd realize if you attended management meetings occasionally. You're skating very near the knuckle and if you can be bothered to return to the office, I'd like to see you asap."

She said "asap" as if it was a word, not A-S-A-P. Stupid cow. Save, repeat or delete, my mobile asked. Easy one.

"Hello, it's me, Maggie by the way, can you give me a ring when you get a chance."

Then there were a couple more message-less missed calls from

Maggie. I put on a toweling robe and wandered into that big marvelous room of Ivan's, with its kitchen and the installation that had so seduced me that night only nine days ago. He was nakedly putting sugar into our teas. He was naked happy person and I felt overdressed, like a reverse of the classic panic dream about being the only nude person in a room full of besuited others. A laptop was lying open on the coffee table with another of Ivan's magical blooming installations flowering upon its screen.

"I like your screen saver."

"It's my site, my blog. You're not the only one, you know."

I noticed the laptop's lack of spewing guts and ports and frowned.

"It's wireless," he explained. "It's brilliant, you don't need to plug in a modem or anything but can use it anywhere in the house. I could sit in the bathroom with it if I wanted. Now that's truly portable. It works by . . ." He stopped on seeing me put my head to one side. "You think I'm nerdy, don't you? What will you tell your friends about me? That I'm an artist or a consultant or an entrepreneur? Or will you tell them the truth, that I'm a computer spod?"

"I'll tell them you're a techie, my sexy techie." We had got onto the we're-going-to-introduce-you-to-our-lives point after just one night. I was just pulling him down toward me when my phone rung with a "private number."

"It's me, Maggie. Didn't you get my text?"

"Hello you, no I didn't. I mean, I did, but I haven't opened it up. Sorry, things have been a bit . . ."

"I can't really talk," she said weakly. "Everyone in the ward is listening."

"Ward?"

"I'm in hospital."

"God, are you OK? The baby?" I stood up, now robeless.

"We're fine. She's fine."

"She? A girl? You gave birth? You're not due until next month."

"Emergency Cesarean. I got these terrible pains yesterday afternoon and a bit of bleeding and they told me she was distressed. So was I by this point, as you can imagine. Not to mention Mick. Still," she said, sounding brighter, "this is what celebrities do, whip it out a month early so as to save their figure and their relationship but not going through that belly-expanding last bit and the vaginal messiness of a natural birth. I asked them to give me a Cesari-tuck while they were at it." She laughed and then groaned. "I can't laugh, it hurts the stitches so much. I'll never laugh again."

"But what about your baby. What about her?"

"She's fine. A bit small but I think she'd have been a monster, if we'd left her in there. Already over five pounds, almost six, which is really almost normal. No fine, good, in fact, no tubes sticking in or out of her. None of that bag-of-oranges look that premature babies have. She's beautiful. If a bit yellow. Bag of lemons perhaps."

"Shit, you're a mother. You're parents. You're amazing, both of you. All three of you."

"I've got to go now," she whispered.

"But wait, what's her name?"

She giggled delightedly and then moaned again. "Ouch. Izobel."

"Yes, but what's her name?"

"That's it, that's her name."

"I-S-A . . ."

"No, I-Z-O-B. It seems like the spelling that will get her noticed in life. We're in for a few days, please come and see us. But promise not to make me laugh."

Izobel, a name to get you noticed. Izobel, whose job is about to terminate, whose love life has been a disaster.

Izobel who is, what was it Alice had said, "funny and pretty and stuff." Izobel, who has been reborn on the same day as her 5 lb namesake has come into existence.

Epilogue

To: mail@izobelbrannigan.com
From: maternitymaggie@hotmail.com
Subject: what to wear

Hello my fellow non-nine-to-fiver, have you got an outfit sorted for wedding of the century? I'm almost back to my prenatal weight but everything's in a different place, boobs where stomach was, stomach where knees were, head in the clouds, hand down the diaper dispenser etc. Camilla aka Herod has made it very clear that although the guest list stretches to 200, little Iz is not invited to the big day and I'm terrified about going without her as she's become my kind of creepy ventriloquist's doll that I speak through. I have no identity beyond her, what will I talk about? Argggh, M xxx

To: maternitymaggie@hotmail.com
From: mail@izobelbrannigan.com
Subject: re: what (not) to wear

Ah, just get drunk and know that you're a hundred times more interesting than the other guests. As token ex at the banquet, I have to look disgustingly chic. Am thinking of blowing one little trickle more of my PR O'Create redundancy hush money or Married Man's lucrative freelancing fund on an inappropriate frock. You can take the girl out of PR but you can't take the PR out of me—I may be a penniless psychology student, but damn it I'm not going to dress like one. Anyway, I wouldn't worry what you wear, as flatmate of the bridesmaid, I can assure you that you can't look worse than Becksy who's thrilled at the prospect of looking like a Garruda Air hostess with tubular full-length skirt and matching bolero jacket. So clever of Camilla to have six wan crappily dressed versions of herself beside her so that she looks like the lead singer with an ugly backing band. Love, big Iz

To: mail@izobelbrannigan.com
From: maternitymaggie@hotmail.com
Subject: re:

Ooo, get you, back in the knife drawer. Are we quite as happy about Frank's marriage as you say you are? "I'm so happy for them, no really" blah blah. Methinks the lady doth protest too much.

To: maternitymaggie@hotmail.com
From: mail@izobelbrannigan.com
Subject: re:

Most evil phrase in English language begone. How many times have I been cursed with going through the lady doth protest pantomime. You fancy him, no I don't, ooo methinks the lady doth protest, no I don't, yes you do you're protesting too much etc. etc. Not that it's a problem now as it is totally clear that I only have eyes for one man. As you know, Iz's six-month birthday marks the far more important half-year anniversary of my love and me. The first of many I'm sure. But don't get me started on the wonder of Ivan . . .

To: mail@izobelbrannigan.com
From: maternitymaggie@hotmail.com
Subject: re:

Bless, I don't know which of the three of you is cuter. Are you expecting anniversary gifts? I've already spent a fortune on two hand-painted plates from Camilla and Frank's wedding list. So unfair, why don't Mick and I get anything for being monogamous?

To: all
From: alice@licesmith.de
Subject: hello from Germany

Hello all, just a quick e-mail between moving house, meeting so many fun Berliners and starting the new job (very very high-powered as well as highly paid!! Huge technical skills shortage so if anybody's hot on Java, get out here!) to give you all my new e-mail address. E-mail me anytime though am so busy can't say I'll be quick to reply ;-) . . . Germany's great and am really loving life and feel like everyone's much more positive than back in rainy old England. Camilla, have a brill day—shame the wedding's so small as I'd have loved to join you all. E-mail some photos of it and all the news soon.
( ) Alice

To: ivan_hotmailaccount@hotmail.com
From: mail@izobelbrannigan.com
Subject: Fw: hello from Germany

Hello sweetheart, please find attached message from weirdie Alice. She doesn't give up, does she? And do you think she realizes that her e-mail address looks like "lice smith"? Oh well, why should we care? Apart from the fact that, I suppose, I wouldn't be e-mailing you now and seeing you tonight if it weren't for her.

Any supper requests? Big kiss, I x

About the Author

Like my heroine, I was bored one day at work when I decided to Google myself. Unlike Izobel, I found absolutely nothing; well, lots about a realtor, poet and lawyer called Christina Hopkinson, but I had to delve pretty deep before I got to me. But I did think to myself, "Wouldn't it have been weird if there had been a site devoted to me and my life?" and from there I developed the plot of *Cyber Cinderella.*

I was often bored at work. After being educated in Cambridge (school), Oxford (university) and Madrid (nightclubs), I wasn't qualified for much other than the usual media job that sounds a lot more glamorous than it is. I decided to stop waiting for a big fat redundancy payoff and chuck in my job to give writing a go. I got reemployed as a receptionist and typed fast and furiously in between answering the phone in a singsong voice.

Over the following twelve months, I got married, got pregnant, got published and moved house. I now live in London and divide my time between the differing demands of toddler and typewriter. I'm working on my second novel, as well as contributing features on health and parenting to British newspapers such as the *Telegraph* and the *Guardian.*

Get in touch with me through www.christinahopkinson.com.

Christina Hopkinson

5 Reasons Why Googling Yourself Is a Very Bad Idea

1. It's like reading somebody else's diary. You wade through lots of boring stuff that's not about you and, if there is anything actually relevant, it's always negative. I found the gem "Christina Hopkinson clearly needs help" on a message board in response to an article I wrote in a newspaper. To which the other contributors all agreed!

2. The shame of looking yourself up and finding you're not on it at all. Or you are—but it's only as an eBay buyer or seller.

3. Your discovery that an ex has put pictures of you up on the Web. And you're at a hugely unflattering angle, with your bits hanging out. Or your ex has posted your photo on a don't-ever-date-this person site.

4. You find other people with your same name that are much more exciting than you are. Like the friend who got obsessed with the person of the same name who'd won the Social Entrepreneur of the the Year award. She wondered, could it have been me? Should it be me? Then she wanted to change her life. Then she realized she never would. Then she wanted to watch daytime TV in a slump of depression for the next ten years.

I Googled what would be my married name, Christina Carruthers, to find that somebody else had already bagged that domain name and created the site www.christinacarruthers.com. What's more, I'm completely outflanked in the glamour and makeup stakes by the rival Christina—reigning Miss Gay Dupont Circle of America and competitor in five—count 'em—five Miss Gay America pagents.

5. Googling leaves a trail of technological slime easily followed. Oh, the shame of being caught looking yourself up. Worse, the shame of getting an emergency visit from the men from your work's IT department for having accidently logged onto a porn site when curiously looking at your namesake's Swedish Web link.